THE BLAZING STAR

BY

IMANI JOSEY

WISE
CREATIVE · PUBLISHING
Ink

ISBN 13: 978-1-945769-16-0
eISBN 13: 978-1-63489-924-6

Library of Congress Catalog Number: 2016947140
Printed in the United States of America
First Printing: 2016
20 19 18 17   5 4 3 2

Cover and interior design by Steven Meyer-Rassow

Wise Ink Creative Publishing
837 Glenwood Ave.
Minneapolis, MN 55405
www.wiseinkpub.com

To order, visit www.seattlebookcompany.com or call (734) 426-6248.
Reseller discounts available.

To Mom, for loving words

To Dad, for believing in mine

LIGHTNING STRIKES

"What is that on your head?"

I whipped around. Dad's eyes were wide saucers. "Hair," I said, panting. I slipped my book bag off my shoulders and let it drop to the floor. The sprint from the bus stop in the thick, May humidity was brutal. I did, however, make it in time.

"I see that." My father rose from the seat he'd patiently occupied backstage in the auditorium. "But there's less of it."

I appreciated the hum of the air conditioning before speaking again. My dad made his way to a roll of paper towel situated between refreshments on a nearby table. He tore a sheet and handed it to me. "Thanks," I said, taking it and dabbing my moist brow.

"I didn't want you to sweat your hair out," he mentioned of my pressed locks.

"I'll wrap it tonight." My breathing evened before I flashed a smile. "Do you like it?"

"It's not that I don't like it, Portia." He eyed my 'do and cocked a brow. "It's different. You and your sister usually—"

"We always look like the twins from *The Shining*." I crumpled the paper towel and strode toward the heavy curtains framing the stage.

"That's an old movie."

Peeking through the gaps revealed the restless faces in the crowd. "I like old movies, Rich."

"We can be on a first name basis when you pay bills," he grumbled as I tossed the used paper towel in a trash can. I called my father by his first name sometimes to get on his nerves and other times to shift topics without him noticing.

I glanced back as he shook his head. I wasn't successful this time. "I cut my hair a little. We don't have to look alike all the time."

"Well"—he added the last of his commentary—"it does look nice."

Scheduling a hair appointment before my sister's early-morning ceremony wasn't a great idea, but I was going to look how I wanted on the day I'd dreaded for almost three years. My denim capris hugged my round hips, one of the features I was proudest of, but the gloss I haphazardly smeared on my mouth during the bus ride was gone now. The haircut was as good as it was going to get. My hands ran over my clipped strands as the house lights dimmed.

A pale light shone on a row of seats onstage in front of red, velvet curtains. After a few moments of awkward silence, the eight members of the Academic Decathlon team walked on. Applause followed as they took their seats, my twin sister Alexandria at the head of the line. A white, pleated dress flattered her frame.

I flinched when a hand landed on my shoulder. I hadn't noticed my dad approach. He patted my arm and smiled, a gesture that had put me at ease as long as I could remember. "Don't be nervous for her," he said. "She's been practicing all week."

His focus returned to the stage, but mine remained on him. Neither Alex nor I resembled him much, aside from his wide smile. He did have a great head of hair, thick and lightly salted, and a beard the envy of lumberjacks worldwide. Needless to say, single moms brought him casseroles at PTA meetings. Our principal waltzed toward a podium in the middle of the stage. My dad whispered: "Ready?"

"To stand behind Alex and hold a trophy? Who even suggested this?"

"Your principal wanted Alex's family involved in the presentation," he said.

The citywide smartass competition compared participating schools' scores in math, science, and the humanities. My sister's team had won the Academic Decathlon a week before. My twin's individual scores were the highest, not only of the Eleanor Roosevelt team, but in Cook County. This made her AcaDec's MVP: the Golden Apple champion.

The principal relinquished the podium to Alex. It didn't take 20/20 vision to see she'd waited a long time for this moment. My sister stepped into the light and reached for the microphone, her dark, pressed hair kissing her shoulders as mine had done only a few hours before. "Good morning," she said, as the device returned a claws-on-chalkboard screech. The audience contorted and groaned, but she kept her cool. "Good morning," she repeated. "My name is Alexandria White."

A whistle sang through the auditorium from a group of boys near the back. My father lurched forward to poke his head through the gap in the curtains. "Is this a school or a damn construction site?" he growled.

"*Dad.*" I tugged him back.

"The *mayor* is here."

I peered around his shoulder as a staffer beelined toward the fuss. "The teachers got this." I tugged again. "Those boys will stop, and Alex won't. Just . . . watch her."

I somehow angled my father back toward his elder (if eleven and a half minutes counts) daughter's speech. The spotlight swallowed Alex, but nothing short of the apocalypse would stop her. Since we'd set foot in Roosevelt, she'd toiled to be AcaDec's first Golden Apple champion in over a decade, the first African-American Golden Apple champion ever.

It was time to hail Caesar.

"Please welcome the mayor of our fine city," Alex said, eyes cast offstage. "Mayor Wendell Price!" Mayor Price emerged from the opposite wing to thunderous applause. He was a rotund man with an effortless smile, the kind of politician you liked no matter his stance on the issues. Alex moved to the side as he took the podium.

"Good morning! And thank you, Alexandria." His baritone sailed over the shower of acclaim. "Don't applaud me. Applaud these young people. This is academic excellence before you."

He turned toward Alex, who beamed back. She'd wanted this award for almost as long as I'd dreaded her winning it—having beefed up her pursuit this year. For my twin, the Academic Decathlon was the sun, blotting out everything and everyone.

"And this young lady . . . It's been twelve long years, but we have a Golden Apple champion." His gaze shifted to Dad and me.

Show time. A teacher waiting backstage brought me Alex's trophy. Where they'd been hiding it, I'll never know. She placed the thing in my arms and backed away with a wide smile. It was more bronzed than golden and too big to hold gracefully, so my father helped me manage its weight. The crowd electrified as we walked onstage carrying the statuette of a golden apple on a funky vase. My dad handed it over to Mayor Price as my gaze met Alex's. Her eyes were as wide as our father's had been.

"This is more than lightning striking," said Mayor Price. My twin's focus jerked back to him. "This is hard work and dedication. Alexandria White is our Golden Apple champion!"

Both the principal and the mayor presented the trophy to my sister. My dad and I clapped as she glanced at us again. Her teammates popped up from their chairs to crowd around her, stealing her attention once more. I wasn't sure if she had just won the Academic Decathlon MVP or the Miss America Pageant.

The coronation took only a sliver of the Monday morning schedule. When the formalities wrapped, reporters and administrators swarmed Alex and my father, giving me the break I needed. The genius society Mensa inducted my sister as their youngest local member before we hit puberty, and there'd been a lot of these functions between then and now. I'd learned to sneak out or sleep with my eyes open at all of them.

I made my way to my locker, stomach in knots. As I unlocked the metal door, I knew the knots had nothing to do with the hair I'd hacked off. They came from the inevitable finally happening: Alex was the Golden Apple champion, and she'd want to keep twinning. She loved matching our clothes and hair, going to the same parties, having the same friends. Twinning was so important that she'd insisted that whichever prestigious school she attended, I'd attend as well.

The title of Golden Apple champion boasted impressive spoils, one being a scholarship to the University of Chicago. She now had the academic muscle to ensure that wherever she got a scholarship, her twin would also. It was a notion I considered sweet until last month, when I started applications for schools in

DC and anywhere else as far away as possible.

"*Poooooorrrrrrtiiiiaaaa.*" My name slithered out of Jaden's mouth like Parseltongue. A junior, like me, he was in a few of my classes and had pleasant enough features. They contorted, however, during his daily creepiness. Jaden's last name was Watson, which usually placed his locker about three down from mine. He used that proximity to his advantage. "Nice cut," he said as I glanced at him. His brows lifted in the way that made me want to shower. "And nice pants."

"Jaden," I said. His eyes traveled the short length of my capris. "They let you out of your cage today?"

"I don't know why you're so mean to me." He tsked as I rummaged for my history notebook. Luckily, it sat on top of a pile of folders in my locker. "If you play your cards right, you can have this body."

I snatched it before slamming my locker door shut. "Wouldn't you rather leave it to science?"

Short bursts of laughter sprang from behind Jaden as I unzipped my book bag, threw the notebook inside, and closed it once more. Jaden grimaced and turned as Jason Jones walked up wearing track pants and his letterman. "You've got a way with women," Jason said, slapping Jaden's shoulders, maybe a little too hard. Jaden shrugged from Jason's reach and stalked off, mumbling under his breath.

I threw my book bag on my shoulders. The laughter died down as Jason leaned against the locker opposite me. "Nicely done, Miss White," he said.

I smiled. "Where are your people?" I asked of the usual throng that surrounded him. "You can't be seen speaking to someone without a fancy jacket."

"Cheese stands alone." He glanced in the direction of Jaden's departure. "I was going to help you out, but you didn't need me."

"It's the thought that counts," I said. For all her success at twinning, Alex and I only shared one class during our time at Roosevelt: seventh-period Cultures and Civilizations (née history). It sentenced two types of students to its drudgery: juniors who needed the requirement and seniors who hadn't deigned to take it as juniors. Jason Jones was the latter.

His gaze traveled to my hair. "You're different today." I touched my locks. "It's nice," he added. "What did you think of the ceremony?"

What did I think of Alex's moment, one that made it painfully obvious we didn't want the same things, that we weren't twinning? "It was nice," I said.

He smoothed his green track pants as my eyes danced over him. The floor-to-ceiling windows amplified stray light bouncing off Jason's bronzed skin. The track team must have started their practices outside again. Curly spirals of hair hinted at his mother's Afro-Cuban roots. "They deserved it," Jason said, with an easy grin. "I'm never going to win a Golden Apple."

"Neither am I. But Alex is your tutor, so there's hope for you." The grin slipped into his signature smile, a megawatt flash of white teeth. My chest tightened. The crush was my indulgence into the utterly ridiculous, spanning exactly thirteen months, seven weeks, two days, and twenty-seven minutes. It marked my discovery of this exception to the human genome studying in my living room. Alex tutored him oblivious to her favor with the universe.

I held his gaze too long, and heat bloomed across my neck. "I saw your dad in there," he continued. "I was going to say hi, but he looked busy with the—"

"Attention," I said.

"Right, the last time I was at your place he asked me about

schools and I was undecided. I wanted to tell him I got accepted to State with an athletic scholarship."

"That's great," I said, even if I didn't wholeheartedly mean it. As a talented athlete at a school known for academics, he'd inevitably attend some institution for free. But the thought of my remaining year at Roosevelt without him was about as enticing as a lobotomy. "I still have to figure out where I'm going."

"Oh, I thought you'd go to U of C," he said, confusion tinging his voice. "That's where Alex is going, right?"

I shrugged. "I guess."

"Twins do different things?" he asked in mock surprise. "What do you have next?" his voice was too rich for anyone not hosting a late-night radio program. "I'll walk you over."

I stifled the blush that barely showed through my brown skin. I gripped my book bag straps. "I'm heading to—" *Dear God, what have I been taking all year?* "French."

"I was heading toward the language lab anyway," he said, mouth twitching up.

The knots in my stomach became a twist in my chest as we began the trek. I didn't understand what had changed. Jason and I never said more than a joke about Alex tutoring him, nor did he ever find a need to defend me from creeps like Jaden. He never walked with me. He never looked at me like *that*. "She's really excited, isn't she?" Jason asked.

I hadn't been listening. "Who?" I replied, having forgotten everyone I'd ever known. "Oh, Alex. Right. She worked hard. We're really proud of her."

"I bet," he said. "Hey, look." He'd already started toward a nearby stairwell where a staffer impatiently secured a poster to the wall. Though ripped at the edges, the colossal advertisement read *A Moment in Time* in orange and blue font, the school colors.

Under the headline, a silhouetted couple danced on a cloud. I'd hate them if I didn't want to be them. "Oh," he said. "Are you going?"

"To senior prom?" I almost choked out. "I'm a junior, in case you forgot."

"I assumed a senior had asked you."

My laugh was edged. "I'm not that cool and even if someone did, it wouldn't be right for me to go without my sister. Twin thing."

"You both have a line of guys waiting to take you."

I slowed my pace. "We didn't plan on going."

"We'll just have to do something about that," he said. Words almost tumbled out of my mouth: *What will we do? WHAT. WILL. WE. DO?*

The bell rang. "Class," I managed.

"I'll see you guys in seventh," he said, before disappearing toward the language lab.

All day I was light, feminine, as if whatever I touched would turn to sighing flowers. The giddiness was mine to command and impossible to contain. I spun it on a spindle. I washed it through my hair. I rolled back and forth on it like a cat on warm laundry. I'd had a very promising walk with Jason, my own lightning strike, one that hinted that he might actually invite me to his prom. "You're smiling," Alex said as I took a seat next to her in history.

"No, I'm not," I lied.

"Yes, you are. Something's up," she said, and focused on me. "Is that why you . . . ?" she pointed to my mane.

Nope, not answering that. "You like it?"

Her expression was steady. "I have to get used to it," she said. "I didn't know you had a hair appointment. We usually go together."

"I didn't know you had a fancy pin," I said, and pointed at the new brooch at the collar of her dress. In addition to the ugly trophy, she had also received a more attractive, apple-shaped pendant that shimmered against the white fabric. Alex also shone.

As fraternal twins, *similar* would be the best way to describe us (making Alex's fixation on sameness kind of masochistic). We did have the family bend to our noses and small chins, but Alex stood an inch taller, and unlike my chestnut eyes, hers were a mosaic of hazel and gold. Without the trademark specs, her shining eyes were striking against her skin.

"Nowhere near the same thing." Her face lit up. "Oh, yeah. Someone from U of C was there." She wiggled her brows at me. "Confirmed both scholarships are in the bag now."

"Nice," I said, my voice pancake flat.

Her smile slipped into scrutiny. "Portia, something's up."

I only shook my head. "You're too smart to be this dumb," I replied.

She rolled her eyes and shuffled papers around on her desk. "Whatever makes you happy," she said as guilt nipped at me.

My twin focused on her notes and papers, unaware that I still watched her. I needed to tell her we weren't going to college together, and although the timing wasn't idea, I needed to do it now. I reached out and tapped her shoulder before I could tell myself not to. A harrowing rush of fear and anxiety welled between my ears.

"Miss White and Miss White." Jason's textured voice grabbed my attention. Alex had also turned at the greeting, and we angled ourselves toward him simultaneously.

Alex spoke first. "Hi, Jason, how are you?" she asked.

He pushed through the rows, sitting a few seats over from us. "I'm good, and congrats! Saw you up there today with the Golden Apple."

Alex nodded in thanks and pointed to her book bag. "Gotta get ready," she said before turning to rifle through it. Her ritual required five minutes to prepare for every class, come hell or high water.

But *I* hadn't turned away yet, and neither had Jason. His eyes on me, he smiled a big, toothy smile. "Portia White," he said, with a wink. Air escaped my mouth, a long sigh from an untied balloon, as he turned to address another classmate on the track team.

"Class!" Our instructor, Mr. Pomey, rose from his desk to write on the chalkboard. We jumped at his voice and waited straight-backed as he finished writing and faced us. Of the younger teachers, only he wore a daily tie accompanied by one of his myriad pairs of suspenders. He tugged at the day's blue bands, his auburn hair shaking as they snapped back to his chest.

"Ye hath entered this temple of learning to thine own risk and peril," he said. Mark Pomey liked outdated language and odd word pairings—anything that no one would say in real life. Always good-natured, he never accepted we weren't paying attention, opting to wax poetic about Byzantium as we vandalized our desks with magic markers.

He picked up a few midsized cardboard boxes that had been sitting on his desk. "I can't hold everything for this presentation." His eyes scanned the audience. "Portia!" he called out, interrupting my less-than-appropriate daydreams of Jason. "You have a new hairdo."

"I do," I replied.

"Am I boring your new hairdo?"

"Never." Another lie.

"Then why don't you come to the front? I need you to hold one of these boxes. It's not heavy," he said as I slowly unfolded from my seat. "Expeditiously! Don't dawdle!" When I met Mr. Pomey by the chalkboard, he said, "My assistant Portia will help us prepare for Friday's excursion." He handed me the smallest of his cardboard boxes. "The museum trip concludes our study of ancient civilizations. Seniors, I'll enter your grades sooner than everyone else's. But if you cut on Friday, I will also cut your grade in half."

A stark groan emitted from the room's graduating contingency. Mr. Pomey laid both of the boxes on his desk again and pulled from the largest a dark case with nicks denting its exterior— some sort of acrylic—from years of use. "What's that?" I asked, casually slipping my box onto the desk as well.

He ignored me and scanned his audience in dramatic suspense. "Believe it or not, before I came to Roosevelt, I studied archaeology. I met my wife, the curator at The Field Museum, on a dig in Israel where we studied trade routes. The artifacts in this box are on loan from the museum for our research." He flung a piece of cloth at me. "Since you put your box down, think fast!"

By some miracle, I caught it. My frown deepened. I held up a flimsy headdress that could have belonged with a Halloween costume. "This didn't come from a dig," I said.

"Okay, it isn't authentic, but what would you call this if it were really from Egypt and not Taiwan?"

"A nemes crown," Alex chimed. My sister's voice was a quick snap through the classroom. Mr. Pomey's eyes found her amongst the students. He shot her a look as she feigned innocence. She always had the answer, but it didn't always stay in her head. "Alex, please."

"I'll raise my hand next time," she said.

He sighed, relenting. "Well, can you tell us more?"

Don't threaten Alex with a good time. "It would be the royal headdress of the Egyptian nobles," she said.

"And who would be Egypt's highest priest and noble?"

"The pharaoh."

"Indeed." Mr. Pomey nodded and turned to address the audience. "Many of the pharaohs ruled Egypt from modern day Luxor, which in ancient times went by the name Thebes or Waset. The nemes crown was the famous striped head cloth worn by the pharaohs. They wore many crowns, but this one you most often see in movies."

"With a snake in the front, right?" Alex asked. "Oh, yeah." She lifted her hand as he sighed.

"Yes. The snake was a fierce cobra called a uraeus. Now, the nemes crown tied at the back of the head, leaving lappets on either side of the face for ceremonial clothing. Okay, Portia, you can put that down." I did as I was told and turned to leave the front of the room. "Wait for a moment," he said, halting me.

"There's more?" I asked.

"Of course," he replied. "Now, cover your eyes and hold out your left hand." I smirked and followed orders as he dropped a cold object on my palm. "Okay, you may look." My eyes drifted to a small, blue ornament fashioned like half of a round beetle, engravings on its shell.

I wrinkled my nose. "It's a bug."

"It's an Egyptian scarab," he corrected me. "Well, part of an Egyptian scarab. It is solid lapis lazuli, a material highly sought for this bright shade of blue. It would be considered a token of good wishes among the aristocracy," he said as I flicked a nail over the inscription. "Be careful with that. I can't get another one at the mall."

I frowned and turned my focus to the tiny figures on its back. "These are hieroglyphs?" I asked of the marks.

"Yes, the ancient writing style," Mr. Pomey said. "We would need an Egyptologist to translate that." He continued with facts about the scarab, turning back to my classmates. My eyes danced between him and the ornament until his words ran together, muffling as if underwater. *Enunciate,* I wanted to tell him—we had that kind of relationship—but my mouth was the driest sand. My heart raced as needling ripples spread across my palm, tiny pinpricks followed by pulsating heat.

My classmates watched Mr. Pomey, oblivious to my discomfort as the scarab's shine amplified to painful brilliance, its blue like gleaming waves crashing overtop each other. And in this blazing sheen the tiny figures on the scarab, the ancient hieroglyphs, became comprehensible script. *To my beloved, the blessings of Amun,* I read, as that uncomfortable heat ignited me from the inside out.

A blurry figure scrambled to meet me at the front of the room, trying to catch my gaze. More than her face, I could see the pendant gleaming against her white dress. Alex squeezed my shoulders, her voice thick and heavy to my ears. "Let me take her outside, Mr. Pomey. She needs air." She deftly removed the scarab from my hand and placed it in the artifact box.

"Yes, of course. Someone get Portia a tissue," he said to my classmates. *A tissue?* My tongue touched my lips, and the metallic kick of blood danced in my mouth. I locked on my twin's sparkling eyes as someone extended a Kleenex.

"Here," Alex said, pressing it to my nostrils. She ushered me toward the exit, but a wave of nausea and dizziness slammed me first. Heavy, frenetic pressure knocked me off balance, and neither of us could carry all of my weight. I sensed my body falling fast to the ground.

But before I did, I was in the air. He'd caught me and hoisted me up like a princess bride (or pirate wench) as his clean scent filled my nose. I clung nearer to him than I'd been in thirteen months, seven weeks, and whatever assortment of days. It didn't matter that Jason was rushing me to the nurse's station.

ALEX'S DAY

"You don't have to do that," I said. Alex rolled her eyes before putting a makeshift fan down. She'd been treating me like a wounded soldier in a war movie since we got to the nurse's station, and my roiling gut and achy limbs couldn't distract me from the onslaught of her neuroses. "What?" I asked, adjusting the tissue lodged in my left nostril. My sister stared as if I was wearing a Portia mask.

"How do you feel?" she asked. I frowned, knowing that she didn't want to ask how I felt. She wanted the *who, what, where, when,* and *why* of everything she'd just seen. She usually fussed when my dad or I got sick, but today was entirely different.

"I'm fine," I said.

She narrowed her eyes. "Your temperature's a hundred degrees. You're not fine."

"I'm *better,* then."

She grunted before asking, "Do you want to go home early? The nurses will okay it."

I shook my head. "No, I'll wait through your last class. If this happens again, I'd rather not be home alone." She nodded, adjusting the compress on my forehead. I placed my hand over hers. "Really. You don't have to do that. I'll be okay."

She slipped her hand from beneath mine. "I don't get it," she said, thoughts spilling over. "The nurses think you had a panic attack, but that doesn't explain the nosebleed or the fever." Nothing bothered Alex more than the rare occurrence of not understanding something. "What happened back there?"

"I don't know. I remember getting to the nurse and bits and pieces before that."

"You couldn't hear yourself when Pomey gave you the scarab? Well, you definitely slurred," she chuckled, before seriousness set in. "But you read it."

"Read it? I was too busy dying, thanks."

"No," she pressed. "Pomey put that thing in your hand and you looked at it." She stood as if recalling an academic text. "He kept talking about the scarab and Friday's trip. But then he stopped because"—she peered at me through long lashes,— "you were making noises. Your back was too straight and your eyes traveled back and forth over the hieroglyphs on the scarab. You murmured in some language. I'm not sure what it was."

The scarab's gleaming light, blue like waves under a summer sky, flooded my memory. I dropped my gaze. Digging the pieces from my memory intensified my headache. "I don't know."

"Poor Jason had to find another shirt. He wasn't safe from your nose bleed."

That part I *did* remember. Jason scooped me up as my legs gave out, carrying me to the nurse's station. "Of course he wasn't," I replied.

"He was a good sport about it," she said. "He even stayed a few minutes while the nurses checked you."

I laid my head back on my pillow with a deep, contented smile. "Good to know."

I exited Roosevelt to bright sunlight. My ailing body welcomed its rays as I crossed the parking lot. Anything was better than the sterile nurse's station. I usually met Alex by our car after school, a blue Honda Civic named Cecile. We alternated driving days, and today my twin had the keys.

"Cecile, my love," I said, leaning against the driver's side door. "I'm ready to get out of here." But Alex was nowhere to be seen. Though I'd hightailed it out of the nurse's station, she probably thought I'd remained, waiting for her to fuss some more. I grabbed my cell and sent her a quick text—*By Cecile*—before sitting on the curb nearest the car.

The frantic scuff of sneakers on pavement reached my ears, coming from the west end of the parking lot. Despite the west end's proximity to public transportation, no one with a sense of self-preservation ventured to it. Sasha and Smith Graham, sister bullies better known as the Grizzlies, guarded it like the bridge in "Three Billy Goats Gruff." Only a freshman would be stupid enough to wander over there.

Though I normally would have stayed put, I'd already unfolded from my seat and moved. Smith's sneer cut through the air as I approached the west end. "This would go a lot faster if you just handed over the phone." I shook my head. As I figured, a dumb girl with a freshman ID tag clipped to her shirt had strayed, and Smith and her sister batted her around like maniacal kittens with a ball of yarn. Their father was a former NFL defensive lineman, and with a noted community businesswoman as their mother, the pair could have easily been the most well-liked girls at Roosevelt. Instead they slummed it as parking lot bullies, stealing phones for the fa-la-las. "I told you," said the freshman, clutching her book bag. "I don't have a phone." Smith, the larger of the two, shoved the girl against a parked car. Sturdily built at five foot eleven and six foot one, the running joke was that the Grizzlies could have been birthed by their father alone. The freshman, by contrast, was a scrawny collection of brown curls, knees, and elbows. She wore jeans and a blue T-shirt, ill-fitting hand-me-downs faded through generations of wash cycles.

A yank to my arm diverted my bout of self-righteousness. "The hell are you doing?" Alex's eyes bored into mine. "Those are the Grizzlies!" Her chest rose and fell violently, causing her Golden Apple pendant to gleam as if sending some sort of code. I diverted my eyes and pointed at the freshman. "What?" She snapped her gaze to the altercation before returning them to me.

"You're saying this is okay?" I asked.

"I'm saying I like my teeth," she said. She tugged at my arm, dragging me back toward the car. "She'll learn not to walk over here until the Grizzlies graduate."

I shrugged out of her grasp. "Just give me a second," I said.

"*Portia*," Alex growled, and I turned on my heel and approached the scene again. My measured advance went unnoticed until I was officially an intruder. Smith and Sasha exchanged amused glances at my interruption before Sasha grabbed the freshman and flung her to the ground.

Smith spoke first. "What do you want?" she asked as her high ponytail bobbed. Her voice grated against my eardrums. She always sounded like she was cursing, no matter what came out. "I have room in my bag for your phone, too," she warned, folding her arms.

Before I could speak, Alex slipped her arm around my waist and tugged me again. "Don't mind her. She's not feeling well today," my sister said. She pulled as hard as she could, but despite being slightly bigger than me, I had determination on my side.

"Relax," I said to my sister.

She searched my eyes, mouth almost agape. Portia didn't jump into people's fights, especially losing battles. My twin blinked fast, but her grip loosened. "If that's what you want," Alex said, and moved aside.

I strode past the Grizzlies to the battered freshman, my sickness second fiddle to a strange bout of excitement. Adrenaline shot through me as I extended a hand to the girl. She stared with wide-eyed fascination. "You okay?" I asked, pulling her up.

Blood from a nasty scrape on her knee stained her jeans. I began to ask about it, but a tug on the collar of my shirt, a jerk only Smith could do with such strength, distracted me. I dangled in her grasp. My sister rushed in, but Sasha blocked her with impressive speed. She grabbed my twin's shoulder and yanked her back. "I guess she's a hero," Sasha snorted, digging her fingers into Alex's shoulder. My twin yelped in response.

Smith twisted a knot of my shirt, tightening its hold around my neck. "I always like heroes," she said. "Don't you?"

"Yeah, especially breaking their noses," chimed Sasha. Though I'd stood on the sidelines of schoolyard fights, I'd never been the main event. But Sasha had grabbed my sister, and both Grizzlies were picking on a freshman who couldn't defend herself. Instead of fear, white-hot electricity sang through me, spiking to dangerous levels at Smith's touch.

Turn, my instincts said, so I clasped Smith's hands and whipped around to face her. Smith gaped at my speed, and I relished the surprise and confusion etched on her face. My limbs were the instrument of my instincts, synched to muscle memory I couldn't recall earning. "Break my nose," I told her.

Smith's grip loosened. "Wait, what?"

"Break my nose, Smith." A surprised chuckle escaped my throat. Her gaze flicked to Sasha, whose pointed look encouraged her to get on with it. I used the moment to slip out of her grasp. Didn't matter. Smith nodded at her sister and swung toward my face but my urge to evade was lightning-sharp. She howled in frustration and barreled forward like a bear: claw, scratch, protect pic-a-nic basket. Dodging her again wasn't taxing.

Sasha's arm tightened around my neck before I remembered she was there. She had let go of my sister in order to help her own. "I'm going to kill you!" she said with the desperate strength and shrill of her sister, the elder Grizzly.

Smith now blocked Alex as I spoke to her sister with as calm a voice as I could muster given the grip on my throat. "Let me go, Sasha," I said. She responded by squeezing tighter, so I dug my heel into her foot. She shrieked, reaching down as I turned and shoved her. She bounced off a nearby car, yelping as her skin scraped against the pavement.

"Enough!" Smith shouted. I turned to her. She'd left the guard of Alex and stood near enough to strike me. But instead of trying, she dragged her feet in trepidation. "Relax," she whispered, not wanting anyone to hear the surrender. I evaluated myself, still in a defensive stance. "Just leave Sasha alone."

I pointed toward the freshman. "Will you leave *her* alone?" I asked. Smith nodded once. I withdrew, and Smith scooped a whimpering Sasha from the ground. Over my shoulder, Alex stood where the Grizzlies had left her. Her dress had a few wrinkles at the shoulder, but her face was emotionless. I approached her and pointed to Cecile. "We should go," I said.

She said nothing, turning toward the car as I followed in silence.

The excitement and electricity dulled as we made our way to Cecile, and sickness settled anew with each step. *Just make it to the car*, I thought. "Hey, wait!" someone called out to us. I kept walking, but Alex stopped. I turned to see the freshman trailed us, Miss Knees and Elbows.

I'd seen her clothes during the fight but hadn't noticed much else. The freshman approaching was smaller than me by a few inches (maybe standing 5'1" or 5'2"). But it was her skin that now held my attention. I thought I knew every shade of brown, but this girl's skin was the deepest ebony I'd ever seen, clear and perfect as a starless night. Despite her skin's beauty, I was positive she'd gotten plenty of shit about it.

"Hi," she said when she reached us. Her eyes and tumbling curls were as dark as her skin. She was a perfect onyx doll. Worry colored her expression when she caught a good glimpse of me. "You look sick," she said before I could compliment her.

I pursed my lips. "I'm not."

"You're sweating a lot."

"It's May. It's hot." I shook my head. "Who are you? Why were you over there anyway?"

"I missed the 132 bus, so I was catching the 126." I nodded, needing no further details. Both the 132 and 126 ran through the Randos, a public housing complex about thirty minutes from school. Formally known as the A. Philip Randolph Homes, the city tore down most of the Randos' original buildings to make room for condo construction pushing south. My dad had some clients there, and Alex and I sometimes tagged along. Of all the Chicago neighborhoods, it wasn't one you waltzed into or out of willingly. "I forgot about the Grizzlies," she added. "I'm Selene Samson."

"Try to remember them next time, Selene."

"Looks like they should remember you." Despite my delirium, my mouth tugged upward. "Why did you help me?" she asked.

I shifted under the gaze, growing sicker by the moment. "Because it wasn't fair," I replied.

"She's Portia and I'm Alex," my sister said, by way of an introduction. "And you're right, she is sick." She placed her hands on my shoulders. "I need to get her home." She opened the passenger door and started ushering me in.

"Okay," Selene said as I climbed into the car. She backed up as Alex closed the door behind me and walked around to the driver's side, in more of a hurry to get home than usual. I checked the rearview mirror as we pulled away. Selene remained, watching me.

Dad was late. He normally got home around seven o'clock or so, but it was nearly eight. He had a small, private law practice in the South Loop, handling wills and divorces mainly, and I wouldn't have minded his tardiness if Alex wasn't ignoring me. We drove twenty minutes in absolute silence after my tangle with the Grizzlies, and she parked me on the couch the moment she could. There'd be no fussing. She only checked in every now and then to ensure I hadn't keeled over.

The alarm beeped three times, as it always did when the front or side door opened. He was back. Alex sped down the stairs toward the kitchen entrance before I could hobble off the couch. She was a flash of white, still in her dress from the ceremony. "There she is," Dad said as Alex flung her arms around his neck. I shuffled in behind her. My twin had taken the contacts out, and her frames made her look like herself again. "The Golden Apple champion!"

"There've been a lot of calls since we got home," she said.

"I bet you'll be in the *Times*," he said before angling his head. "What's that?" he asked, pointing toward her shoulder. Her ceremony dress didn't cover enough of her shoulder to hide the bruise Sasha had gifted her.

Alex angled away from him and stammered through an explanation, one I interrupted. "I got in a fight," I said.

Richard turned and nearly gasped as he took me in. It wasn't for the hair this time. The dizziness and nausea had died down, but I must not have *looked* any better. "What's wrong?" he asked.

"She got sick in class today," said Alex.

"So Portia got sick and in a fight, but Alex got beat up?" he asked us.

"But no one's pregnant," I added.

"*Portia*." He massaged his brow. "Neither of you thought to call me?"

My twin said nothing. Instead she stared over her frames, peering straight at me for the first time since we'd gotten home. *Cutting your hair. Fainting in class. Fighting the Grizzlies. Tell me what's going on,* her eyes begged.

The house phone rang. Alex shook her head, ending the stare down. "I'll get it." My twin disappeared from the kitchen.

"I didn't say you could go," Richard yelled after her, but it was too late. He sighed and returned to me. "You're not usually one for fights."

"Today was different, I guess."

"Did the administrators see?" I shook my head. He nodded. "All right, let's get you to the couch. You look . . . bad."

"Just what a girl wants to hear," I said.

He got a good grip on my shoulders and led me back to the sofa. "You want something? Soup? Tea?"

"No, I doubt it would help much," I said.

He nodded but, before taking a seat, announced, "Oh no, someone knocked it over." My brows creased as he scooped up a statuette—a small woman of solid ivory—on its side by the entryway. Paintings, figurines, and sculptures from the corners of the globe filled the room, pieces he'd collected in his days before children, or gifts from friends who knew his tastes.

"I'm sorry. It was probably me. I was all over the place when we got home. Did I break it?"

He picked it up. "No, it's tough. It's been over there since we bought the house. I doubt anyone could actually break it." He came to my side holding the piece, inspecting the craftsmanship.

"You like that one?" I asked.

"One of my favorites." The statue's white arms cradled a nursing baby. She smiled down at the infant with exaggerated features. "It was a gift from Mrs. Evers. I should remember where it's from," he said with a regretful sigh. "It hasn't been that long since you've seen her."

An elderly woman came to mind, though I'd only met her on a handful of occasions. Mrs. Evers was a shapely woman with reddish-brown skin like cinnamon and eyes that never quite settled on one thing or person. Like Selene, she also lived in the Randos, but it was the old woman's restlessness that always freaked me out, despite her generosity with the peppermints in her purse.

"She bought that for you?" I asked, suddenly wondering how she afforded something so precious and valuable. Rich only nodded, so I didn't press. Instead I said, "She was sick the last time you mentioned her."

"Yeah, she's not doing too well," he said to my apologetic eyes. "Diabetes. But she gave this to me around the time your mother—" A tremor of pain shot through his eyes. *Passed,* he couldn't say. Instead of continuing, he shook his head—his way of redirecting the conversation. He placed the statue down. "So why did you get in a fight?"

"The Grizzlies were picking on a freshman. Two on one. It sucks."

"So you and Alex jumped in?"

"*I* jumped in," I said with a laugh. "Alex was trying to get me out." I nudged him. "Are you mad?"

"Depends. Did you win the fight?"

I grinned. "Yep."

"Alright, just don't make a habit of this." He placed the statuette on the floor. He seemed like he had something to say. "I admire how you've handled your sister's attention. It was a big day for the family, a big day for her."

"So?"

"So," he mocked me. "You have big days coming up, too."

That's why my sister had to get me a scholarship. That's why I'm always Alex White's twin sister.. "I'm not good at anything," I mumbled.

"Of course you are. There just aren't trophies for everything you're good at, like ass kicking apparently." He thought about it a moment. "Unless you want to do MMA."

I couldn't help but laugh. "*Dad.*"

He took a moment before speaking again, thoughtfully running a hand over his beard. "It's been weird between you and Alex for a while, especially since Alex really threw herself into the Golden Apple stuff this year," he said. "Or maybe it's typical for girls at this age. I just feel like you two don't see it."

"See what?"

He searched my face. "You're both bright, resourceful girls. What terrifies her—things like jumping headfirst into something new, something unexpected, lights you up." He nodded toward my hair. "Where you doubt how talented and clever you are, she's always stepped into her gifts. You complement each other."

I shifted from the full heat of his gaze. "Dad, spare me," I said.

He nodded and eased back. "You're the only sisters you've got." He stood as Alex yelled after him from another room. "I've been beckoned. Let me know if you need something." I nodded as he left.

I maintained my vegetative state on the couch all evening, breaking it only to consume saltine crackers and Sprite. My sister's phone calls continued well into the night, long after my father decided to turn in. He'd left it up to me if I felt well enough to go to school the next day as the clock turned to 9:45. I decided against it and flipped channels from my pillow fort.

The doorbell rang, but there was no stir in the house. "Door!" I yelled to whoever would answer. It rang again. No responses. I rolled my eyes and begrudgingly left my fort. My hands gripped the walls and steadied my walk down the narrow entryway. I made it to the door a few moments later than I should and peered through the keyhole.

I snapped the air into my chest and swung the door open. *You're. Kidding. Me.* Jason Jones stood before me like a desert mirage. He wore his letterman again, but jeans instead of track pants this time. He scrubbed his face. "Hey, Portia," he said. "Sorry it's so late."

I feigned bravado, leaning against the wall as if it wasn't the only thing keeping me upright. "It's okay. What's going on?" I asked, though enough thoughts flooded to drown him out. I was right. He wanted to take me to his prom. He wanted to bend down on one knee, vow his love, and cue a mariachi band.

"How are you feeling?" His eyes traveled the length of my body, and I shifted under the scrutiny. "You look a little better."

"I'm a lot better. Thanks," I said with a smile.

He returned it. "Right. So you're probably wondering why I'm here." My smile turned greedy, expectant. He swung his book bag around and dug in it, soon producing a notebook. "You left this when you were sick in Pomey's. I figured you'd want it back."

"Thank you," I said as he handed it to me. "And thank you for taking me to the nurse. I heard I ruined your shirt."

"I have a lot of shirts," he said quickly. My cheeks flushed as glee warmed my limbs. "I wanted to make sure you had this for the trip on Friday, if you were still going." I tilted my head, trying to read the stall in his voice.

"Jason?" she called out. I looked over my shoulder; my twin stood in the hallway. She'd changed out of the wrinkled white sundress into leggings and a pink tank. I rolled my eyes. *Oh, now she can talk.*

"Your sister left her notebook in Pomey's today."

"That was very sweet of you." She approached us. "We didn't have time to get our affairs in order. I was going to make sure she had everything tomorrow."

"It was no problem really." He smiled. I smiled. We all smiled. "So I have to admit something," Jason announced.

Finally.

"What?" I asked.

"I didn't just come by to bring your notebook, Portia. I was actually thinking about our conversation earlier." Alex's gaze drifted toward me, part of her signature *you-withheld information* face. "Portia said you two weren't going to prom,"

Jason continued. "You guys can't stay home for prom."

"Why not?" she asked

Between the sickness and anticipating his invitation, something in my brain shut off. Words tumbled out of my mouth. "Because *we're* going," I said to Jason. "After we spoke this morning," I added quickly, "I kind of figured you wanted to go with me."

Jason's eyes snapped to Alex's before peeling themselves to mine. "Oh shit, Portia—"

"Don't you want to go?" I asked

"Yeah, but . . ." he trailed off, his embarrassment quick, obvious, and for me, unbearable. "I asked my friend Brandon— Brandon Ellis—if he was taking anyone. He said he'd like to take you."

Maybe it was the ringing in my head. Maybe the heaviness in my chest cut off the oxygen supply to my brain. For whatever reason, my ears had deceived me. "What? Who?" I sputtered like a rusty tailpipe. "Why?"

"Brandon's a good guy," Jason said. "He was going alone, and he said he's liked you for a while now anyway." His voice dropped an octave. "I thought the four of us could all go together."

And then I understood.

"You like *Alex*?"

He turned to my twin for help, but she was as dumbstruck as he. Jason angled toward me. "I'm sorry, Portia." There was no light or sound. There was only time standing still, thick and heavy, blotting out my adolescence.

Alex patted Jason on the shoulder, the dismissal the flustered boy craved. "See you tomorrow," she cut in, putting us out of our misery. With an apologetic nod, he couldn't retreat fast enough and neither could I.

The door hadn't closed when I hit the landing step. "Portia, wait," Alex called after me. I turned to glare at her, hands on my hips like a petulant child. "He was only trying to help us."

"Help *us*?" I turned to glare at her. "You failed to mention that Jason Jones loves you."

A beat passed before Alex spoke again. "I kind of thought you knew, since he was over here all the time for tutoring."

"I obviously didn't know."

"Yeah," she said. She picked at lint on her leggings that wasn't there. "Anyway, we just decided to be friends. I couldn't have a boyfriend with all the decathlon work this year." *Jason Jones isn't a boyfriend. Jason Jones should be displayed in art galleries under track lighting.*

"Oh yeah, we wouldn't want anything to get between you and your precious Golden Apple." She dropped her gaze at the cheap shot, but I was too humiliated to apologize.

She sighed and rubbed her head, trying to think her way out of the embarrassing situation at hand.

"If I knew you liked him—"

"I don't like him!" Skeptical-twin face replaced her embarrassment. I hated that face.

"Okay, okay." She paused. "Do you need anything?" she asked, as my feet grew antsy. I shook my head. "Well, before you lie down, I want you to know I'm really sorry if that hurt your feelings."

If?

She was brilliant, nice, even beautiful with those eyes of hers. Not hard to see why Jason would like my twin. She'd be the belle of the ball at Jason's prom, another Alex day. It was always Alex's day.

"Actually," I said, "I want you to know you can keep that scholarship."

She narrowed her gaze. "What are you talking about?"

"The scholarship to U of C," I said. "My applications are already in. I'm going to school on the east coast." She stood like a statue, blood draining from her face. I whipped around towards my room. "Without you."

SUDDEN DEATH

I *shouldn't have said that,* I thought a while later. *Shouldn't have said what? The truth?* I shook my head. I should have said it. Just, not like that.

I turned on my side, drowning in guilt, self-pity, and whatever strain of Ebola I'd contracted. I tossed and turned in bed and could have just kicked myself for being an idiot. I'd missed the outcome of a very basic equation: Alex and Jason were attractive people spending a lot of time together. Of course they *liked* each other. I rolled onto my back and blinked away the image of them sharing the last noodle of a spaghetti dinner.

A thick shower persisted outside my cracked window, moving a breeze across my sticky skin. My room still glittered, despite the evening's dimness. We lived in a multi-unit off Lake Shore Drive near Hyde Park, where the lights twinkled despite the rain, and cars raced by into the wee hours of night.

"Hi, Mom," I whispered. I hoped the greeting would find its way through time and space to her. I hoped all the greetings I had whispered over the years did. Alex and I had photos and fuzzy memories of our mother, Sandra, but as we entered our teens, those pieces were less satisfying. A rare autoimmune disease took our mother when Alex and I were six years old. In my memory she's always bedridden, but smiling, with a big laugh that filled up a room.

I imagined that on a night like this I would have sought my mother's advice. If she had lived longer, this would be expected of mothers and daughters. She probably would have stroked my hair and listened to me sob. She would have told me it would work itself out. She would have said she loved me, and so would someone else.

The latch on my door clicked. I rolled my eyes and turned toward my window. "Leave me alone, Alex," I said, with my back to her. "Get out." My sister didn't respond. I prepared a full arsenal of expletives to clarify my point. But I'd be the only one to hear them. When I glanced at her, the door was ajar. And no one stood in the entryway.

"Hello?" I asked as my desk lamp began to flicker and died.

The evening dimness blackened still. My heart rate sped as I could no longer see my hand, let alone the streetlamps' glow. I called out again, feeling as if I was lost in the darkest cave when vivid light pierced the nothing. The beams shone onto the bedroom walls, taking the shapes and lines of exotic animals.

Elephants roamed grassland flaring their trunks. Prey dangled in the teeth of a tree-climbing leopard. A crane's long beak snapped a snake in two and devoured the pieces. Water flowed through the grasses beneath them, and the sun hovered above like an angry ball of fire. The fireball swelled as the waters steadily rose, threatening to drown or burn them to ashes.

It vanished, and the room was black again. As I clutched my stomach, racking my brain to figure out if I'd ever hallucinated before, the blazing light shone again in the form of curious, little eyes before me. A thin cat slinked into sight, its coat of undulating gray and silver, and settled on the edge of my bed. Its eyes were an incredible green, more brilliant than the jeweled collar at its neck and the bronze ring in its ear. A purr hummed in its throat. "We're dog people," I whispered. "How did you get in here?"

Though my heart still raced, I extended my hand. It inclined its head toward my fingers as every light in the room flicked on. My heart slammed in my chest. Where my feline companion had been was nothing but my apparent lunacy. I glanced around my bedroom before turning back to the window and laying down, the evening breeze soothing my thudding heart.

"I know you don't feel great, but you can't wear those in the museum." Mr. Pomey told me this nicely enough, so I took my sunglasses off. "Thank you," he said. "You know missing the trip wouldn't have affected your grade, Portia. I'm not so inhuman as to disregard illness."

"I wanted to come," I said with a half smile.

Mr. Pomey patted my shoulder, his ginger hair ruffling in the wind. "Well, all right," he said, and returned to ushering the students. "This way in." He strode toward the museum entrance wearing a T-shirt and jeans instead of his trademark suspenders. I smiled at his youthful jaunt. If I didn't know him, I'd mistake him for a student.

Contrary to Mr. Pomey, my walk could mark me as a senior citizen. And I'd never felt as old as I did counting the steep rows of stairs to enter The Field Museum. The worst of my sickness had passed, but bouts of achiness remained. I peered at the landscaping. A reservoir snaked around the back of the museum with tall blades of marshy grass, speckled rocks, and mud on either side. It was pretty, though obviously man-made, fitting with the whole ancient-world-in-the-modern society-motif. For a moment I wondered if I could hang out there for the duration of the trip before I turned back to the stairs. This climb wouldn't help me feel better. *I wanted to get off the couch*, I reminded myself. *I can do this. One stair, two stairs, three stairs.*

"Grab the railing, Portia," a sophomore girl called to me. I turned and nodded quickly. *Thanks, Person I've Never Talked To.* It wasn't the first time a relative stranger had spoken to me since I'd returned that morning to Roosevelt in infamy. After asking about my well-being, everyone wanted the graphic details of my sickness. The combination—fainting spells and speaking in tongues—scared my peers to fascination, but I had no answers for their barrage of questions.

I made it up two rows before his crisp scent gave him away. *Dammit.* "Do you need help?" Jason asked, materializing from almost nothing. It was our first exchange since Monday. We had caught eyes when I arrived at the buses for the trip, but his expression immediately turned apologetic. If anything was worse than losing Jason, it was receiving his sympathy. I shook my head. *Just let me go down with the ship.*

I entered the museum without an escort. Mr. Pomey hopped up on the lobby benches of the vestibule, followed by a pale-skinned woman with raven hair and a taller girl who couldn't be much older than Alex or me. "Everyone, please come this way to hear our curator!" We trudged forward for instructions. The dark-haired woman gave Mr. Pomey a small smile. "Remember, be nice to my wife," he added.

She turned to address us. "Good morning, everyone!" she began. Her hair was tied in a single twist that swung across her back like a pendulum. "My name is Mia. I'm the executive curator here as well as Mark's *much* better half," she teased.

Whistles. Mr. Pomey shook his fist at the students as Mia continued. "To my side here is Cassie, one of our interns for the upcoming summer. She started this morning, so I'm happy to see her jumping into the swing of things." Cassie, whose hair was almost as red as Mr. Pomey's, waved shyly. "Now, a show of hands of those who'd rather be anywhere but a museum today?"

Bold hands shot up as the crowd hummed with chatter. My hands weren't amongst them. Mine were folded across my rib cage. Alex was nearby, and Jason as well.

Now more attuned to their body language and nuanced flirting, I could see how I missed it before, how I thought they were only friends. They were incredibly discreet. Discretion wasn't much of Jason's forte, so I assumed the tactic to be Alex's idea. This year's attempt at the Golden Apple in particular had strained our relationship, and I wondered what else she had kept from me over the last months.

But I couldn't undo what I'd learned about them, and to keep from throwing up in my mouth, I stayed close to the front. "I figured," Mia continued. "Despite that, I still want to thank you for coming to our little outing. I know Mark threatened your grades. I promise to make this as painless as possible, and maybe it'll be a little fun, too, as you're already learning about ancient cultures.

"That being said, consider yourselves archeologists for the day. My staff has hidden candy treasures around the museum for a scavenger hunt. We'll give you lists, and whoever finds ten pieces first wins the grand prize. And I'm telling you, the prize is awesome."

Mia wagged her finger. "But you have to bring all of your items back intact within an hour." She held up the papers and pencils. "Now, please, break into groups of three." *Threes?* I groaned as I grabbed supplies. It wouldn't be a day of unbothered wandering after all.

"Partner?" Alex asked as she approached me.

I peered at my sister as if she had three eyes. "Where's Jason?"

"Don't be like that," said Alex.

"Fine," I grunted. "Partners." We started toward the exhibits in the silence I hoped would last the day. But Alex drew a long breath, preparing to say something she'd practiced.

"We're not going to prom," she said.

Hello, elephant in the room. "I don't care what you two do."

Cue skeptical-twin face. "Then why have you been avoiding me all week?" she asked.

"You avoided me after the Grizzlies," I countered. "Besides, I'm sick. I didn't want you to catch it."

"I just didn't, and still don't, get what happened with the Grizzlies. And you didn't want me to catch it? You're a terrible liar, Portia," she said as her mouth thinned. "And you especially can't lie to me." She shook her head. "We're not going, and I wanted you to know that."

My relief was less satisfactory than expected. Alex's shoulders didn't slump, but her taut face only highlighted her exhaustion. She'd sacrificed a lot to become the Golden Apple champion since we'd started at Roosevelt as freshmen. My twin had hauled herself away to her room on Friday nights to study, burning bulb after bulb out of her desk lamp. A focus that never wavered meant no homecomings, no movies, and no bowling with friends.

I couldn't be the reason she gave up another weekend. "Look," I said to my shoes. "You should still go."

She stopped midstride, eyes snapping to the side of my head. "I should?"

"Yeah, you should," I said. I nudged her to keep walking. Alex's teeth were on the larger side, and she exposed both rows in a smile. "I'll just deal with it."

"So does that mean you're going to take the U of C scholarship, too?"

"Oh," I paused. "No, I still want to go to DC."

Her sudden brightness dimmed. "I see," she said as Mr. Pomey called out to us.

"Alex, Portia, is there anyone else in your group?" he interrupted as we neared our first exhibit. I was grateful he'd distracted us from our conversation topic, but two in our group was plenty. Alex and I searched each other for the perfect lie, but Pomey was too fast. "Great." He turned toward the benches and waved someone on. "Young lady! Please, this way."

I'd forgotten some of the freshman history classes were on the trip until Miss Knees and Elbows, Selene Samson, approached. "You can join Alexandria," Mr. Pomey said. He pointed to my sister. "And that's Portia." Selene nodded to us. She was less tattered this time, torn jeans replaced with a yellow sundress and sandals. The dress was too big on her waist, though. Another hand-me-down.

"I like your haircut, Portia," Selene said to me. "I meant to say that the other day."

My Monday feelings—confusion, ache, odd power—intensified at the sight of the freshman. The way she watched as we pulled away in the parking lot cemented her as a piece of the puzzle I hadn't yet placed. I wasn't happy to be reminded of my crappy Monday with her presence. "Thanks," I said sourly and walked towards the exhibits without either companion.

Alex was aghast. "Hi, Selene," my twin said, some paces back. "Don't mind her. She's not herself this week."

We had an hour, so I channeled my sour mood into the hunt. I wanted to claim the prize—whatever that may be—and my single-minded focus soon afforded us a steady lead. Mia and the museum employees had passed out baskets to the teams of students, each big enough to hold the candies at each exhibit. Lists of the participating exhibits lay at the bottom of the containers with mini pencils to scratch off names.

Alex spent most of her time behind me, chatting with Selene about school and the weather. The three of us perfected our system of staying out of each other's way. That changed, however, as we passed a Mesopotamia exhibit en route to our last hunt location. Mesopotamia was less a storefront exhibit as it was a narrow, roped-off hallway lined with priceless artifacts.

Selene abruptly stopped and placed her basket on the floor. Alex and I did so as well, watching her yellow dress disappear down the hallway. "That's Mesopotamia," Alex called after her. She scooped up Selene's basket. "We're looking for Turkey."

"Just a second," Selene yelled back. I glanced around. *Where were the security guards?*

I rolled my eyes. "We can look at the exhibit after we get the prize," I called out. But she was too far out of range, or she just ignored me. "I'm going to Turkey," I said to Alex.

"Come on. Let's bring her back." Alex patted my shoulder. "I don't think she has many friends."

"I am not following her."

"Then follow me," she replied. "Unless it's to U of C."

I cursed under my breath as she walked away, and I followed. "It's not the same thing," I said when I caught up to my sister.

She shrugged. "Not really, but kind of." Her eyes traveled ahead. "What's she doing?"

When I turned toward the freshman, she was paces away from us, busily unhooking the rope to the Mesopotamia exhibit. The hallway was dimly lit, with the exception of the track lighting displaying the artifacts. "Hell if I know," I said.

Alex walked toward her. "Selene, what are you doing?"

The freshman, now wandering down the forbidden hallway, turned slightly toward my sister. "Looking for something," she said.

"What are you looking for?" Alex asked.

"I'll tell you when I find it," she said. I sighed at Selene's non-answer, and Alex frowned at me. She then tried a different approach with Miss Knees and Elbows. "So . . . um . . . you transferred?" she asked as Selene peered in, through, and around the cases.

"You knew that already," said the freshman. She touched the case of a small alabaster comb.

Alex arched a brow. "I figured," she continued, focusing on the freshman again. "No one goes by the Grizzlies who knows better."

Selene's eyes raked the glass case of each artifact. She then darted her head to the side as if she was expecting something to be waiting there for her. She did this a few times, an odd dance to witness. "I transferred in January. Still learning the rules," she said. "Everyone says you're really smart, Alex."

The width of my sister's eyes meant this was outside of their established polite conversation. "I'm no smarter than anyone else," Alex flustered. Though it was no secret, Alex was never comfortable acknowledging her academic prowess. She was the most gifted student at Roosevelt, but it was rarely discussed over the lunch table. It was just a part of her: *Alexandria White, junior, smarter than you.*

"Yeah, right," said Selene, and I snorted. It was probably my first good chuckle in three days. The girl could see through Alex's bullshit, and I had to give her credit for that.

My sister shot me a nasty look and checked the time on her phone. "If you're looking for something, we can ask the curator for a list of the items in the exhibits," she said. "But let's head back. We can probably still get one of the prizes."

This wasn't a motivator for Selene. "I can meet you two there," she said dismissively. I laughed outright this time, albeit a darker one. As annoyed as we were, she was equally bothered with us.

"Fine by me," I said.

I turned, but Alex grabbed my arm. "What are we going to tell Pomey?" she whispered at me.

"It's a museum, not an alley," I replied.

She huffed before approaching Selene again. "Was there something online you saw? I promise you Mia knows where it is."

"Everything in here must be thousands of years old," she said, by way of an answer.

I sucked my teeth. "Just tell us so we can get out of here."

She stopped scanning to focus on me. "I'm looking for your scarab, Portia." It took a moment for her words to process, but when they did, my back went ramrod straight. Selene's mouth twitched up as she continued, "I heard about what happened Monday before you came to the parking lot. I heard you got sick, that you had to be carried out of class." *Why didn't I let the Grizzlies demolish her?* "And that you can read the scarab I'm looking for."

"She didn't read anything," Alex's voice cut in. "Don't be ridiculous." I glanced at my sister, who only days before also believed that I read the scarab. She wasn't going to admit that to Selene, however.

I turned back to the freshman, wanting to say something caustic, but I couldn't speak. Worse yet, her gaze was as it had been in the parking lot, as if she could see right through me. "Come on, guys." My sister's voice was firm. "I can hear the other teams. Let's go."

Selene stuck out her hand for her basket, and Alex slowly gave it back to her. The freshman began toward the last exhibit as if she hadn't just continued the week's pattern of weirdness. We watched Selene go, and I clutched my basket until a side caved in.

Once back with the other students, it wasn't long before Mr. Pomey flagged my sister down. Her distracted gaze indicated that she still thought about Selene, but neither of us wanted to say much more about her. She turned to me, eyes indicating Mr. Pomey's direction, but I shook my head. "I'll hang out here," I said. She nodded and walked toward Mr. Pomey, Mia, and the intern, Cassie.

When she'd left, I stood a while, watching as students moved about me. My foot repeatedly tapped the ground. Not talking about it didn't keep my conversation with Selene from replaying over and over again in my mind. "Hey," a voice said, interrupting my thoughts. I jumped. Selene stood beside me with a knowing grin. "Didn't mean to scare you."

"Shit, Selene. You can't just do that."

"Sorry."

"Yeah, whatever." I caught my breath. "So why did you say you were looking for that scarab?"

I expected her to play dumb, but she didn't. "I debated telling you when you first got on the bus today," she began. "I didn't know if you could handle it. Now I *know* you can't."

"Can't handle what?"

She rolled her dark eyes. "You know you read that scarab," she said. "And I know it's in the museum."

"Stop being dumb," I snapped. "You act like you were on Monday."

Her eyes fluttered as she surveyed floaters nearby. "You're not exactly fun to be around, but you helped me and I wanted to help you," she said. "I dreamed about the scarab finding you here."

"*Finding* me? An inanimate object is looking for me?"

"I'll explain." I let her pull me to relative privacy. We found a shrouded corner. "I've always had these dreams. I know the type because I have a shitty headache when I wake up after them. They're never very clear, but I always feel like I know something I shouldn't afterward."

"I usually have one every couple of months or so," she continued, "but the minute I set foot in Roosevelt, I had the dreams almost every week. The migraines were crazy. It was like my head was splitting open." She blinked. "Until Monday when I met you.

"That night the dreams were clear for the first time. I saw Mr. Pomey returning the scarab to the museum. They put it in an office somewhere near that Mesopotamia exhibit. I thought if I got to it first, it wouldn't find its way back to you and make you sick again."

"Why are you saying this?" I asked, eyes locking with hers before narrowing. "Do you think it's funny?"

She held my gaze. "I also saw what happened during your class." Her voice fell to a whisper. "'*For my love,*'" she said. "'*The blessings of Amun.*'"

My shoulders dropped as she stepped closer. I stuck my hands out to block her. "Back up," I warned, creating distance from us. "And don't follow me." She held her place as I turned away. Without a glance back, I pushed through the crowd, searching for Alex. Nothing could get me far enough, fast enough.

I found my twin near the front. I debated telling her about Selene, but the hollow pit in my stomach encouraged my silence. "Hey, I turned in our scavenger hunt stuff," she said. "We probably won't get a prize, but maybe there's a participation prize."

I nodded as Mia climbed onto the bench, her snake-like braid swinging back and forth. "Can I have everyone's attention?" she asked, and directed Cassie, who stood nearby, to hand her a stack of papers. Once received, she waved them. "I have the winners! Now, the team that found ten artifacts in the least amount of time is . . ." She glanced down slowly, dragging out the anticipation. "Jason Jones, Robert Grand, and Brandon Ellis!"

Jason, flanked by Brandon and Robert, made his way toward Mia's bench. My body shook, but I joined the applause. "But . . ." began Mia, holding up her index finger. "What was the goal of being an archeologist today? To bring everything back intact, right?" She scanned the three young men. "Which of you gentlemen will account for the gummy worms from the Turkey exhibit?"

They exchanged bewildered glances until Robert slumped his shoulders and raised his hand. "We had turned it in. I thought I could eat some after you saw we found them," said Robert.

"Nope, I'm sorry, guys. It's the first lesson of being a professional. No matter how excited we are about our finds, we can't just do what we want with them. This is why I chose tempting candies as our medium today," said Mia, with a wink. "But you won't leave empty-handed. Mark, can you hand them the bag of gummies? That's the best I can do."

Mr. Pomey handed over the consolation prize as Mia returned to her sheets. "Now, who are Marisa Hightower, Emma Fisher, and Diana Gonzalez?" A group of sophomores near me shot their hands into the air. I didn't recognize them and assumed them to be members of another history class. "You ladies also did an excellent job. You brought everything in intact like actual archeologists. But . . ." Mia poked out her bottom lip. "You only found nine items on the list. You needed to have all ten. That will land you ladies with the honor of second place."

Mia held her papers tight as she turned her attention back to the crowd. "So, I'm sure you all want to know who the winners are," Mia called. "They are . . . Alexandria White, Portia White, and Selene Samson! These ladies found everything on time and returned the artifacts intact, displaying the skills of true archeologists. Claim your prize, ladies!"

Alex grabbed my arm and pulled me up onto the benches. Selene met us there and at the sight of her, Alex stiffened and I moved as far away as possible. My twin swallowed hard and looped her arm with mine. This time Selene didn't make eye contact with either of us. "Twins!" Mia exclaimed. "How cute is this!"

She clapped her hands, not allowing me time to dwell on the edged dynamic between Selene and us. "Now, I told you the prize was awesome, and I'm going to deliver! The three of you will receive museum goody bags and fifty-dollar Visa gift cards."

Everyone applauded as Mr. Pomey distributed the prizes. I began to hop off the bench, but Mia placed her hand on my shoulder. "Not so fast," she continued. "I have another treat for the leader of the group. Who led this awesome win?" My sister's name washed through the audience in excited murmurs.

"Portia!" Alex yelled to everyone's shock and nudged me forward.

Before Mia could continue, Cassie waved for her attention. She bent so Cassie could whisper in her ear, and nodded. "Everyone, you'll have to excuse me for a moment." She looked to Cassie. "You grabbed the box from my office?"

"Yes," she replied quickly.

"Then you can get us started here. Well, Portia," Mia said, and turned to the three of us on the bench. "I have another surprise for you. Everyone close your eyes. Cassie, help her out, please." We did as we were told. Our eyes shut against the echo of Mia's shoes clacking down the hall.

Cassie's shaking voice filled the air. "In my morning of working here, I've realized how much Mia wants to make history tangible. But I'm glad a girl won because a boy probably wouldn't have wanted this necklace, even if it is really old and beautiful." A few seconds passed before Cassie draped something heavy around my neck.

The clack of Mia's shoes scrambling back into the foyer jerked all of our eyes open. "No, Cassie!" she yelled. "Not that one. You grabbed the wrong—"

Mia's voice drowned out as my eyes snapped down. She'd fastened a chain around my throat. From it dangled both halves of Monday's scarab, fitted together in a single pendant. I'd love to say I smashed it into a thousand pieces (with no apology to the museum). I'd love to say that after we left, I caught reruns on the couch all evening. I'd love to say I watched Jason take Alex to his prom a few weeks later.

But that never happened. No sooner had the scarab touched me than heat tore through my body again. It was wild electricity, my limbs like crackling wires. I reached for my sister as her image broke into shards of light. Maybe the museum shook, maybe it was just me, but as she grabbed my hand, Selene surprisingly took the other. It was my last vision as this sudden death reconfigured every inch of me in writhing pain.

THE DANGER YOU SEEK

The symphony was strange. Frogs croaked in a marsh as birds splashed their feathers in nearby water. Crickets chirped. Balmy night air hung above me while I spread my limbs against the soft earth. I hadn't opened my eyes, but I was on some sort of bank.

I didn't get the luxury of opening them one at a time, however. Voices carried toward me, so I blinked them wide and sat up. In the shroud of night, it was difficult to make out anything but the calm waters flowing beyond the marshes, the museum's reservoir. I narrowed my eyes, trying to make out the lights that should glint from the top of the Field. But there was no museum behind me or cars speeding by on near empty streets. Or streets.

What happened?

I racked my brain, but my head only responded by throbbing as two men marched into sight. I lay back down on my stomach to watch them. They were close enough to hear but far enough to overlook me in the dark. The pair wore soldier-like clothing: leather gear, thick sandals, and swords dangling at their sides. And one was not happy.

He spoke quickly while jabbing his pointer at his smaller companion. But the echos that reached my ears were in a language I'd never heard. I listened to the rhythmic discourse until a single word I understood broke through. "Who . . . ?" one asked, followed by a string of foreign words. The small taste of English compelled me to inch forward despite the mud. As I did, something heavy dangled from my neck. My eyes traveled down to the scarab necklace from the museum.

I inhaled sharply before tucking it in my T-shirt and continuing. The closer I got to them, the more words I could make out, but their voices also turned into a sharp, vibrating commotion. This was a hammer to my already throbbing head. I tugged at my earlobes as pressure mounted in my skull. Finally, as if on a descending plane, my ears popped. I gripped the sides of my head to ease the sting, but when I finally let go, the men's words were no longer alien.

What the hell? I thought. *Why can I understand them now?*

"Why did you leave the boats?" the smaller of the two asked. "We've gone too far upriver."

The larger grunted. "Because I don't know who the bigger fool is: you for suggesting this or me for going with you."

"Neither," said the second, smaller man as his companion turned away. "You can't just leave. We have yet to travel to the southern border."

"We've been north for weeks and found nothing. We should report this to the capital before embarking on new travels."

"Procedure be damned," said the smaller man. "My father is dying and our borders weaken by the day. The Kushites want a moment like this."

The larger man stepped forward. "Have you forgotten your responsibilities here?" The smaller placed a hand on the shoulder of his companion, who shrugged it off. "You seek danger by leaving in this way."

"I don't," replied the smaller man. "Your worry is excessive." Silence wedged between them. When it became obvious the smaller man wouldn't budge, the larger turned from him and slipped away into the purple night. The other watched him go before striking at the ground. Grass and dirt flew about before he took a deep breath and trudged on, presumably back downriver.

Wait, I thought as he stalked away. Maybe this guy could point me toward help. I propped myself on my hands and knees, though they sank further into the mud. My head swirling, I wasn't too surprised that as soon as I manuevered to my feet, I fell back down, landing on a patch of sticks in the grass. They snapped under my weight.

The sound cutting through the quiet may as well have been thunder crashing in a summer storm. Still within hearing distance, the soldier immediately stopped. His hand found the hilt of his sword as he looked about him. "Who's out there?" he called. "By Ma'at, I won't harm you if you are peaceful."

I sat in the mud for a moment, holding the sides of my head to steady it. My fingers massaged my temples before running through my hair. Thick texture greeted my hands, my short hair having reverted to its springy coils. I'd laid in the mud and dampness too long. *So much for my press*, I thought.

"I know you're there," he called out again. Instead of unsheathing the weapon, he now crossed the muck, coming closer to my hiding spot. I sighed and finally pulled myself up. In the evening glow, we stared at one another.

He wasn't very tall, and the soldier get-up was even stranger at close range. A brown pectoral plate rested over his chest and shoulders, a thick animal hide stitched along his ribs. He wore a belt at his waist, supporting a heavy kilt of bronze plates, and braided sandals on his feet. He seemed to be as confused by me as I was by him. In fact, he'd stopped midstride as I pulled myself up, eying the peculiar girl covered in mud. "A maid?" he asked finally.

"Maid?" It was all I could think to say.

"Why are you out here alone?" He glanced over my clothes. "And what are you wearing?" I didn't get a chance to answer as rustling in the not too far distance disrupted us. The figure of another man, not the one he'd been speaking with earlier, emerged from the shadows downriver and trudged our way.

I would have asked if he knew the man, but the abrupt wariness on the soldier's face said he did not. He turned to me before jabbing his pointer toward a cluster of large rocks on the outskirts of the muddy terrain. "Go," he said. "Hide."

I did as I was told, head momentarily clearing under the threat of danger. I crouched down behind the boulders and, once safely hidden, craned my neck around the side to watch the goings-on. The soldier drew his sword as the other man finally emerged from the shadowy distance. He wasn't what I or the soldier expected.

The man's dirt-caked, bony limbs poked through ragged clothes. "I feared you were lost," he said, voice like gravel. He opened his palms flat out in submission and nodded. "Soldiers rarely stop here."

The solider sighed and put the sword away. "I am not lost."

"You're not? I had hoped to steer you correctly for pay. Your sword is iron, a true rarity. You've been compensated well for your service." Everything about this guy gave me a bad vibe, but the soldier regarded him with mild interest. At least until the beggar drew a small knife from his rags. "You should not have stopped here."

"I've sliced figs with better knives," the soldier said. "Leave now and I will not harm you."

"Assumption kills many fools," the thief said. "I will slit your throat and collect that marvelous sword as you bleed dry."

The soldier laughed. "We are not evenly yoked."

The thief switched the dagger to his other hand. He bent his knees, ready to lunge before abruptly stopping. "You're right," he said, tucking the knife back into his rags. "We aren't." A less shabbily dressed man emerged from a patch of foliage near them and took his place beside the small thief. This man was a giant wall that rushed forward and scooped the soldier up like a misbehaving child.

"You've met my son," the thief gloated. "And I would say we are now equally yoked."

GIFTS FROM SWENETT

Despite the grip of the Wall, the soldier's graceful, agile movements were sophisticated enough to draw his sword. The small thief tsked in disbelief, but the advantage remained with the Wall. He landed a short blow to the soldier's ribs and, as the soldier gasped, knocked the sword from his hand. He gripped the soldier's neck as his father delighted. "Fight, young man," the thief chimed. "We will be wealthy *and* entertained."

Street smarts dictated that you call the police when something like this happened, not get involved. But my track record—and disdain for two-on-one fights—compelled me to help the soldier, apparently calling on whatever I'd experienced in Mr. Pomey's class and the parking lot with the Grizzlies. Warmth spread through my limbs again, but instead of slicing through me, it hummed beneath my skin.

The warm energy tingling in my limbs pushed the headache even further away, making my body the better version of itself, stronger and more precise. Heart pounding, my instincts again gave clear instruction: *use your resources.* Still crouched, my fingers wove through the grass as I soon discovered that this portion of the bank was littered not only with speckled rocks but also with jagged ones. A particularly sharp one caught my attention, so I snatched it up and unfolded myself. Focusing on a clear line toward the altercation, I let it fly.

And winced at the subsequent crack of bone. The thief hit the ground with a shapely welt on his forehead, visible even from where I stood. His son tossed the soldier aside almost reflexively, letting the soldier use this dumbfounded panic to his advantage. His movements were songlike. He grabbed his sword, turned on his heel, and plowed the butt of his weapon into the Wall's chin.

More cracking bone.

More flinching.

More thuds.

The soldier's gaze darted around before he jogged to my hiding place. "Did you . . . ?" he began as I came around to meet him. Before I could answer, he shook his head and urged me on. "Let's move from here," he instructed before trudging away from the unconscious Wall and his equally unconscious father.

We didn't stop moving until welanded in almost a foot of spiky reeds, still muddy but further away. He stopped for a moment and placed his hands on his knees. Strangely, since I'd thrown the rock, I hadn't felt entirely terrible. "Did you throw that rock?" he asked again, catching his breath. I nodded. "How did you throw like that?"

"I just did," I said, still somewhat shocked that I could understand him and he could understand me.

He eyed me. "That was very brave, but a woman shouldn't be out like this."

"Lucky for you I was."

He arched a brow and, of all things, laughed. Like my mother's, it was a big laugh, an absorbing laugh. "No wonder you're out here alone. Your people must have cast you out," he said. "Where are you from?"

"Like what side of the city? South Side." I flicked my eyes around again. *Still no museum.* That familiar throb pulsed through my head. I touched my temple. "Are we far behind the Field? Where did the buses go?" I asked as a wave of sickness passed through me, springing from my throwing arm. This was becoming a pattern: sensation in my limbs, crazy new skill, and sick as a dog.

I clung to the thick leather covering his shoulder as my legs buckled. Nausea and lightheadedness primed me for collapse, but the soldier didn't allow it, clasping his arms around me. *Pirate wench: take two.* My head swirled as his voice was drowned out behind my eardrums. The world went black.

Sunlight flooded my vision. "Good morning," Soldier-Guy greeted me when I opened my eyes. I'd been lying on some makeshift mat of marsh reeds, still near the water, but not in the mud this time. I sat up and glanced around. Still no museum. Still no Lakeshore Drive. Only billowing plants were near us, their slender leaves shaking in the wind.

I was also greeted by ubiquitous, unmerciful heat. I fanned myself before rubbing my eyes. "Hey," I replied. My ears rang, but at least the pressure in my head was gone.

"I've never seen someone sleep so long," he said.

I tugged at my ears. "How long was I out?" I asked. "It felt like minutes."

"About a day," he said, coming to my side. He'd ditched the leather pectoral, and was now wearing some sort of linen tunic beneath his skirt of shifting metal. "Are you thirsty? I carried water for my journey, but unfortunately no food." He extended a brown pouch with a nozzle on the end.

"Drink," he urged. I wanted to hand his ugly bag back in favor of a bottle of water, but the burn in my throat wouldn't allow it. I unfastened the nozzle and gulped down lukewarm liquid. "And I've never seen anyone drink so fast."

"It's really hot," I whined. "The last thing I remember was asking you if we were far from the museum."

"I don't know what it is you're searching for, but we're further downriver. It was better to move. You don't know who is watching, as we discovered."

"You dragged me while I was asleep?"

"Carried," he corrected. Smudged remnants of dark makeup rimmed his eyes. His brown hair was cropped short, as if it had been shaved a week or so prior, and his skin was a tanned, warm brown. He could easily be my year or a senior at Roosevelt. "And your ornament is lovely," he added as I touched the scarab necklace. No pain this time. "That is a very rare lapis."

"Cassie . . . Mia wanted me to wear it." For a moment I wanted to ask if he'd lost a bet due to the Goth look, but didn't, in favor of reaching for more water.

"I had something similar once." He came to my side and stretched his hand out. "May I?" I unfastened the necklace and handed it over to him. "This is from Swenett. I can tell by the smoothness of the shell. And Swenett's known for its beautiful stone, but they also make incredible wings for these trinkets."

I shook my head. "It doesn't have wings."

He fiddled with the scarab. Light gleamed off its blue shell, which lacked the dents it once had in Pomey's class. It was, in fact, shining and new. "There it is," he said, before pressing its sides. I jumped when two glass wings popped from either side of the scarab's body, gold encasing shimmers of glass.

"That's gorgeous," I said as he smiled.

"Mine was a falcon," he said. "I kept it until my child lock was cut. This Cassie or Mia"— he struggled with the names— "must have thought highly of you." He tucked the wings back and handed the necklace to me.

"They just worked at the museum," I said, and fastened the necklace again. "It should be right back here, but it's not. And Lake Michigan should be over there, but it's not." I fanned myself. "And it's so hot, I can't think."

"Keep drinking," he said, nodding toward the pouch.

I sighed and picked it up. "What were you and that guy talking about last night?" I asked when I stopped drinking. "You were talking to someone before those guys jumped you. You said you were leaving?"

"*Jumped* me?" He laughed. "I'll assume you mean the man before the thieves. He was . . . is a trusted friend. He didn't want to accompany me, or for me to travel alone."

"Then it's dangerous." I took another swig. "Why would you travel alone if it's dangerous?'

"My father is dying," he said, more freely than expected. "He is an important man, and when important men die, everything must be in order."

"Why?"

"Other men want to be important. Unrest is more dangerous than solitary travel." He thought for a moment. "So what is wrong with you?"

"Why would something be wrong with me?"

"You are not well," he said.

I coughed as if on cue. "Summer cold. Nothing to freak out over."

"Plague begins with a cough," he said incredulously. He straightened his back. "*Is* there plague where you come from? Is that why they cast you out? Tell me now."

"*Plague?* That's a little dramatic. This isn't *The Ten Commandments.*"

He didn't laugh. Instead he shook his head and repeated, "Do you have plague?"

"No." I scowled at him. "And if you were so afraid of plague, you would have just left me."

He diverted his eyes a moment before looking back to me. "You didn't leave me when you could have," he said, voice softer. "I had to return the favor. I had to keep Ma'at."

"Ma-what?"

"The order and balance of everything," he said. "How do you not know Ma'at? Where are you from?"

"South Side," I repeated. "Remember? Hyde Park specifically. Some people don't really think it's south, you know, in comparison to the Hundreds, but—"

He shook his head again. "I assumed you were from a sepat near Waset as you dress your hair like a local woman, even if it's long."

"I *just* cut my hair."

He ignored me. "But the people of Waset keep Ma'at and your clothing . . ." he continued. Confusion trimmed with disgust reached his eyes as he regarded the dried mud and dirt on my clothes.

I brushed at my T-shirt. "So I'm muddy. Look at you. Is this some sort of hobby? Ancient war reenactment?"

"My clothing is worn by the most valued of soldiers. And you will faint again if you leave that on."

"I won't," I lied.

"Your brow says otherwise," he said. I frowned and wiped my forehead. He was right. I was caked in mud and drenched in sweat. He eyed my jeans and Nike sneakers, a gift from Richard. "What is this exactly?" He reached for my pant leg to inspect the material.

I jerked away. "Hey, pal, no touchy."

He snapped his hands high in surrender. "I meant no harm. I've never seen anything like it."

"They're jeans," I said, like he deserved a dunce cap. "Denim." He played with the word before asking, "And what is your name?"

"What's *your* name?"

"I asked first."

He sighed. "I am Merenptah."

Roosevelt was one of the most diverse schools in the city, but I'd never heard a name like it. "What does that mean?"

"It means that I am beloved of Ptah." *Ptah? Waset?* His hand gently touched my forehead and I jerked away again. "No harm," he said quietly. I eyed him as he placed his hand on my forehead once more, checking for a temperature. "It's not just the day. You are hot with fever." His fingertips lingered on the side of my face.

I shivered. "I don't know what's going on," I said. "I was at the museum, and now I'm here, and I'd just like to call my dad or my sister. I need to find a cell phone." I shook my head. "Or just get a grip."

"It's the fever clouding your mind. But I will help you find this museum or phone." He stumbled over both words as badly as he did Cassie's name. "Or whatever you need," he said. "I promise."

Despite my body's aches, something in me softened, and I nodded. "Are you sure you won't tell me your name?" he asked.

I shook my head as he smirked. "Well, we should return to the city. What you seek is more than likely there."

He stood and dusted himself off. I attempted to follow suit, but my limbs weighed me down. I wobbled like a children's toy. "Maid," he said, stradying me.

I frowned. "I'm not known widely as 'maid.'"

"You have refused me your name, so it is only proper to call you maid." He squeezed my arms.

I dragged my eyes up to his. The coal-black irises had the depths of worlds behind them. "This is all for Ma'at?" I asked.

"You have kept me from a dishonorable death," he said. "It would be my honor to do the same for you."

I smiled at the odd compliment.

"Look!" he said. "I have cured her sour disposition. My debt is almost repaid."

"Not quite," I said. He squeezed me again before mulling over his few belongings. I watched, holding my arms. Something new nagged at me, keeping the smile at my lips, and I knew it wasn't plague or fever.

WHERE WE PART

We neared the capital's edge by dusk, taking a back road dense with bending tamarisk trees to avoid unwanted attention. The plant's slender branches bloomed with soft pink petals, casting a delicate blush across the sky. During the walk, Merenptah relayed that the capital was the city of his birth; a thriving metropolis cleaved in two by what I once assumed to be the reservoir behind the museum.

Until my dad's catchphrase about assumption rang clear in my head: *you know what happens when you assume? You make an ass of U and ME.*

The foliage surrounding the water never gave way to street signs and pavement, just wild overgrowth in the thick, moist heat. The Field never met my sight. And although Merenptah seemed decent enough, I didn't know him to trust him. If we didn't near civilization soon, I'd have no problem kneeing him in the balls and making my own luck.

Where are we going? I asked about every five minutes.

Though he groaned more than a few times, he never changed his answer. *Waset.*

I don't know what Waset is, I'd reply. We grew so frustrated with each other that we unofficially agreed to silence.

The sun sank in a bed of shimmering rose and gold when finally, the bending plants gave way. Our path grew wider, with deepened tracks in the dirt from overuse. The apex of a massive structure stretched above the trees in the near distance, prompting my heart and feet to accelerate. "Wait," Soldier-Guy called after me, but I moved down the pathway until two enormous stone walls greeted me. *Was this the entrance to the city? The modern metropolis?*

Large wooden torches were affixed to the walls with thick straps. I choked back a cough as smoke from the charred resin burned my nose and eyes. "What is this?"

Merenptah caught up to me. "You should conserve your energy until we get you help." He pointed toward a gap between the walls leading inside. "We can go into the city here," Merenptah said.

He gently encouraged me forward, but my heels plunged into the soft ground. My definition of a city involved steel and concrete, Michigan Avenue and lost tourists. "What is this?" I asked.

"We're just outside of Waset."

"For the millionth time, I don't know what Waset is," I shouted. "I just need to find a train or Google Maps, or whatever else can take me home. I've been a good sport. I've walked with you all day. Now just help me get home!"

He blinked quickly. "I know that your fever is causing you duress," he said. "But I'm only taking you into Waset, the capital"—he patted his chest—"the city that is my home. Here you will find the best care and a way back to your sepat. But out there, alone like this, you will die."

I howled in frustration. "What the hell is Waset?" My eyes skipped over to the illuminated murals spanning the walls. I'd been so preoccupied with the stone I hadn't noticed what was painted on them.

No.

"These are two of Pharaoh's many walls of proclamation. See how he tramples his enemies with his chariot?" Merenptah approached with caution. "Most of us find them inspirational. What's wrong?"

I snapped around to him. "Waset is the capital of *what?*"

"You are not well," he replied, as I searched his face. "The Two Lands," he finally said. "Reigned over by our great Horus Lord, Pharaoh Anen. It is the year of the Scorpion." He took a breath. "Egypt."

The words crashed down, colliding with me like every unexplainable moment to this point, the unexplainable that veered now into the impossible. They swam through my memories, one of Mr. Pomey with his stupid Egyptian almanac, telling us the time of the Scorpion was three thousand years ago. My eyes flicked to his sandals, metal kilt, and the dried kohl around his eyes. It wasn't a costume.

You're in Egypt, Portia. The words rang in my head until I found myself screaming. "That's not true!" I yelled. "Forget it. I don't need you. I'll find my own way." Despite the churn in my stomach, my feet flew from this horrifying, new reality. I wanted to go away to DC for college, not ancient Egypt for the rest of ever.

I didn't know if he was behind me and I didn't check. My pathway led inside Waset, weaving me amongst a cluster of short, flat homes. I tried to kick the run into high gear, but my energy reserves had depleted. My limbs were heavy things, unab;e to fight against gravity

It was then that I had my answer of Merenptah. He followed me in a jog that sped up as I hit the dirt floor. Memories of Mr. Pomey holding up the fake crown danced across my mind. I thought of the weeks and weeks he'd taught the civilization, the mummy movies we'd watched, and the stories we learned of Anthony falling on his sword and Cleopatra's asp.

And Merenptah wasn't an eccentric, well-meaning stranger. He was a soldier, dressed for the times. I was the one who didn't belong.

He shook me. I opened my eyes as he slipped his arms around my torso to help me up. "Let me go," I said weakly.

"Then steady yourself and I will gladly let you walk alone."

"You're crazy." I tried to ease myself up, but couldn't. "I have to get home."

"Let me ensure your safety in the balance of Ma'at. Then I will leave you for someone you find sane."

"Okay," I said, after a long moment. "I'll . . . it's alright if you help me."

He smiled. "Thank you. Her feather would find my heart heavy if I left you before I should."

"I don't know what's happening," I said as we began to walk down the pathway. He touched my shoulder, and I turned back to his gleaming, dark eyes. In them was a kindness I hadn't expected. Maybe one I'd never experienced.

"You will be safe," he said, though I didn't believe him. I was sick as death in antiquity, and I didn't have my twin or father to depend on. I blinked the salty tears away. There was only me.

We passed rows of homes with flat roofs and tiny windows. They were the mud brick structures from Mr. Pomey's lectures, stout buildings baked in the sun's swelter. But despite the abundance of dwellings, only the pair of us walked outside. "It would be livelier than this," Merenptah said, reading my mind. "But most people are beginning their evening prayers and sacrifices." He glanced toward the sky. The sun had vanished, and the glowing moon claimed its place.

We arrived at the back of a large home with its own wall separating it from the road. It towered over its neighbors, screaming rank and importance. On Merenptah's third knock, an older woman wearing a lively patterned cloth came to the door.

"By Amun!" she exclaimed, pleased yet surprised to see the soldier. "Had I known you were coming, I would have found a proper wig to greet you, Merenptah." She patted her scarf before quickly shutting the cedar door behind her. She nudged us into the shadows of the yard's clustered fig trees and wrapped her arms around the soldier.

When she pulled away, my face flushed hot in embarrassment. Despite the veil of night, the thin fabric she wore was incredibly sheer, leaving little of her body to the imagination. Not so far off for a hit show on some premium channel, maybe. A definite no-no for any self-respecting grandma. My eyes shot to the ground.

"Are you returning from a campaign?" she asked. "You only visit me when you return from one."

"Somewhat of a campaign. But unfortunately, my beloved nurse, I came with more to discuss with you."

Her eyes burned my brow, but I didn't look up. They shifted to my Nike sneakers. She gently lifted my chin. "It appears so. And who is this?"

"I would introduce her, but she has refused me her name. I found her when I was returning to the city." He turned to me. "And this grand woman was my childhood nurse. I don't know how we let her go. I obviously haven't done so in totality."

"You grew into a handsome man and no longer needed me."

She patted his cheek admiringly. Hints of dark makeup rimmed her heavy eyes. "By Amun, she is not well," she said, focusing on the pallow of my cheeks.

"I thought she might have plague," he whispered.

The woman touched my head. "No, child. I have seen plague. She is not well, but that is not the cause. Why did you need to provide her with assistance, Merenptah? I would not call this your best idea."

"I am in her debt," he said, his gaze lingering. Mine returned to my feet.

"I see," she said, eyeing the both of us now.

"You had so many remedies for me as a child. I thought that maybe you could—"

"She'll need more than my tricks. I will take her to the priestesses."

"And I will accompany you."

"Merenptah," she warned. "Let an old woman do this work." He objected, but she only touched his cheek again. "They are surely looking for you." She nudged him.

"We part here, then." He turned to me. "The blessings of Amun to you." I touched my scarab, his parting all too similar to its inscription.

When he'd gone, the woman gently took my arm. "We won't be long," she said, peering back toward her home . . . or, I gathered, her employer's home. "They won't notice if we do this quickly."

We walked as quickly as we could, my escort fighting a persistent limp. "My name is Serepti," she said, long after the time for introductions. Her eyes were focused ahead, and multiple rings jingled in her ear.

"Where are we going?" I asked.

"I am taking you to the Temple of Isis," she replied, letting her hand run across my shoulders. "You're no slave. There are no marks on your back, hands, or legs. And your necklace is expensive. You may even be highborn," she said. "You were lucky that Merenptah found you when he did. There aren't many good men like him."

"He was nice," I managed.

"Whatever you did where you came from, you cannot do here. There is no mercy in the capital." Her warning did not ease the ache in my stomach as I focused on the "quick walk" that actually took about an hour. A speedy trip should have been five minutes. But I came from a world with cars. Between planes, television, and Wi-Fi, my world was small in comparison to that of ancient Egypt.

We'd passed through much of the city before stopping at a long, stone pathway. "The Temple of Isis," Serepti said admiringly. "To be brought here, that is great favor with the gods, especially for the sick and outcast. This is the home of Egypt's great mother. She's beloved by all, from royalty to lowly rekhet."

Colossal sycamore trees lined each side of the stone walkway. Their branches reached at least a hundred feet toward the bright moon, and I shrank beneath them. Serepti hummed contently with each step. By the time we reached the pathway's end, my stomach dropped. We weren't done.

Rows and rows of ascending stairs, much like those at the entrance of The Field Museum, lay ahead of us. With this mystery illness stirring inside me, I'd have to pull myself up, or pass out trying. My escort said nothing as I struggled, offering her arm occasionally.

When we reached the top row, two intimidating walls stood before us, swallowing our bodies in their shadows. The space between the pylons must have led into the temple. I was less concerned with the structure's layout as I ogled the scenes stretching over the walls. Graffiti was one thing, and so was art. These images, much like the walls of the proclamation outside the city, were much more.

Illuminated by bright torchlight, the goddess Isis, a towering woman with outstretched wings and a throne-like crown, welcomed Pharaoh to her home in paints of vivid red, green, and yellow. She didn't smile, but she was gracious, humbling Pharaoh in her presence. My eyes turned to Serepti for instructions, though she didn't speak. She took in the image of Isis as I did, contently humming again.

A guard appeared from the gap between the pylons. He wore a linen kilt that draped to his knees, a detailed belt securing it at his waist. He carried a spear too large to be practical, and a bronze plate hung around his neck. A linen headdress resembling Mr. Pomey's sat on his dome, only the guard's was obviously real. His skin was dark and smooth, and in the dance of the torchlight, he appeared to be in his late teens or early twenties. "The temple is closed until morning," he said.

Serepti nodded to him. "A Medjay watches the temple. The gods are pleased, I'm sure," she said to him. "My apologies, but we are not here to pray. I ask that your priestesses look at her."

Alarm sprang across the guard's eyes. "Wait here," he said, before disappearing inside the structure. As we anticipated the guard's return, my tank officially hit empty and I slid to the ground. The cool stonework kissed my feverish skin as I lay. I couldn't rely on my senses to rightly judge the passage of time, but the guard returned in what I thought to be a hurry. A second pair of feet followed him.

"This is the Lady Tasherit," the guard explained.

"Thank you, Rawer," she said, voice nearly a whisper. The

priestess nodded to Serepti before kneeling beside me. The Lady Tasherit wore a light jade robe over her sheath, perhaps denoting rank more than functionality. I appreciated it. With the exception of Merenptah, and the temple guard, she was the first Egyptian whose clothing I couldn't see through. She wore a heavy, dark wig atop her head with tiny braids and colorful beadwork. It was too severe for her small face, almost making one miss her small, delicate features and quick, kohl-rimmed eyes.

"This child is not well, my lady," Serepti said as Tasherit inspected me. "Her health is a matter for the goddess." I groaned as if on cue. The two women stooped over me as if discussing a bruised melon. *If we just cut the squishy part off, we could still make a smoothie.* Tasherit lifted my chin to better see my face. I didn't know if a weak smile or another groan would be more convincing. I went with the groan.

"Assist her," Tasherit whispered to Rawer. My face contorted at the fragility of her tone. I didn't think anyone would be able to hear her, except maybe dolphins or bats, but the guard must have been used to it. He scooped me up without asking the priestess to repeat herself. This was the third man to carry me in the span of a week, and I was unsure if this was a good or bad sign. As he carried me into the temple, I ganced over my shoulder as Tasherit exchanged whispers with my escort before even she departed.

Rawer wasn't exactly graceful. His choppy stride between the pylons reminded me of Cecile's transmission problems from the winter before. I clutched him in a futile attempt to steady his walk, but soon gave up. The moon shone down as we entered a manicured courtyard. The Lady Tasherit's sandals slapped the hard ground a few paces behind.

I groaned as another jerky step signaled we'd entered a room. Shadows slid over my face. My eyes cast up and a vast, clear evening sky greeted me. It was a ceiling-less Hypostyle hall, ringed with polished, limestone columns like those I'd seen in my textbooks. "Be gentle with her." The priestess's small voice dancing with the music of nightfall.

"Yes, my lady," Rawer replied. I gazed at decorated columns lining an aisle in the middle of the hall. We passed through them like the sycamore trees. I lost track of the twists and turns once we left the room and its columns, the paints on the walls melding together. Finally, Rawer delivered me to a quiet chamber with a constant breeze. He laid me on a hard mat, and I closed my eyes to still the motion in my head and stomach.

When I opened them again, Tasherit sat beside me. A sweet aroma drifted off her her skin, and I tried to speak but my word tangled on my lips. "Shhhh," she said and held a cup whose contents smelled like liquid veganism. I naturally turned away and groaned. She only came to my other side. "Drink this. It will help you sleep. You need rest and strength."

"No," I managed.

"It will help. I promise." Though I didn't know her, something in me believed her. I relented and opened my mouth to drink the wheatgrass-y shot down. As I swallowed it, my eyes grew so heavy I couldn't fathom keeping them open another second. "Rest," she said. "Your journey has taken a great deal out of you, and it has only just begun."

THE KUSHITE

It didn't take a day this time. Instead, I woke up in about twelve hours. Sun poured through the window hinting toward early afternoon. Its rays only added to the warmth in the air, heat that swept across my skin with the slightest shift or movement. I found Tasherit already sitting at my side. She welcomed my consciousness with a tilt of her head—a fascinating talent considering that big-ass wig. She smiled before hopping to her feet and buzzing around the room.

My eyes cast upward where I followed a red and yellow pattern zigzagging across the stone ceiling. When I reached utter dizziness, I peeked around the chamber. If this was the temple's equivalent of an infirmary, there weren't many patients. A child rested by the door and an old man near the window. The little boy couldn't be more than eight, and lay with a short kilt wrapped around his waist. The older man's haggard breaths shook his salted hair. Everyone else scurried about without making eye contact with Tasherit—temple servants assumedly.

As I turned on my side, a woman of average height burst into the chamber. With a round face and bright eyes, she couldn't have

75

been more than eighteen or nineteen years old. Her clean-shaven head gleamed from light pouring through the windows, and she hastily wove between the servants. Her path was a direct route to Tasherit.

"My lady," the woman almost shouted, though acutely within hearing distance of everyone in the room. Tasherit winced but continued working while the new woman's braided sandals slapped the stone floor impatiently. "My lady!" she screeched again.

"Lower your voice, Bekmut," said Tasherit. "This is a place for healing."

Bekmut nodded too low for mere agreement—deference maybe. "My apologies, my lady," she strained to whisper. "Sound is welcomed when we rehearse the goddess's hymns and incantations." Bekmut peered around, her kohl-rimmed eyes flittering until they rested again on Tasherit.

"But I have good news," Bekmut continued, her tone spiking again to a screech. Tasherit groaned in kind. "That beastly merchant Neben from Swenett brought servants to the temple this morning. More help is always a blessing, especially considering the festivities. You of all people should be thrilled."

Tasherit's voice was airy but firm. "I don't need help."

"Of course you do. Lady Sikara will be giving you more duties with"—her hands waved in circles—"the Lotus Ceremony, the presentation, dressing every one of those hundred girls. And you also go to the market every week with the rekhet."

"Only until our cook can have servants again," replied Tasherit. "It's nothing I can't bear."

"You're a madwoman. How are you going to do all of that *and* perform your healing duties without servants?"

"Bekmut—"

"Just come with me to inspect them," she insisted.

Instead of returning Bekmut's gaze, Tasherit glanced my way. "Some other time."

Bekmut scowled. "If you don't choose, Ramla will take them."

"The old cook wouldn't dare." Tasherit sucked her teeth. "Her Holiness forbade it until the season of Peret. She was wretched to her last servants."

"Her Holiness rarely goes to the kitchens," said Bekmut.

"Be that as it may"—Tasherit placed a hand on Bekmut's shoulder in finality—"do not fear for my work. I am fine." Defeated, Bekmut turned to leave. I listened until the clack of her sandals disappeared down the hall. Once she'd gone, Tasherit shook her head and ambled to my side. I attempted to sit up, but pain tinged my nerves. "You were listening," Tasherit said as she eased me back down, a simple gesture drenched in memories of Alex.

"What else am I supposed to listen to?" I asked.

"You should listen to your body as you regain strength," she said. I shook my head. As much as I was surrounded by mud brick walls, I was also at the nurse's station at Roosevelt under those sterile paper sheets and a polyblend blanket.

"Tasherit?" I asked.

Her brows drew together. "Are you in pain?"

"No," I replied.

"Then don't speak," she said before gliding over to the child by the door. She knelt to place a linen compress on his forehead. Sweat beads rolled down the little boy's face as she cooed at him. Maybe he had the plague Merenptah mentioned, though I doubted they'd try so hard to rehabilitate him if he did.

As she worked, Bekmut's news danced in my ears. A merchant from Swenett had come to the temple. I touched the scarab again and my fingertips soon felt tiny buttons on the side. I pressed them. The scarab's glass wings popped out and glistened like a kaleidoscope. "Tasherit," I called out, pushing the wings in their slits.

She caressed the boy's cheek before returning to me with two cloth dressings. Her eyes flicked to the lapis scarab, but she didn't mention it. "Yes?" she asked softly.

"Who is Neben?" I asked.

"A merchant," she replied. "From Swenett. He finds servants for noble homes and the temples in the city. Kind of an oily man, but that is their business." A particularly damp compress found its place on my forehead.

"I would like to meet him. My necklace is from Swenett, and I want to ask him about it. Maybe he knows something that could help me."

She eyed me. "The goddess must heal you. And you look like a woman of Waset," she said, sounding like Soldier-Guy. "Swenett is in the south. You don't wear your hair like them. And your clothing certainly wasn't from the south."

"Wasn't?" I peered down for the first time to notice my jeans, T-shirt, and even my Nikes were gone. I was wrapped in the soft, lightweight linen she and Bekmut wore, some sort of tunic dress. And like everything else, I could see through it. I shifted a bit, but Tasherit wasn't interested in what I was (or wasn't) wearing. "What did you do with my clothes?"

"We burned them," she said. "They were damaged and . . . strange." Tasherit thought for a moment. "How about this: when the goddess heals you, I will take you to speak with Neben." My eyes brightened, but she held a hand up at my glee. "Only when you are well."

"Okay." I smiled. My eyes returned to the boy. Maybe he

wasn't sick. Maybe he fell through the rabbit hole as well. Tasherit touched my face, beckoning my attention again. "But until then you must stay quiet and rest."

My eyes flicked to the scarab. "Okay," I repeated. "I just want to go home."

I slept as if it was my job as the days crept on. The air was hot and steamy—May back home, and what Tasherit called the Shemu season here.

Every day I asked Tasherit if I could speak with the merchant Neben, and every day Tasherit told me to rest. But lying on my reed mat forced me to comb memories of my last day in Chicago, my last moments in the future. That endeavor always led back to the scarab around my neck. But even if I figured out how or why it brought me to ancient Egypt, the answers didn't guarantee a way back.

When my thoughts weren't on merchants and bug jewelry, I worried about my dad. He might be more accustomed to divorce proceedings than time travel, but he was the wisest person I knew. If anyone could explain the unexplainable, it was him.

I imagined Dad pacing the living room floor, re-dialing my cell, and cursing Mr. Pomey's negligence. Did my family assume something unthinkable had happened? Or did they believe I wanted to abandon them?

About a week into my stay, Bekmut flew into the infirmary again. This time her head was covered with a wig holding more braids than Tasherit's, and malachite amulets dangled around her neck and wrists. "My lady," she said to Tasherit, who was busy cleaning up the little boy's reed mat. The goddess had apparently healed him enough to return to his parents, who lived in a sepat—something like a county—nearby. "Please come quickly. I can't find Her Holiness, and I don't want Ramla to harm the child."

"What child?" Tasherit asked. She wore the same wig as during Bekmut's last visit, but with a plain tunic.

"One of the servants Neben brought last week," Bekmut clarified. "Ramla took the child for herself in the kitchens since you didn't claim one."

Tasherit gasped. "Did you tell the guards?"

"I did, but you must come since Ramla already called Neben back to the temple," Bekmut said. I sat up in my bed as she spoke, my heart beginning to race. *Neben was back.* "If he can take the child. Ramla is trying to force her toward those stoves and burn her hands."

"By Amun . . ." Tasherit began to run.

"That's why I told you to claim a few," Bekmut shouted, chasing after Tasherit. I scrambled out of my bed to follow Bekmut's voice. I'd give myself the clean bill of health needed for this meeting to happen.

The priestesses piled into the kitchens first. Heat billowed from the cooking area from the multiple cone-like stoves baking bread for the day. I assumed you'd have to bend to put dough inside the small mouths of each. A cacophony of shouts clamored around us.

Aside from the priestesses and me, the room already contained three people: a tall man in a shendyt—the kilt I'd grown accustomed to Egyptian men wearing—and a round woman with a green head wrap and sweat beads pouring down her face, and a screaming girl darting, of all places, *behind* the baking stoves. Fanning herself under the kitchen's swelter, Tasherit slid her wig off and handed it to me. Tightly braided hair framed her face.

"Be useful," she whispered as I tangled my fingers in the wig's beadwork.

"By Amun," Tasherit exclaimed, and glared on the round woman. "Ramla, stop this." The old cook ignored Tasherit, reaching once more for the servant girl. The girl was so tiny she'd successfully wedged herself between it and the back wall despite the hungry fire inside. "The goddess frowns on this."

"This rekhet Kushite dropped my food." Ramla reached again toward the stove before withdrawing her hand. "I don't know how you withstand this heat, but by Amun, when I catch you . . ."

"*Ramla*." Though Tasherit's voice was soft, Ramla addressed her this time. "You shouldn't forget that the goddess loves and is beloved of the rekhet."

Ramla waved her off and turned toward the man at the door. He was only mildly interested in the display, and he swatted at a fly buzzing around his ear. "Neben, are you prepared to take her back?" Ramla asked the waiting merchant. "You should help me get her."

"As far as I'm concerned, she is still yours," he said. He slammed his hand on his skin. "Got the little monster." He glanced up at Ramla finally and belched before saying, "Only in working condition. If you burn her like the other, I will have no use for her." He smoothed his floor-sweeping kilt.

What a prince, I thought, rolling my eyes. "She will be able to work," Ramla said, and focused her disdain on the stove blocking the girl from view. "But she will learn not to be so clumsy in her next home."

"Then, my favorite customer, I will have her only if you can catch her." Neben belched again before laughing outright.

"Oh, by Amun," Bekmut said. "Stop this, Ramla. We still need help in the temple. Give her to the Lady Tasherit. You are not to have servants, remember? This is ordered by Her Holiness."

"You forget, girl, that I prepare the meals for Her Holiness." Ramla darted, catching the girl by the sandal and dragging her behind the stove. The girl shrieked as Ramla held her tight. "Ah!" Ramla yelped. "This rekhet made me burn my hand." She yanked the servant up. "Caught you."

My heart stopped. Where my eyes had been on Neben, they were now fixed on the onyx doll dangling in Ramla's grasp, the freshman I'd once saved from the Grizzlies in the parking lot. Her curly mop of hair hung longer over her eyes than I remembered, and she wore a pleated linen sheath fastened over her right shoulder. Sheer terror marred her face.

I dropped Tasherit's beaded wig as blood rushed to my hands. "Selene!" I shouted, darting past both Tasherit and Bekmut and nearly knocking them down. Like in the parking lot, my movements found an incredible grace, allowing me to wrench the freshman free of Ramla's grasp. She hid behind me.

Burning and tingling had followed the blood flow to my palms, and the friction of releasing Selene was excruciating. The surfaces reddened considerably, but I held my position. If Ramla wanted Selene, she'd have to move me first.

"You dare touch me, rekhet," Ramla yelled. My face flushed as I trained my unflinching gaze on her. The old cook blinked rapidly at my nerve. In the spasms, her green eyes flashed a shade of violet so deep and unnatural I stumbled back.

Selene steadied and when I caught Ramla's stare again, her eyes were as they had been. I glanced at the priestess, never letting my gaze completely leave Ramla.

Tasherit approached me as if I was a wild animal, which in the moment was accurate. "Lady Tasherit, unless you plan on helping, stay where you are," I warned.

Bekmut dashed out of the room to find guards, I assumed. Ramla, surprisingly, stilled. She glanced at Neben who read her expression. "If you wish to return her, Ramla, Lady Tasherit, I will be at the market until high sun," he said with a nod, and disappeared.

Tasherit straightened her back and peered around the room. "Stop this." Everyone turned to her. "Ramla, you are not to have servants. That is the rule of Her Holiness, and it stands." She peered between Selene and me. "And the both of you will come with me."

BEFORE HIGH SUN

"How didn't you get burned?"

Selene was quiet as we weaved through the painted halls behind a wordless Tasherit. "Good to see you, too." Sarcasm edged her voice.

"Oh, sorry." I thought for a moment, and rephrased. "I'm really glad to see you and thank God that lunatic didn't burn you."

Her eyes softened. "That makes two of us." She peered at me before clasping my hand. "I thought I was the only one here," she whispered. She squeezed my palm. It sent a tinge of pain through my hands, still red and sensitive to the touch. I winced and gently broke from her grasp.

"Hurts," I said.

Selene motioned that I should still show her my hand, , though her shoulders trembled, a reaction to the strain of working under Ramla. I held my palm up. "Why's your hand red?" she asked, taking in the crimson splotches across the surface. I nursed it a bit. "What happened to it?"

"Don't know," I said. "Started in the kitchens."

Before she could speak again, we followed Tasherit into a narrow chamber meant for one or two. My eyes danced around the stone walls and east-facing windows. Light poured onto a mural of the goddess adorned in flowing green robes, a purring cat at her feet. An inclined bed with carved, lions paw legs sat in the corner. A cedar table was positioned next to it with a plate of honeyed cakes and pomegranites.

We stilled as Tasherit stood in the middle of the room tapping her foot, distracted by her thoughts, before addressing us. "My name is Tasherit," she said to Selene. Her hand slid over her head absentmindedly until she frowned. "Where is my—"

"I left it down in the kitchens," I said of her wig. "Sorry. I think your braids look better."

"The goddess means to test me for some reason with you. It seems you are well today." Her eyes traveled to Selene. "And you know the Kushite?"

"Selene," she said. "My name's Selene."

"Kushite?" I asked them both.

"Nubian," Selene replied. "That's what they've called me since I got here—because of my skin apparently, and how long I wear my hair."

"But everyone here is pretty damn bronze and brown." Selene shrugged as I turned back to Tasherit. "Are you going to throw us out, Lady Tasherit?" I asked.

"Of course not," she said. "These are my chambers. You can rest here until I can get the carts ready."

"Carts?" Selene asked. "Why do we need carts?"

"I normally go to the market before the sun gets too high and they put all of the food away until the day cools. I'll just have two tasks today."

"What two tasks?" I asked.

"Food," she said. "And finding Neben so you can speak with him." I had all but believed the likelihood of seeing him again was small, that I'd have to renegotiate with Tasherit. "He said he'd be at the market."

Selene's back straightened. "I'm not going back with him or Ramla."

"No," I said to Selene. "Neben has information we need." I pulled the scarab out from beneath my clothing as her dark eyes widened. "Yeah, it's the scarab from the museum. And I was told it's from Swenett, just like Neben."

Tasherit cut in. "If you know a Kushite," she said, "then I may have been mistaken. You may be from the south."

Selene watched the gleam of the scarab, new and pristine around my throat, before turning toward Tasherit. "Why are you helping us?" she asked the priestess. "She's just a rekhet and I'm a servant."

"We're all servants of the goddess, and the goddess loves and is beloved of the rekhet," she said, much like the speech she gave the cook. "I'm not Ramla. I told your friend she'd speak to Neben, and she will." She took a moment to think. "I will check in with Rawer on the market carts and return shortly." She turned on her heel and left the room.

When Tasherit had gone, Selene walked to one of Tasherit's windows and gazed out. A small breeze shook the coils at the top of her head. The freshman took a deep breath and glanced back to me. "You're sure about her?" Selene asked.

"Tasherit? Yeah, she's good people, I think."

Selene tugged at her linens. Nervousness and distrust colored her gaze. "Ramla wasn't a good person," Selene said.

"Did the eye thing happen a lot?"

She wrinkled her brow. "What eye thing?"

"Her eyes turned purple when we were in the kitchen, when I was blocking you from her."

"I didn't see anything," said Selene. She turned from the window to lean against the wall. Light glowed against her beautiful, dark skin. She was a piece of the world I had left behind. She was the only thing that made sense.

"A fishing family found me by the Nile. They call it the Iteru," she added, without prompting. "They had too many mouths to feed and turned me over to Neben. Said I would go to the palace as a servant." She shook her head again. "Ended up with Ramla."

"A soldier found me."

Her lips tugged upward. "You win. The last thing I remember is the museum, and then there was this drop in my stomach and I landed in all this water. I had to swim to the top. That water turned out to be the Iteru." She played with a dangling curl before glancing at me, smile turning wicked. "Was the soldier cute?"

"That's your question? You don't want to know how I got here?"

"I'm sure it's similar. Besides, it's a perfectly good question that deserves an answer."

I rolled my eyes. Maybe this was what it was like to have a little sister. "*Selene.*"

"I'll take that as a yes."

I scrubbed my face. "Were you sick when the family found you?" I asked.

"No," she said. "I've never been sick, not even a cold."

"I was so sick they pretty much rolled me into the temple of Isis."

"Sexy." Selene's laugh bounced off the reliefs of the goddess on the wall. I joined in until Selene angled her small torso toward the door. Tasherit stood in the entryway, a new wig on her head.

"She's freaky quiet," said Selene.

"The carts are almost readied," replied Tasherit. "Come with me."

We rode into the busy marketplace in the bed of horse drawn cart. Men and women haggling prices for goods made way for us while their children squealed and ran in the city streets. The pungent stink of horses, mules, and other beasts of burden clogged my nostrils. Selene stayed near to my side and jumped at any sudden movement, whether a passersby or a blowing leaf. *Ramla did a number on her*, I thought, feeling awful.

As we made our way into the commotion, Tasherit was more focused on the task at hand: ordering for the temple staff, and sending servants back to the cart with huge baskets of supplies. She'd replaced the wig I lost in the kitchens with another, lighter than its predecessor and with malachite and ivory beads cascading down its sides. She'd also changed into a jade sheath to become Ancient Egyptian Tinkerbell.

Finally the cart stopped and Tasherit hopped out. She whispered something to Rawer as he helped me out and turned to Selene. His eyes brightened. "You are well?" he asked her. It was the first time he'd spoken outside of his work overseeing the guards in the temple. Tasherit buzzed nearby, speaking to the three servants who'd also made the trip, but I stopped to watch him.

Selene nodded. "I'm okay," she said, almost as surprised as me.

He took her hand and helped her off the cart. "You wear your hair in the Kushite style," he said. "Many of the Medjay men, working in the palace or the temples, are Kushites."

"Okay," Selene said.

His gaze lingered on her. "It is nice to be reminded of home," he said, and turned from us. Selene smiled as Tasherit came back to us. "I will finish the purchasing while Rawer goes looking for Neben," she said. "I want you two to stay by the cart."

"Can't we go with Rawer?" I asked. *Since he likes Selene.*

"I'd rather you stayed by the cart. We're familiar with the market. Let us handle this." She started rummaging through some supplies on the cart, plucking a large woven basket to carry. Tasherit's face tightened as she examined the basket, inspecting the sides for weak spots.

"If you won't let us go with Rawer, could we at least help you?" I asked. "Why do you have to do all the shopping anyway?"

She struggled with a big cart before stopping. "The temple grows much of its own food in our gardens, but whatever we don't grow we get from farmers and merchants here." She sighed again. "The job *should* go to the kitchen staff. But as you saw this morning, the kitchen staff is not at its best. Ramla burned her last servants and isn't allowed to have any help until Peret, the planting season. She's too old to scour the markets alone."

"What does that have to do with you?" asked Selene.

"I volunteered to help. Ramla is a superior cook, and it's the only reason we put up with her tempers."

"You're nice," Selene said. "My grandmother might say you're too nice."

Her eyes flicked to Selene and then back to the task at hand. "Perhaps," she said, and disappeared with the servants that had also ridden with us.

A rolling cart passed Selene and me with two mules pulling an array of luscious pomegranates, figs, and melons. We stepped back to protect our toes, but as it passed us, Selene plucked two figs. "You're supposed to pay for that," I said when she handed one to me.

"Yeah, well, I'm supposed to be in English class right now," she said before biting into the fig.

I glanced around. "If Rawer doesn't come back soon, we should just go look for Neben ourselves. But I'm sure he'll be back for you."

Selene slurped the fig juice dripping down her chin. "Who? Rawer?"

"You're gross," I said of her slurping. "Yeah, him. He looked at you like he knew you."

"He seemed nice. And this is so good . . ." she said of the fig. I knew what she meant. I'd had little of the sweet plants during my recovery in the temple. The rest of the Egyptian cuisine I'd sampled tasted strange, between the spices they used and lack of butter and sugar. I must have gone through sugar withdrawal during my recovery period, but biting into a sweet fig was otherworldly. As I watched the locals scurry, I couldn't help but wonder if I might run into Merenptah. If he were here, maybe he could help us—

"What are you thinking?" Selene said. I jerked my eyes to hers. "You get this gaze-y look when you're thinking something. You did it in the museum a few times." She studied me. "You were looking for that cute soldier, weren't you?"

"What? No! I was looking for Neben," I lied. She smacked her lips in skepticism. "I should have left you with Ramla and the Grizzlies."

"For the Grizzlies, too late. For Ramla, too soon," she said with a shudder.

"Sorry," I said. "But I wasn't thinking about Merenptah."

"Oh, Merenptah is his *naaaammmmme*." She made a googly-face at me. I sucked my teeth and turned away, her laughter swelling behind me.

More men and women of Waset passed us by. These people were the labor class of Egypt, buying and selling goods for their families, or perhaps the houses of their employment. Most were clad in simple tunics instead of the finer weaves of dress, the long sheath Bekmut preferred, or a fitted, strappy style Tasherit called a kalasiris. My eyes jumped from face to face, watching women in dark wigs bobbing down the pathways. Occasionally a higher class woman would pass us, nonchalantly fanning herself with a long plume.

I snapped out of it when two figures approached us. One was Rawer, walking with the urgent yet dignified stride of a Medjay; the other was Tasherit. Servants no longer trailed her, as they appeared to be loading the cart. "That was quick," I said as both the guard and Tasherit found a place in front of Selene and me.

"We found Neben," Rawer said. "Or at least, an associate of Neben."

Tasherit cut in quickly. "The dockworker who prepares his barge for travels to Swenett," she said. "He was making purchases for the trip and said the merchant is not here. He didn't come to the market like he said. He went to another household." She glanced toward the clear sky. "He should be back tomorrow, so we'll return. You may stay with us in the temple tonight. Let's pack up the items and return."

I nodded and we made our way to the cart. Tasherit inspected the baskets of dried meats, herbs, and spices the servants packed neatly on the cart. Once she finished, we all squeezed in the packed bed, and began our trek back towards the temple. The wagon wobbled in the dirt road as we moved forward, but I was far from my days of nausea. I held firmly to the sides, watching people conducting their business as we made our exit. I vaguely heard Tasherit speaking to Rawer in the background. "Which house?" she asked the guard.

"House Neberu," he replied. "Neben went to the architect's home. His wife and children are returning from their northern estate for the festivities. Actually, these look like their litters coming now."

"I'd imagine Neberu is in the city often," said Tasherit. "There's always a tomb construction to oversee." We jerked forward as the mules pulling our cart dug their hooves in the ground. The abrubt stop allowed a long procession of horses, mules, and litters to pass.

Tasherit turned to Selene and me with a hopeful expression. "This is good news. House Neberu is not far. He will certainly return to the market. We'll get an audience."

"Can't we just go to the house?" I asked.

"No, Her Holiness would have to write to them for that. It'll be faster, I promise you, to speak to Neben in the market."

I nodded before exchanging a glance with Selene. We'd find a way to House Neberu tonight, even if we had to sneak out. In the meantime, we watched the caravan. The family must have been very wealthy, for it took more than a few minutes to pass. I spotted what looked to be the last three carts, probably carrying servants. "I don't know what servants or wares he'd be able to barter there," said Tasherit. "They are stocked."

"I doubt he's bartering," said Rawer. "Neben is a cousin of Neberu."

High sun was soon approaching, and heat beat down on our brows. "I see the end," Selene said, eager to get back to the temple out of the swelter. As the last wagon passed, I caught the silhouette of a girl. Her hair was no longer pressed straight and she wasn't wearing her glasses, but I'd know my twin anywhere.

Alex.

I almost flung myself from the cart, stopped only by Tasherit's quick reflexes. I'd barely seen her hand move before she grabbed me and held on tight. "You must stay still," she said. "We have too many provisions to let any fall out of the cart."

"What's wrong, Portia?" Selene asked. I lurched around as she spoke, listening to no one. Alex's wagon had passed into the distance. My sister was alive, here with Selene and me. In that last moment at the museum, when the world shook and broke into light, we'd all touched hands. *Was that enough for the scarab to get us here?*

As our mules pulled us toward the temple, blood flowed to my hands, tingling as they had in the kitchens with Ramla. But for the first time, pulsating heat filled my entire body. I flicked my eyes to my hands and saw they glowed bright white.

The hum of electricity rushed through me, white-gold sparks through my skin. They danced on fingertips. I suppose I should've cared about my fingers going all electrical outlet on me, but I didn't. I didn't care without Alex. The cart lurched forward, and I staggered, grabbing the side—the *wooden* side—with my sparking hand. Maybe the boards were brittle from their days traveling in the heat, or maybe my sparks were hungrier than even fire tasting kerosene. Whichever was right, the sparks turned into flame, spreading beneath my hands, devouring the cart's panels, and finally engulfing the cart itself.

My next memory is of Rawer ripping me off the cart. He tossed me to the ground before returning to the wreckage to help others. I lay in the dirt, awed by the flames that stretched toward the sky. The shouts of the men and women dousing the fire surrounded me. Rawer unharnessed our mules, which ran wild around the frenzy.

Tasherit appeared before me, face half covered in dirt. Her beaded wig was gone and her breathing was ragged. I backed away from her, but she snatched my hands.

I struggled against her as she adeptly flipped them over. The white glow was gone, replaced with damaged, blistering skin. She inspected my feverish palms, touching one lightly. I yowled and snapped my hand back. Her blazing eyes met mine. "You did this," she whispered.

MY LADY

The ride back to the temple was marked with uncomfortable silence. Rawer arranged for us to travel with two laborers who'd been working on a nobleman's tomb nearby. They were heading to the temple anyway for something called the evening prayers. As we moved against the setting sun, the bed of their small wagon shoved the three servants, Selene, Tasherit, and me together in the most awkward way possible.

Crickets and frogs sang in the tall grass beside the road as the rickety cart arrived at the temple's kitchens. Torchlight in the doorway illuminated the dirt smudged over Tasherit's face as well as her round, wigless head. *I'd made her lose another. Damn.* We caught eyes briefly. She'd announced my guilt at the market but nothing more. I had no idea if she was mad about the cart, or repulsed by what I had done. And if the latter, was she upset enough to kick Selene and me onto the streets?

Rawer hopped out of the cart first and then turned to help Tasherit. The priestess nodded to the laymen graciously, if tight-faced, before addressing Rawer. "Please help these men to the evening prayers," she said of the tomb builders. "Unload the cart," she instructed the servants, "though there's not much left after the fire." I gulped. Only Selene and I were left. "And you two follow me."

She strode into the kitchen entryway past the mosquitoes and pests buzzing near its torchlight. Selene and I exchanged glances before following. Selene stiffened as we entered the small room with busy stoves at work. They weren't nearly as hot as before, but that didn't assuage Selene much. Luckily, Ramla was nowhere to be seen. Bekmut, however, flew in wearing another heavy wig and a translucent kalasiris. A fine green wrap hugged her shoulders, and the kohl at her eyes glittered with flecks of gold in the style of the city's noblewomen.

"Lady Tasherit," said Bekmut. "You took a long time. Did you find Neben?" She stopped herself when she took in the dirt caked on our skin and clothing. "What happened?" she asked Tasherit. "And where's your wig?"

Tasherit peered around her toward a long hallway instead of answering. She then placed her hand on Selene's back and ushered her toward Bekmut. "Take the Kushite to the baths to get cleaned up," Tasherit instructed the priestess. "We had trouble in the market."

Bekmut stammered. "But where are you going?" she asked as Selene's eyes skipped between Tasherit and me. I nodded at her as if to say it was safe, though I wasn't completely sure.

"Please," she said to Bekmut. Tasherit wrapped her hand around my wrist and tugged me on through the narrow hallways painted with images of the goddess and winged Mut. Once out of hearing distance, I spoke up. "You can let me go. I'll follow you," I said. "And I'm sorry. Whatever I did, I'm sorry."

Tasherit's stride slowed to a stop. "Show me your hands again," she said, and I did so delicately. She inspected my injured palms for a moment before saying, "Hide those." I wanted to ask why, but instead folded my arms across my chest and tucked my hands beneath them. *Who'd care if my hands had blisters?* I wondered as we moved again.

"We're going to the evening prayers," Tasherit announced as we passed other priestesses who, like Bekmut, took in our disheveled appearance. It was a stark contrast to their cleanliness. Though we weren't nearly pristine enough, Tasherit appeared to be respected sufficiently that no one stopped her.

We left the hallways and landed in the courtyard enclosure from my first evening. The living quarters of the priestesses were on the left side of the temple, with the infirmary on the right, and the open courtyard wedged between. Eager men and women made their way inside. "What is this?" I asked.

"This court and the next are open to all the people of Waset," Tasherit said. I marveled at the inner walls of the courtyard were paintings of Pharaoh sacrificing a bull to the goddess leapt from the stone. "The Prayer Hall is next. It is where they bring offerings," Tasherit said as we bypassed the worshippers. "And where the morning and evening prayers are conducted."

"Oh," I said. Maybe if Alex and I had some sort of religious affiliation, I would know what to expect. But Richard wasn't churchgoing, and thus neither were we. While my friends endured itchy tights and Easter recitals, there was no Sunday school for us (or baptisms, synagogue, mosque, bat mitzvahs, or pilgrimages to Mecca). My father saw religion more as a study in human behavior than doctrine. But to the men and women filling the courtyard, holding oil lamps to light their way, the gods were real and tangible, infusing every aspect of their lives.

I entered the hall behind Tasherit. Large columns guarded the room as much as the Medjay fading to the back with bronze swords. Memories of Rawer's rickety stride from my first evening in the temple filled my mind. The Prayer Hall was the Hypostyle chamber.

"Why do the columns look like plants?" I asked, admiring the pillars as we took to the center aisle. The tips of each column caressed the ceiling like shy leaves.

Tasherit looked at the columns as if she'd never given it much thought. "They are fashioned like papyrus, or lotus, or any other plant you'd find in the Iteru's marsh," she whispered. "Now, no more talking."

My eyes drifted to the men and women spilling into the hall to give the goddess their obeisance. From the outskirts of the chamber, priestesses hummed their hymns to Isis, and whispered incantations to invoke her favor. When we reached the front, Tasherit motioned for me to come closer. "We will just stay long enough for . . ." She peered around. "Perfect, it's starting."

The crush of bodies made the room hot and stuffy. I could now appreciate the lightweight material and general nonchalance toward nudity in Waset. Large ebony altars at the head of the room, square blocks carved and decorated on their sides. My eyes trailed behind the altars to a set of latched doors.

A few moments later, the room grew smaller still as servants led a modest procession down the hall's main aisle, followed by high-ranking priestesses with robes of green. Despite the dance of color, my eyes focused only on the woman anchoring the parade. A hush moved through the crowd as she passed, her swanlike neck elongated.

"That is Her Holiness, the High Priestess, the Lady Weret," Tasherit said. "She will conduct the evening prayers." My eyes returned to the gazelle-like High Priestess of Isis. If she managed to live about three thousand years, she could easily play forward in the WNBA. Above her finely woven robe, extravagant gold jewelry adorned her neck and ears. A metal headdress resembling an elegant ibis covered the rest of her head. Its green-painted feathers splayed around her face. She moved gracefully, with her left arm at her side and her right hand unseen, tucked into her robes almost like a sling. Some temple patrons knelt before her, but her eyes never wavered from the altars.

After the grand entrance, the ceremonial activities involved chanting and lighting cones of incense. As the High Priestess worked, Tasherit left my side and spoke to another woman, whom I'd noticed flanking the High Priestess earlier. She wore no wig. Instead her hair was tightly braided, with tiny beads woven between the plaits and stacked high.

She approached me with Tasherit as everyone else focused on their prayers. My instincts told me to straighten. Though she wasn't dressed particularly different from any of the other priestesses, and couldn't be more than about twenty-two years old, nothing about her said she was to be taken lightly. "This is the girl?" the woman asked. Her voice was low and sharp, and she didn't regard Tasherit with deference. I assumed that she outranked her. Tasherit nodded. "Then come, and do not waste my time."

Tasherit wasn't just reserved. She was also a secret-keeper. There weren't two great ladies, but three. Tasherit was third in command of the temple, and the respect the other priestesses gave her now made sense. The holiest woman was the high priestess, Weret, and following her in rank and importance was the woman Tasherit fetched from the prayers: the Lady Sikara.

We convened in a large chamber whose mud brick walls curved on all sides. Within, the Lady Sikara hurled words like *insolence* and *brazenness* from behind a dark, wooden table sporting alabaster jars of oil. She held her ire in until we were away from the temple patrons, but now in private, she had no reservations. "Tasherit, you do not disturb the evening prayers for *anything*," Sikara said, gripping the sides of her work table. "Especially when you look as if you've rolled in mud."

Tasherit's arms stayed neatly at her sides as she weathered the priestess's rant. I trembled in a wicker chair beside her, digging my nails into its sides and avoiding direct eye contact with either of them. "I know, my lady," Tasherit began, in a respectful timbre. "But there are circumstances you must understand."

"Do you *not* understand that such impertinence dishonors the goddess? It's ridiculous—"

"*My lady*!" Tasherit insisted. Of all the lady's features, Sikara's chin was the sharpest, and she jutted it in the air at Tasherit's outburst. "We came to you at this regrettable hour," Tasherit began as Sikara stepped in front of the table. "We came to you at this regrettable hour because we need to speak about the events of today."

Sikara flicked her hand. A gold cuff, fashioned like a bending stalk or wheat, gleamed with the motion. "You told me your cart burned down. Just replace it."

Tasherit turned to me, eyes insisting I stand. Mine shot to the floor. "Please," she said. "Rise." I rocked onto my feet. Tasherit came to my side and gently took my hand. She then delicately laid her palm against mine, which still needled my tender nerves. "It's beneath her skin, my lady," she said to Sikara. "You'll feel it if you touch her hand. I thought I'd sensed heka in her before, but nothing of concern. I was wrong. It caused her to burn the cart down."

Sikara, curious now, swept her robes back and strode closer to us, to *me*. My breathing hitched, unsure what was beneath my skin that she needed to examine. When we finally stood face to face, she no more than an inch or two taller, she indicated that I show her my palm. I inhaled deeply before doing so.

Sikara's index finger moved across my skin. Her touch was lighter than expected but still sent a painful shiver through me. I yelped and withdrew my hand before we locked eyes. The gaze that met mine was stunning, prettier than even my twin's. Gold specks glowed through her dark irises like hungry embers in ash, and she regarded me with raw fascination. I held her stare, watching those embers crackle.

"Heka," she said, more calmly than before. "Tasherit, please." Tasherit bowed gracefully and slipped out of the room. When she'd gone, I once again became that bruised melon in the market—though perhaps now a *unique* bruised melon. Sikara stepped away from me, returning to the business at her table. "Only heka achieves what you did," she said.

"Heka?" I asked, inching closer. "What's that?"

She nodded toward a closer chair. "Sit there," she said, and continued to work with the oils, muttering over the row of containers. I followed her instruction. "Heka is magic," she continued.

"There's no such thing," I said despite the evidence to the contrary: my hands glowing white, sparks shooting out of my fingertips, a scarab that knocked me flat on my ass, and, of course, being in ancient Egypt.

"Do you know who I am?"

"You are the Lady Sikara," I said, with all the formality I could muster. I dipped my head as Bekmut had deferred to Tasherit. Sikara wiped her hands on her robes and maneuvered from her table. I fought the urge to sink in my chair as she neared.

"But what else did the Lady Tasherit tell you?" Sikara asked as she knelt before me, extending her hand toward my throat. I flinched away, but she shook her head. "Be still," she said, and I held my body in place. Her hand clasped the scarab necklace for a brief moment. "She's told you nothing?"

I shrugged as she moved away, opting to lean against the table with her arms folded. "I conduct the prayers if Her Holiness is indisposed. And as a priestess, I am a student of heka. When used correctly, heka helps people. It protects them." She straightened. "Follow me," she said, a general in all but military gear.

She glided out into a central hallway not far from the temple's first courtyard, and I trailed her like a cocker spaniel. I caught the glances of curious servants and priestesses in cream and jade linens. Carrying their wares and trays, the temple folk's treatment of the priestesses carried sharp distinctions. They nodded to Tasherit. They bowed to Sikara.

The corridor led to the Prayer Hall, which emptied as the evening prayers had concluded. We walked its main aisle in silence before reaching the latched doors dividing public and private worship. She opened them and swiftly crossed the threshold. We soon arrived at a chamber larger than the one we'd left but smaller than the Hypostyle Hall. My eyes danced around. The servants had already lit the oil lamps in preparation for her arrival, casting a soft glow on the angles of the room. "Are we in the sanctuary?" I asked, despite myself. The sanctuary was a private place of worship, one of the most important rooms in the temple.

"We're near it," Sikara said. "What are you called?"

"Portia," I replied.

Her nose wrinkled. "A foreign, unflattering name," she said, not even attempting to say it back. I frowned. "And you are from where?"

You wouldn't believe me if I told you. "Swenett," I replied. "I think."

"Hmm, yes, that trinket around your neck is from the south." She glanced up at me. "Though you look like you could be from a local sepat." A beat passed. "And Tasherit says you travel with a Kushite."

I shifted my weight. "Selene," I said. "And a sister, who is at House Neberu. I need to get her out of there."

"I see." Sikara folded her arms. "For reasons I do not know, Ma'at has deemed you worthy of heka. I rarely see this outside of the priesthood." I began to protest, but she shook her head. "Don't lie to yourself or me. It's in you. It's in your ka, to be exact."

"Ka?"

"Heka is a gift from the life spark in your soul."

It was all a little too otherworldly for me. "Wait, you're saying when my hand freaks out it's because of my *soul?*"

She sighed. "I felt it, as did the Lady Tasherit." She waited a beat before beginning again. "Your gifts can be of use to this temple, but you don't know how to control them. I assume burning my cart was unintended as, judging by your appearance, you were still inside when you set it aflame."

"Accident," I managed.

"This is the instruction room for priestesses. Swenett isn't far, but I am unfamiliar with the particulars of their education. You'd have to learn to properly address the gods of Egypt in the fashion of Waset. If the priesthood interests you, you may reside here to train as a scribe, and eventually a priestess. The Kushite may stay as well as long as you are serious about this work, and I will inquire about your sister in the architect's employment. Though I'll attempt to advance your remedial education, know our upcoming ceremonies require my attention as well."

She'd help me get Alex back. "Okay," I said. quickly "And do you mean the ceremonies Bekmut was talking about?"

"Prince Seti will be married to the princess of the Hyksos in the next season, Akhet, less than a month away. The Hyksos are people of the Delta. Those arriving here will do so from their capital of Avaris. They have particular wedding ceremonies, beginning with the Lotus Ceremony. We have been preparing for months."

She walked to the door and opened it, indicating that our time together had ended for now. "Have Tasherit retrieve food for you and the Kushite from the kitchens, and bathe. We'll resume our work in the morning." When I crossed the threshold, her voice called out again. I looked over my shoulder as the priestess said, "This will not be easy."

BELIEVE IN MAGIC

Selene and I dug into our plates of honeyed bread, cheese, and pomegranates. The air grew thick with moisture as the days slipped into Ahket, the flooding season of inundation, the most important of the year. I'd been studying for weeks and had gathered that, if we were at home, it would be about July. Alex and my birthday was on July 16th, and the thought of turning seventeen without my twin made me ache almost as much as my recovering hands.

Though my studies were crucial to getting her back, I'd grown impatient over the weeks. To her word, Sikara was slow in her inquiries to House Neberu amid the wedding preparations, and if she couldn't hold true to her promise, Selene and I would have to find Alex on our own. We'd already scouted a path to House Neberu that cut through the wheat fields adjacent to the temple, avoiding main roads leading deeper into the city. We'd also found a rickety cart near the stables, and a horse—long in the tooth—that would probably go unnoticed.

When my thoughts didn't revolve around the circumstance, magic, and my sister, they sometimes drifted to the kind soldier that saw me into Waset. I wondered if Merenptah had made his trip south or if he stayed somewhere in the city. I wondered if he'd stroll into the temple to pray, or maybe to see if I was alright.

Selene and I had taken over Tasherit's chamber. While I studied with Sikara during the day, the freshman helped Tasherit in the infirmary. Apparently she was a natural in whatever Tasherit did to heal people.

This morning, we ate as if someone would take our breakfast away. "What?" I asked as Selene chuckled to herself.

She nodded toward her food. "Ramla made this," Selene replied. "She had to feed the filthy rekhet. It's kind of funny."

"As long as it's not poisoned," I said.

"Tasherit said she wouldn't dare."

"Ramla's eyes turn purple," I said.

"Nobody saw the purple eyes but you. Stop with that."

"They did," I said. "And for that, you never know what she might do. So you and Tasherit are buddies now?"

"I like working with her. She's nothing like Ramla. She's too nice," she said with a smirk. The morning sun poured in through the chamber's windows. "That's why we're eating and sleeping in her bedroom." She took a bite of her pomegranate before announcing, "Sikara sent a message."

I almost dropped my food. "How did you hold that in so long?"

"You mean in the five minutes since the trays got here?" She laughed. "We're going to House Neberu tomorrow. Tasherit is taking us."

"I thought she'd never look into it. It took her almost all of Shemu. I'll tell

tell Rawer this afternoon."

Selene squeezed my arm. "We'll get Alex. She'll be fine," Selene said. I exhaled as the freshman pushed a tendril of her hair out of the way. It grew so long and coiled that Tasherit trimmed it weekly. The trims were Selene's compromise with the third great lady, who begged her to braid it down or shave it off. I still wanted to keep mine short, which Tasherit considered the proper way of a city woman. "Though, if it gets crazy, we might have to break Alex out with your heka. How is it?"

"Okay, I guess. I haven't seen the sparks again, but the glow is enough to be convincing," I said. "Sometimes I still don't believe all this, in the magic."

Her lips thinned. "Portia, your hands glow in the dark. Magic is the *most* logical explanation."

I sucked my teeth. "Are you still dreaming about the scarab?" The freshman diverted her gaze before I nudged her. "This is the part where you say words related to the question I asked."

She cracked a smile that stretched into a sigh. "I'm just not sleeping great. There's a lot in my head. And I miss my grandmother." She angled toward the wash of morning light, which illuminated the bags under her eyes. I didn't understand grandmothers and grandfathers and all that, as I'd never had either. But I did miss my father and my sister. That longing we shared.

"You lived with her?"

"Yeah, and I have siblings. They're a lot older, so it was really like . . . just us, you know? Things made sense when my grandmother explained them. Like when my head hurt so bad I couldn't think or neighborhood kids gave me shit."

"What for?"

"Being darker than them," she said. "A southerner, a *Kushite*. And my name. Not a lot of *Selene's* around the Randos." She shrugged. "But my grandma helped me keep my dreams straight." She smiled, but it faded. "I started having those dreams again when I got to the temple."

"Every night?"

She nodded. "I always see the same woman, though I never remember her face. And she shows me the same thing."

"What's that?"

"Creatures, bugs that look like your scarab, but worse," she said. "They crawl across the sand on these long, pointy legs while the wind howls. The sky is pitch-black, and there's just this army of clawed things turning whatever they touch to ice." She looked up to me. "Yeah, ice. It doesn't make any sense."

I touched my scarab necklace, unsure of what to say. "Why can't these prophetic types give you instructions, like Ikea or something?" I asked.

"I think it's more fun for them this way."

After breakfast, I toiled through my lessons with Sikara. She also insisted I work with the famously overdressed Bekmut, practicing songs for the first wedding festivity: the Lotus Ceremony. Hymns weren't exactly my thing, and the hours drew on as I waited for both the lessons to be over, and the next daybreak when I'd see my twin. When I returned to Tasherit's chambers at dusk, I curled into a ball on my reed mat, praying that Ra's trip through the underworld would be quick, and the sun would burst in the sky soon enough.

Soft fur rubbed against my leg. I shot up and scurried to the end of my bed to find a cat. Its fur was thick velvet, as beautiful as its brilliant green eyes. The bronze ring in its ear jingled, and the cat's warm purr tempered my racing heartbeat. "*You*," I managed. The cat stretched with disinterest. I rolled my eyes and scooted closer, sitting cross-legged. It took this as an invitation to jump onto my lap.

I rubbed its spine, its fur carrying hints of temple incense and jasmine. "What, cat?" I asked. It wriggled before dropping down from my lap and sauntering into the pitch-black hallway. As I followed, the cat mewed somewhere, and the torch ignited on the wall at my side. "*Shit*," I said, grabbing my chest. The miw—cat in ancient Egyptian—waited a few paces ahead.

It mewed again in feline disapproval before prancing away. I inspected the torch, the only light in the hall, before turning from it and following. It wouldn't be an isolated incident. The next torch kindled itself, while the flames of the first flickered and died.

Finally, the cat stopped next to one of the largest windows in the temple, with a view of the main courtyard I'd never stopped to admire. The cat hopped up on the sill and walked back and forth, still purring, still taunting me. "What are you doing?" I asked the cat. It arched before taking a step away from the window, floating out into the night. We were on the ground level, but that didn't stop my eyes from widening as it hovered in the air. It took another step, and another, until it sat down on nothing.

Let's add floating cats to my list of supernatural encounters. The cat mewed as if to say, *Follow me.* I peeked over the windowsill. It wasn't a long way down, but enough to twist an ankle if I wasn't as graceful as she when suspended in air. "I only get one life, thanks," I whispered.

It purred again, laughing at me, and took a challenging step back. Its fur bent in the night wind. *Come on*, its searing green eyes said. "Fine," I grumbled. I placed one shaky leg onto the windowsill and reached out for the demanding feline. "I can't believe I'm doing this."

A hand yanked me back from the ledge, and I toppled onto whoever grabbed me. Instead of cursing, however, my poor cushion clasped their arms around me. "Portia! God, what were you doing? Were you climbing out of the window?"

Worry, a natural state of being for my twin. "It's ground level, Alex," I gasped. "I can't breathe."

"Oh, I'm sorry." She let me go, and we scrambled to our feet. If my heart was thrumming before, it hammered now. I snapped a quick look out the window. Of course the cat was gone. When I turned back to my twin, I almost burst. I'd gone so long wondering what I'd do in this moment but now my mind went blank. *Should I break into song? Find a mariachi band?*

I opted to stare. The girl before me looked like my sister, but her skin was kissed by the sun since I'd seen her last. And long ornamented braids framed her face where pressed tresses from the Golden Apple ceremony had been. She wore a linen sheath and a dark, hooded cloak to conceal herself in the night. "You haven't worn braids since we were kids."

She ran her hand over her cornrows. "They don't exactly have flat irons or hot combs yet," she said, with a small laugh. She twisted the fabric of her cloak in her hands, and her light eyes found mine. We were a pair of modern girls moonlighting as ancient Egyptians. Her eyes glistened with unshed tears, the same as those welling in mine. "I never thought I'd see you again," Alex finally managed.

I pulled her in for the hug this time. "I know," I said. "I've missed you. How did you get in here?"

"Snuck in. Wasn't as hard as you'd think, even with those big guards running around." Her eyes danced quickly around the temple before returning to me. "And I've missed you, too. Are you okay?"

"I'm fine," I said. "Are you alright? How did you know where to find me?"

"I'm a servant at House Neberu, watching their children. The women gossip, and I'd heard some local talk about new priestesses at the temple when visitors described one, a Kushite they said, who sounded just like Selene. I didn't know for sure, but I had to check it out. I had to try."

Guilt crashed down on me. Did I try hard enough to get to her? Sure, I'd pestered Sikara for a safe route to House Neberu, but were my heka studies distracting from us all getting back home? "I saw your caravan a couple weeks ago," I said. "We were coming to your house tomorrow to find you and speak to Neben."

"That drunk moron left yesterday, and he made such a mess with his antics, I don't think they'd accept new visitors until after Akhet, even from the temple. I'm glad I came. You may have gotten turned away."

She thought for a moment. "I don't exactly remember what happened after the museum, but when I woke up I was in a cart on Neberu's caravan," she said. "Apparently they'd just stopped at a watering hole. I was lying out at high sun, so they checked me to see if I was dead. I opened my eyes and they saw the color"— she didn't like talking about her eyes as much as she didn't like admitting she was smarter than everyone—"and said they were the shade of their wheat, that it was favored by the gods. Or something." She waved her hands. "I snuck out this morning and ran here all day. One of the other servants is covering for me."

I touched her face. "Where are your glasses? Can you see?"

"When I woke up here, I didn't need them," she said. "How did you get here?"

"A soldier found me on the Nile bank. I was sick, so he brought me here for help. I've been studying heka as a scribe—well more like an apprentice."

"Heka?" Alex asked. " . . . magic?"

I wrinkled my brow. "How do you know about heka?"

Alex shrugged. "I don't know. The same way I know about anything else. Answers just . . . come." She narrowed her gaze. "There's no such thing as—"

"I know, but we're in ancient Egypt. Selene is in ancient Egypt. And I burned a cart down." I willed the blood to flow to my fingertips, the tingle to burn beneath my skin. Soft light shone through my skin, casting away the darkness. "With my hands."

She took a step back. "What is this?"

"Answers aren't just coming to you?" I asked, snappier than intended. I shook my hands and the glow disappeared. I softened my voice. "Sorry. It's heka." I pulled out the scarab from beneath my sheath. My twin blanched. I didn't know if she could handle any more surprises. "It's exactly what you think it is," I said.

"You believe it and heka"—the word came out clumsily— "brought us here?"

"I do, but I'm more interested in how they could get us back."

"What are you studying with the priestesses?" she asked. "If its magic that got us here and magic that'll get us back, then we need to know everything we can from the people who teach you about it."

Footsteps in the near distance grabbed our attention—Rawer's men on a nightly guard round. "We have to think of our real life," Alex whispered. "We have to think about Dad." Guilt washed over me. The footsteps were closer. "I'll come back tomorrow night. Sneak some scrolls out, and we'll go over everything you learn. We'll find the answers."

"The scrolls are in hieroglyphics, but I will read them to you."

She was quiet. "You don't have to. I can," she stammered, "read them, too. And speak some Hatti and Akkadian." I began to ask more questions, but she spoke before I could. "When I got here, I just could."

"And you don't believe in magic?" I asked. She pressed her mouth into a line and then threw her arms around my neck. Alex squeezed me tightly before dashing down the hall as quietly as she'd slipped in.

TO BE EXTRAORDINARY

I smoothed my jade wrap before entering the chamber. It fell nicely over my kalasiris, finely woven and more sheer than I preferred. In the weeks since I began working with Sikara, I thought that once we got past Egyptian Gods 101, we'd tackle my ability to spark electricity from my hands and set things on fire. We didn't, so I practiced on my own during stolen moments, always commanding the glow but never the sparks or fire.

Akhet had arrived and the Nile was rising. The air turned hot and miserable, especially as the temple kicked into high gear. Tasherit, Sikara, and—I assumed—the elusive High Priestess all prepared for the Lotus Ceremony. They spent hours on end plucking the lotus blossoms, blessing them, and distributing them to the local households.

The afternoon before the Lotus Ceremony, Sikara studied a scroll as I entered her classroom. Most Egyptians outside the priesthood couldn't read or write, and Sikara was particularly learned for a woman of the time, even a priestess. "How did you find the prayers this morning?" she asked, without peering up.

I sighed. Every day I waited for our lessons to divulge the source of my heka, as well as how to use and channel it. So far, Sikara's lessons hadn't gotten me closer to controlling my abilities. "They were good, like yesterday," I said.

And the day before that.

And the one before it.

"I pulled some texts for you to review. They're on your chair," she said, pointing to a high-backed, wicker seat. Again, I sighed and walked over to inspect them, wondering how many I'd be able to tuck in my robes to study with Alex that night.

I gathered them up and took a seat. The scrolls assisted my understanding of the baffling history of Egypt. Modern countries were only a few centuries old. I'd arrived in Waset about three thousand years before my actual birthday. By then the civilization was already three thousand years old.

I scanned the text, curving my back to inspect some of it. "Don't slouch," Sikara snapped, still without glancing at me.

I narrowed my eyes at her and returned to my papyrus scrolls. My gaze drifted over my wrist, a little swollen from the previous evening's labor. "My arms are sore," I mumbled of my work assisting priestesses in the prayer hall. We inspected patrons' offerings before setting the best aside for Her Holiness's private sacrifice. My arms most appreciated the gifts of the elite: jewels and finely woven linen. Laymen brought weighty containers of beer, and many of them were arriving for the Lotus Ceremony.

Sikara glanced up from her scrolls before abandoning her work to sit beside me. "Our service isn't glamorous. We prepare the offerings. We tend the statues. We wipe dust from their mantels until our arms burn. We even prepare for occasions like the prince's wedding, making fans and weaving grass baskets and blessing lotus blossoms. And have you mastered the Hyksos style of wrapping linens for the ceremonies?"

I nodded, stifling an eye roll. "Yes, I have."

"Good," she said, and stood. "Then today I want you to do it again."

"Do what again?" I creased my brow. "Practice the Hyksos wrap?"

"No," she said. "I want you to recreate your heka."

My breathing hitched. "Here?" I stammered. "*Now?*"

"Do you have something better to do?" I shook my head as my eyes fell to my palms. I failed each time I tried to reproduce the heka beneath my skin. Sikara folded her arms expectedly. "What is the issue?" she asked.

I turned to the priestess in defeat. "I can't."

"You've done this before."

"Well, I can't do it now." I sat back in my chair. "Maybe we should break."

Sikara's mouth thinned. "Breaks are for the lazy, not priestesses of Isis."

I diverted my eyes from her scrutiny. "I'm not a priestess yet."

"And you won't be with your inclination to whine."

"I'm not whining. I'm exhausted. I've been learning and cleaning and practicing whatever you want me to practice for weeks," I said. "You don't care that this isn't easy. You just like telling me what to do." I rose from my chair and angled away from her. "Well, I can't do it, Sikara. I'll probably never do it again."

She regarded me for a few painful moments as I shifted my weight. "Are you done?" she finally asked. "Portia," she said, voice softer than it'd ever been, "you are talented, and when a talented person behaves in a lazy way, it's an insult. It's an insult to those who wants the best for them. Most importantly, it's an insult to *me.*"

I turned back to meet her gaze, wishing she'd just called me insolent. Sikara's calm disappointment pricked my flight reflex and my tear ducts simultaneously. "No one is holding you prisoner," she said. "You may leave at any time, especially with this proclivity to sloth."

"I'm not lazy," I mumbled, though she was right. I'd never imagined needing this conversation. Alex had the natural talents. She needed the guidance and coaching, not me. I wondered if she'd ever broken down en route to the decathlon. Had she ever resented her genius and the expectation that came with it?

"Why don't we go outside?" Sikara suggested before we strode out to a private court. The warm sun spread across my face, Ra's sun disk making its way across the turquoise sky. We crossed the yard toward a limestone bench beneath draping foliage. When she stopped a few feet short of it, however, I nearly crashed into her back.

Sikara whirled around to me and clapped her hands together. "What was happening the last time you used your heka?"

I blinked. We'd gone over this before. "I was in the market with Tasherit," I said.

She frowned. "Close your eyes."

"Why?" I asked.

Her eyes only urged me to follow the instructions. When I did, she continued. "You were leaving the marketplace . . ."

"That's when I sat next to Tasherit in the cart," I said.

"And where was it?"

"It was in the road, on the way back to the temple. And then we stopped. A caravan was coming into Waset, so we stayed out of the way so they could pass."

"Good. Continue."

"There were mules and horses and servants."

"And . . ." she pressed.

I saw my sister in a cart at the back of the caravan, but she didn't see me. When I tried to chase after her, Tasherit held me back. I bit my lip. *The caravan pulled away with Alex in tow. She hadn't seen me. It was my opportunity to reach her.* I blinked my eyes open. "I was angry," I said.

"And merely reacting to your anger will push you into actions you are unprepared for. You must be stronger than you've ever been."

"I never had to work this hard before," I admitted.

"And how satisfactory was that?" she asked my abrupt silence. I couldn't say it, but didn't have to. It wasn't satisfactory. *Not at all.*

My breathing labored under mounting thoughts, so many that I barely flinched when Sikara took my hand. She held it before me, where a sole white-gold spark danced at the tip of my pointer finger, my hand glowing once more. My skin flushed and tingled, but even this didn't distract me from the first smile I'd ever seen Sikara display. "It's time to be extraordinary, Portia."

THE BINDING TRADE (PART 1)

A thin trail of smoke seductively coiled in the air. I watched as it gracefully faded to nothing. *Sexy,* I whispered. On my mat of woven reeds, I practiced commanding and snuffing the spark. Though the heka always stung as it sprang from me, I'd done so almost a hundred times since the courtyard. The burning left beneath my skin never impacted its thrill. Besides, practicing was all I could think to do while waiting to meet Alex.

An early curfew came down from the High Priestess the night before the much-anticipated Lotus Ceremony. The ceremony began the royal wedding circus, and as the moon crept higher in the sky, I knew my twin and I wouldn't have as much time as usual. No one was allowed into or out of the temple, save emergencies, at this time of night, but we met biweekly anyway. She always snuck in the hallway with the large window. To me, it would forever be the place cats floated on air.

I snuffed the last spark and rose from my mat. With a glance over to Selene, who was knocked out, I slipped into the hallway. The torches didn't light for me this time, and Alex wasn't in the narrow passageway, so I found the window's edge. I whistled out.

One sang back from the darkness. "Where are you?" I whispered, peering out. "*Alex.*"

"Shhh. Over here, by the courtyard," she called. I shook my head. Rawer's men patrolled the courtyard leading into the temple like the good Medjay they were. Meetings in the holy place, though we'd had them, were tricky. Walking through the courtyard tonight of all nights was impossible.

I scooted over the windowsill, and my feet landed on the cool stones leading toward the temple courtyard. The window was still high enough that I'd need to concentrate to get down. Climbing inside hadn't bothered Alex in the past weeks, and I wondered if the time travel had given her a talent for scaling buildings like Spider-Man.

My sister stood under one of the fig trees clustered near its entrance wearing her traveling cloak. House Neberu must have been very nice or very rich to give her a cloak, or maybe she borrowed it when no one was looking. I never asked. We hugged, though it wasn't tight. "What's wrong?" I asked when I pulled away.

"Let's walk," she said. I scanned the area quickly for any of Rawer's patrolling men. "I already checked for guards," she said. I nodded and we began to move. My sister's elbow poked me a few times as she picked at the cloak. She always fiddled with her clothes when thinking.

"*What?*" I asked again.

Finally, a long sigh came. "We've been going over these scrolls, and there's just nothing in them," she said. "Sure, they talk about how important it is to respect heka, but there's nothing to help us get home. There's no plan."

And my sister was the type to need a plan. For her, everything hinged on knowing what she'd do tomorrow, the day after, and at 6:15 p.m. on Monday of next week. "Is Selene asleep?" she finally asked.

"Yeah, Selene is always out like a light as soon as the sun goes down," I said. "And maybe this will help. I had a breakthrough today," I said. I held my hand up, and the tingle of heka flowed down to my fingers. My palm glowed white before sparks burst from my pointer.

"Shit." My twin near tripped. "That . . . that would burn down a cart," she stammered. She steadied herself and stared at my hand. "Does it hurt?"

My pointer finger throbbed, and I nodded. The aching from all the practice may have affected the spark, as it flickered. "Hold on," I said, trying to make it work again.

My twin chuckled. "You're going to go blind like that."

"Shuddup," I said with a laugh and shook my hand, allowing the glow to leave and return my brown skin.

Sandals tapping the stone pathway caught my attention. I snapped in the sound's direction, willing heka into my hands. It was excruciating, given all my practice and my palms barely glowed. I hoped it would be enough to hold off whoever found us. Instead of a Medjay, a woman of average height emerged from the courtyard's shadows. She wore a green tunic with a delicate weave, but she was without makeup or wig. Her head had gone at least a week past a decent shave. Bekmut was unlike herself.

"I mean no harm," Bekmut said. But instead of her usual loudness, her voice barely carried.

I shook the light from my hands. "You know her?" Alex asked me.

"This is Bekmut," I said. "She's a friend of Tasherit's."

Bekmut continued. "Both Tasherit and I have known about this for a while. She sends Rawer's guards away while you meet."

So we weren't as good as we thought at hiding our meetings.

"What do you want?" Alex asked.

Bekmut studied our faces. "Sisters," she said. "Twins." I didn't know where she was going and didn't ask. "I've overheard your concern. I want to help you."

Alex and I exchanged glances. "Why would you help us?" I asked when I turned back to Bekmut.

"Because you have the favor of the great ladies." Her voice lowered further still, as if she'd thought this many times but never said the words aloud. "Something I've wanted for some time."

"You're Tasherit's friend. You can speak to her whenever you want."

Bekmut shook her head. "You study under the Lady Sikara and, by extension, Her Holiness, Weret." She evened her gaze. "Since I was a small girl, I've wanted to be like Her Holiness," she said. "I was never chosen as you, but the goddess still sang to my ka in her own ways. I never enjoyed being a rich man's daughter," she said, "or wanted to be one's bride." So my guess was right. She was from a noble family. "It's why I joined the temple instead of marrying."

"If you help me," she continued, "I will help you. You need the Guide." *Guide?* I sucked my teeth imagining the men in funny hats showing tourists around the Loop on a double-decker bus. I must not have hidden my skepticism well. "He is a man of great skill and power," she assured me. "Not bound by the heka of Waset or its rules. For this reason, he understands what cannot be understood, which is what you seek. I can take you to him. By the goddess, you will not be harmed."

"But that's this dude's name?" I continued. "Who just goes by *The Guide?*"

Her eyes flickered with annoyance. "He has helped me before," said Bekmut. "And many others in the temple."

I placed my hand on my hip. "But really, *The Guide?*"

She sighed. "You want an unforeseen place, don't you? An unforeseen time? Somewhere far beyond Swenett?" A beat passed. "He can take you there. If there is a want in your heart, he can fulfill it."

Maybe it was her odd soft voice she was using. Maybe it was the way she stared at us. Either way, unease pricked my spine. "And Tasherit's gone to him?" I asked.

"Tasherit is already a great lady. She has no wants," Bekmut replied.

I turned to Alex. "We should talk to Tasherit before we do anything."

"No." Alex touched my arm. "This is a chance we have to take, Portia. And we have to take it now." She held my gaze, that twinkle of desperation staring back at me. It was the same anxious glimmer that took full control of the Secret Santa last year, and the Father's Day brunch months after that. It was the twinkle that made snap decisions when things didn't come as easily. Alex turned to Bekmut. "We'll go," she said.

"Not you," Bekmut replied. "Only the one that summons light and fire." I looped my arm with my twin and tugged her close. *Leave my sister? Hell no.* "Fine," Bekmut relented. "She may walk with us, but only so far." Alex nodded, her eyes holding a new brightness, a sure gaze. Perhaps it was time she stopped answering for the both of us.

Without a decent breeze, warm night air hung around us as we twisted through Waset's empty streets. Most people slept as soon

as the sun set, making it easier to get around undetected. The
thick air remained a companion as constant as the gnats and
mosquitoes savoring Bekmut's sweet perfume. Alex sauntered
quietly at my side, and Bekmut strode a few paces ahead of us.

Even though Bekmut had given us our first real clue about
time travel, no smile creased my lips. I wanted to go home. I
missed our father. Selene needed to wrap her arms around her
grandmother. But the thought of leaving Tasherit and Sikara
tugged at heartstrings I didn't know I possessed. And would I be
able to explore my new abilities in the future? Would I even have
them still?

I narrowed my gaze toward the priestess ahead of us. The hairs
on the back of my neck hadn't lain down since she stepped out of
the shadows. Bekmut's pace slowed, so I called out, "Where are
we going?"

Alex placed her hands on her knees and panted as Bekmut
glanced back at me. "We're here," she replied. "The temple of
Amun."

Waset was a city severed in halves by the Nile. Most temples lay
on the eastern bank, with Pharaoh's magnificent palace in the west.
Pharaoh's grandfather, however, broke tradition, and constructed
the temples of Isis, Amun, and the cow goddess Hathor, near his
home to avoid using the port to send his obeisance. Amun was the
king of the gods, a deity powerful enough to create himself from
nothing and fashion his surroundings from his vast imagination.
Tall, slender trees lined the entryway, and without wind to shake
their leaves, they stood like unmovable watchmen. "Stay here
now," Bekmut told Alex.

"Yeah, yeah, yeah," I cut in. "You need the one with the light
and fire." I pulled the scarab necklace off and handed it to Alex.
Something told me it would be safer with her. "Watch this for

me." Alex fastened it around her neck, and I turned to Bekmut. "Let's get this over with."

The temple of Amun was like that of Isis in design. Behind the tree-guards laid a long pathway and an ungodly amount of ascending stone steps. Bekmut and I climbed them before reaching the mouth of the structure. Two massive pylons honored a man with plumes sprouting from his crown, holding an ankh in his left hand, and a scepter—showing his strength and power—in his right. Painted in swaths of blue, the relief would tower over the proclamation walls at Isis's temple.

As we stood, a guard approached us from behind one of the pylons wearing a cerulean shendyt. Unlike Rawer, this guard didn't show any suspicion at our arrival. In fact, he smiled at Bekmut and pointed us toward the next courtyard enclosed with bending saplings. "This way," she whispered.

"You're very familiar with the temple of Amun," I noted. "The other priestesses rarely leave our grounds." She glanced back at me but said nothing. We made our way through the courtyard and snuck around to the back entrance of their kitchens. From there Bekmut wound me through narrow, stuffy hallways until we reached a chamber for small audiences. An oil lamp burned on a wooden mantle near the door. Darkness swallowed everything else.

"Sit," Bekmut instructed. I found a wicker chair and eased down. She stood close to my side as the heavy scent of myrrh permeated the air. I followed the scent toward another entryway, one now filled with a scribe boy no more than ten or eleven years old. His head was shaven and bowed, and a linen kilt dangled to his knees. When he entered, he lit another oil lamp on an ebony table near Bekmut and me before folding himself into the scenery.

I was suddenly aware that the entryway had filled again. A man standing about a foot taller than the scribe ambled into the chamber at a slow, measured pace. He crossed the floor, his blue shendyt sweeping the ground, before he sat in front of me. "Is this the girl you spoke of, Bekmut?" He'd asked the priestess, but his piercing gaze scrutinized me. Like the boy, his head was clean shaven, and thin lines sprouted at the corners of his eyes.

"Yes," she whispered. "She has heka of fire and light."

I stuck my chin in the air, but that didn't keep my body from shaking. "Are you the Guide?" I asked.

"I am Ankhmir," he corrected. "A servant of Amun and of His Holiness, the High Priest Akoris."

My voice was flat. "So you are not the Guide?"

"I am not," he said. "As I am not the High Priest." I rolled my eyes. *Middlemen and gatekeepers.* "But he can arrange the passage you want," he said. "Bekmut has not told untruths. He has the favor of the gods."

"And what does he want for this favor?" I asked. *Creep*, I added in my head.

"Firstly, proof," he said. "Hold out your hand." I glanced to my side, wishing my twin was there. Instead, Bekmut's unsettling eyes urged me on. I reluctantly stuck my hand out. His eyes traced my red, splotchy palms before he leaned forward. His brow near touched my hand as he whispered an incantation in a language I'd yet to encounter.

Instantly, the creases of my palms brightened, and they burned like never before. "What are you doing?" I asked, trying to wrench my hand back. He didn't answer, however. He continued his spell until my hand glowed so fiercely, I thought it would blot us all out.

And for one incredible moment, it did. The room completely vanished in brightness until everything went black. I panted, eyes darting around until I somehow the scribe relit the oil lamps. The chamber's glow was not nearly as powerful as the light that had a moment ago burst from my hand.

"What was that?" I asked, noticing that everyone but me had been knocked to the floor.

Ankhmir pulled himself up with the help of the scribe. The priest's chair had flipped on its side so his apprentice set is before me again. When the priest sat, he wiped his brow. The light was hard for him to bear. "You didn't think I'd just believe that you had heka?" he asked. "I had to see if it was true."

I held onto my now-throbbing hand as Bekmut pulled herself up to sit beside me. "So what just happened?" I asked him.

His voice was less sure of itself. "The heka was greater than anticipated." My eyes searched the priest and priestess. On the day I entered Waset with Merenptah, I knew that if I had to knee him in the balls, I would. If these two tried that shit again, I'd burn the entire temple down, bum hand or not. "What do you want?" I spat at Ankhmir.

"His Holiness, the Guide, requires the binding trade. It exchanges what you desire most for something of equal value," he said. "You will trade this heka for the passage you seek." He didn't even present it as a question.

I turned to Bekmut, fighting something new and wild and desperate welling inside. "There's nothing to fear," Bekmut said, her eyes soft and calm. Sweat trickled down her face as it did Ankhmir's. "I made the trade years ago, ending an unwanted marriage for the temple life."

My jaw tightened. She'd brought me here. She'd hyped up my sister, my sister who was so anxious to get out of the unknown that she'd thrust me into the completely worse. Bekmut was the reason that I could gain and lose everything at once. I returned to the priest who said, "Return tomorrow night."

"Tomorrow is the Lotus Ceremony. We can't just get a note and leave," I stammered. "Have you ever tried to get past Sikara *and* Tasherit?"

The priest dusted himself off after rising from his seat. "Your temple will dress the bride and her retinue, one hundred maidens if I am to be exact. An opportunity for disappearance might call for a disguise."

The questions flooded from Alex as we made our way back, and though my lips were moving, I wasn't answering with my heart. In fact, I was still shaking. I told her about the priest's suggestion of hiding ourselves in the retinue after the Lotus Ceremony. "Sneak out," she said as we approached the road leading back toward House Neberu. She removed my scarab necklace and handed it to me. "That makes sense." She glanced at the hand I nursed. "Will you be okay?"

"Yeah, eventually," I said and indicated the priestess, who had barely uttered two words since we left the temple of Amun. Her back glistened with sweat now. "It's hot, but it's not that hot," I said.

"Well, she's moving fast," Alex said. "Probably wants to get back before anyone notices."

"Do you think this will work?" I asked her.

She nodded emphatically. "Yes," she said. "I doubt they would notice a hundred and three girls instead of one hundred. Just grab some of their clothes. I'll meet you and Selene at the palace for the presentation ceremony." She hugged me before taking off into the night.

I continued behind Bekmut. Her green tunic clung to her skin as we strode up the pathway lined with familiar sycamore trees.

"Are you alright, Bekmut?" I asked once we reached the top of the stone steps. I jogged closer to find her round face round face and features clenched as I neared. She nodded but didn't turn to me. "Well, thanks," I said reluctantly. "My sister is happy. And I will talk to Tasherit and Sikara about you." "Please," she strained through an odd, gravelly voice. "Let's walk in silence."

Was she really copping an attitude after I met her creepy priest?

"Sure, whatever." I followed her in silence again until her sandal caught a rock or crack in the ground, and I reflexively grabbed her arm to balance her. "Hey, watch out there," I said, holding her tight.

Instead of saying thanks, she whirled around like a predatory cat. Her eyes were no longer brown but this awful, muddied purple-blue. The wash of color swirled with a violence I'd only seen once before—in the old cook's.

"The burning light in you," she began, her voice a terror, seemingly layered in many others. "I've never seen anything like it. It almost hurts; it's heavy on my body." She grabbed my shoulder, her hands cool to the touch despite the sweat pouring down her body, and I yanked free of her grasp. I wrenched away so violently that she staggered against one of the proclamation walls. Arm splayed, she squeezed her eyes tight and she drew desperate breaths.

When she opened her eyes, her irises her brown once more. "I'm sorry," she said, her voice loud and carrying through the night. She picked up the hem of her tunic and dashed away into the temple. I stood, unable to move, watching her form disappear. A death-like shiver crept up my spine.

BELOVED OF PTAH

I was not the ideal servant of Isis, still tired from the night before. My trip to the temple of Amun played over in my head, as well as my encounter with Bekmut near the pylons. As the priestesses stood on the shoreline of the Iteru, I glanced back at Tasherit and Selene, both clad in sheer linen dresses for the occasion. Neither the thick, moist air nor flitting insects appeared to bother them. Bekmut was nowhere to be seen. "Where's Bekmut?" I asked.

"I did not see her this morning," Sikara replied. Though a breeze skimmed the Iteru's shoreline, my thoughts distracted me from the task at hand: tussling blue lotus petals in wicker baskets at my feet. Crowds lined the banks as lightning bugs illuminated the gentle waters beneath it, and the families of Waset gathered near the Nile marsh.

They awaited the first sign of the Hyksos princess and her fleet. Their chatter swelled, intensifying the hum of excitement. Between the heat and my rampant thoughts, I sighed for the umpteenth time. "Focus," Sikara said, swatting my arm with a fan of woven river leaves.

"Focus on what? The water? There are no boats yet." And it was still difficult to see anything but Bekmut's eyes.

"A servant of Isis is intent on her duty." Her arms folded across her chest. A finely-stitched cloak draped her shoulders despite the heat, and dark braids met the nape of her neck. She scanned my work, eying some of my baskets with uneven amounts of lotus blossoms. Her disapproval suggested I rearrange their levels.

"Why is it so hot here?" I asked, moving petals between the baskets by handfuls.

Sikara nodded toward a cluster of servants forming an arc around Her Holiness, Weret. She stood only paces ahead of us, but her distant expression was miles away. Again, she'd tucked her right arm tight in her linens while the other dangled freely. I wondered if she'd recently injured it as her servants fanned her with ostrich feathers. "Would you rather be hot *and* fanning?" she asked. "Your little arms nearly falling off? Why don't you ask the Kushite for help if it's needed?"

"Selene," I corrected her. "And I'm fine." She and Tasherit worked not so far from us, passing out wooden tokens of the goddess to surrounding attendees. Selene's kalasiris blew in the wind as she trailed Tasherit. She held the bag of tokens, waiting patiently with a smile. I was the one in training, but Selene had also acclimated to temple life.

And the binding trade was going to end all that. Guilt pushed down on me, so I did my best to dispel the thoughts. I couldn't get through the Lotus Ceremony and think of the heka I'd exchange, or the priestess's hospitality I'd spit on.

"You are distant today," said Sikara. I didn't respond. My eyes instead skimmed the water front before landing on a raised dais further downriver. A cluster of guards gathered by the wooden platform, and I wondered if Merenptah might be with them, and if he'd be sad to know I was leaving soon. The dais was obviously for the royals, but even though every citizen of Waset was present, the most important were noticeably absent. "Where is the royal family?" I asked.

"They are respecting Hyksos tradition," Sikara replied. "To the Delta, a bride brings her consort his greatest treasures: heirs, a home. She is so special that no one can look on her face until the final day of wedding ceremonies, and she wears a veil until that time. She cannot even be presented to Prince Seti until the sun sets tonight."

"Why is everything here a big deal?" I asked. "So who's going to meet her? All those guards?"

Sikara inclined her head toward the platform. It was no longer empty. Now there stood a throng of men in blue, including the scribe boy and priest I recognized from the night before. I shuddered. At the apex of this grouping was a priest wearing a leopard skin over his shoulder and, like the other holy men of Amun, a shaved skull. The crowd buzzed at his presence. "His Holiness will greet the princess," she said. "He is Akoris, the High Priest of Amun."

I wanted to say I knew of him already. That he was the Guide with whom I'd barter my heka. That I'd met with his viper priest and still shook because of it. Instead I settled on: "Why him?"

Sikara came closer and plucked one of my baskets. In her swiftness, she whispered, "Because he might as well be royalty. You see the great houses of Egypt here today, don't you? You see the rekhet. And you see the priests and priestesses. Egypt is commanded by Pharaoh, but His Holiness interprets the will of Amun.

"Akoris's temple is the richest in Waset," she continued, "and most respected. Traveling dignitaries bring their expensive offerings to Amun during their visits. Pharaoh gives a portion of his spoils after a successful campaign."

"... and also to the High Priest?" I asked. She smiled but didn't answer. "If Amun is so important, why is the princess coming to our temple?"

"Because," she said, "the Temple of Isis is the *second* wealthiest temple in Egypt." Her eyes turned to the High Priestess. "Our lady has sacrificed much to ensure it."

I followed Sikara's gaze. Weret rarely appeared outside of her duties, and being so close to her almost felt like an invasion of her privacy. She wore a small diadem with glistening, green jewels. "The princess will come to our temple this evening," said Sikara. "Her Holiness will bless her before the presentation to Seti."

"Will I ever get to meet Weret?" I asked, lingering on her image a moment longer.

"Don't speak of her so casually. She is the mouth of Isis. She will speak to you only when she would like."

"*When she would like*," I said, though Sikara ignored me. Her eyes fixed on a change in the waters.

"Get your baskets." Sikara pushed my shoulder as I reached for them. "I see them!" she said as the first boats drifted into view. Petals from each side of the river took flight. They swarmed the scarlet sky with blue landing on the banks and waters alike.

Small, crescent-shaped ships of skillfully secured wood led the fleet, each with rowers at the front and back. A handful of young women filled the space between. They wore blue linens trimmed with gold thread, shimmering like fireflies in the morning glow.

And then she was before us. In the middle of the fleet sailed the grandest boat of all, carrying the Hyksos princess surrounded by still more handmaidens. Her wooden ship held a gilded cabin at the center of its deck, easily three times the size of the papyrus-wood boats. Clad in crimson robes, she wore a veil of cascading pearlescent stones secured with tiny netting. It reflected even the smallest glimmer.

Every Egyptian on the banks held their breaths. "What's her name?" I asked.

"Sahdina," Sikara said, without turning to me. "But it will soon be Tuya of the Two Lands."

I scrunched my nose. "Why change her whole name?" Most women I knew changed their names after marriage, but no one changed their full name unless they joined the Witness Protection Program.

"She can't be Egypt's queen with a Hyksos name," Sikara said. "When she steps off that boat, she'll belong to Waset." I grunted and tossed another handful of petals, trying in vain to catch the princess's features beneath the glittering fabric. "And it will be a show of gratitude."

I arched a brow. "Gratitude for what?"

"It is advantageous for the Hyksos to gain Egyptian support," she said. "They will war with the Seafarers soon and can't win without it." She threw a handful of petals out onto the water. They floated atop like lily pads.

"The Hyksos were conquered and annexed by Pharaoh Thutmose many years ago and have lived much like a client kingdom in the Delta since. They have very profitable trade relationships, as their capital, Avaris, is known for a rare tree called the Omnu. The Omnu's spice has a potent healing agent, and its petals are red as the princess's robes.

"But some time ago, ships arrived carrying Seafarers: tattered men and women with no homeland and dwindling numbers. The Hyksos welcomed them only for the Seafarers to discover the Omnu trees and want them for their own. The Hyksos aren't known for their arms, but as the Seafarers were also without weapons, they saw no reason to engage them."

Sikara shook her head. "And then one day it changed. The Seafarers unveiled metal more powerful than Hittite iron. They gained warriors that launched vicious attacks, burning villages, killing men, women, and children until the Hyksos banded together to keep them out of Avaris. There they could hold them off but not defeat them. They needed the might of Egypt, or they would be slaughtered."

Horror rippled through me. *What had the princess seen? What had she lost?* Her boat sailed past us, her straight back indicating her strength. Her neatly folded hands said *grace*. She would spend her life with someone she didn't know, in someone else's land, as payment toward a war debt. And she didn't tremble. I found a new subject. "What is Seti like?" I asked.

"I've never met the prince," Sikara sighed heavily and threw more petals. "What a beautiful girl."

"You can't even see her face."

The princess's ship sailed toward the dais and palace guards to be welcomed by the High Priest. Sikara settled her basket at her feet. "Her prince is the child of Set, the chaos god. I'm sure he lives up to his name."

That afternoon, the servants of Isis filled the temple entrance in flowing dresses of green, awaiting the arrival of the Hyksos princess. They gathered between the pylons with wicker baskets at their feet as the High Priestess stood at the head. Sikara flanked her, still wearing her patterned cloak from the Lotus Ceremony the evening before. Sweat slicked my hands as I struggled with my basket, an oblong thing brimming with linens. I cradled the sides to keep its contents—the traditional Hyksos wrap—in place. Selene and Tasherit waited beside me.

A glimmer cut through the evening's blush. Her jeweled veil twinkled as the princess led her procession up the temple walkway, beneath the arching sycamore trees. No more than a few paces behind her was a slightly older woman in fine but plain clothing—her governess, I'd heard. The princess's hundred handmaidens trailed them solemnly toward our steps. Clad in white and adorned with the pearl stones of the princess's veil at their wrists and ankles, the maidens sparkled like grains of desert sand beneath the sun.

When the procession reached the top of the steps, the priestesses parted behind Weret and Sikara. The leaders of the temple turned before the princess and her maidens, ushering it into the courtyard. The Hyksos imports passed the rest of Isis's priestesses with eyes focused ahead, and at close range, their linen dresses were not only bright white, but woven to translucence.

When all of the handmaidens had entered the courtyard, the priestesses followed them through the Prayer Hall's private doors and funneled into a large chamber. The princess disappeared into a sanctuary to honor the goddess before heading to the High Priestess's private chamber. The handmaidens began to chatter amongst themselves as the remaining women of Isis set down their burdens and distributed linens with the efficiency of the Ford assembly line.

After tucking my last pleated yard around a bored Hyksos girl, it was time. *Go, Portia,* I thought. *Now.* My mind raced as I drifted away from the crowd with my empty basket for the back of the room.

At its edges, temple servants had discarded damaged linens

unfit for the handmaidens. They lay in old baskets draped in shadows. Once I'd meandered undetected, I set my basket down and snatched three lengths of battered material. I tossed them into my basket and looked over my shoulder. The hum of work carried on behind me, and I sighed in relief.

As I returned with my pilfered linens, a hush fell over the room. The princess had emerged in ceremonial dress, robes of rich gold and blue under her sparkling veil. I stared as servants ushered her to the front of the temple, her handmaidens slipping into formation behind. "Why are you carrying that?" My eyes snapped to Sikara, who marched toward me. I placed the basket on the floor and straightened my back.

"Carrying what?" I asked when she reached me.

"*That*," she said, indicating the basket at my feet. "The maids are dressed. We will not need additional provisions at the palace."

I smiled my widest, most innocent smile. "Just in case," I said. She grunted a rebuttal as the High Priestess breezed past us. She exchanged a glance with Sikara, an expression as commanding as a shout, and the lower priestess abruptly followed her. I picked up my basket and found my place with the other priestesses.

The procession left the temple in an excursion like the Macy's Thanksgiving Day Parade. The citizens of Waset crowded the streets, shoving and cheering as the mysterious princess, carried on a painted litter, and her white-clad maidens passed them by. The servants of Isis followed, and my basket grew heavier as we trudged along under the high sun.

Soon we arrived before imposing stone walls, making our way in small groups through its narrow opening. My eyes danced over murals of Pharaoh riding a gilded chariot, conquering his enemies in battle, much like in the proclamation walls bordering Waset. The enclosed palace was a city within itself, what Sikara called the House of Rejoicing. Despite my impending escape, it was a thrill to witness.

The procession traveled a long walkway with limestone statues of the crocodile god Sobek on either side. As they gleamed in the sunlight, I stared like an ancient might regard a skyscraper. Pylons greeted us at the end of the walkway, followed by a courtyard boasting lush fig trees and rows of stairs behind them. The mouth of the palace waited at the end of our travels.

My lungs burned by the time we entered the palace. The servants of Isis followed the last handmaidens through the long, stuffy corridors into Pharaoh's great petition hall, the audience chamber. Here Pharaoh and his viziers took the pleas and requests of dignitaries and everyday citizens, and the room reflected that practical purpose. The wise baboon god Thoth figured prominently in scenes of discernment, flanked often by Ma'at and her feather of truth. Large columns circled its perimeter, and instead of an aisle down its middle, empty space provided a vast floor for petitioners daring to audience with Egypt's highest house.

The audience chamber already bulged with guests when the smell of myrrh flooded my nostrils. Instantly my heart thudded at the ceremonial incense of Amun's temple, taking me back to the night before. Its presence in the air meant robes of blue weren't far away, and if I saw Ankhmir I might actually faint.

I turned in enough time to catch the priests pouring into the space, their heads shaved clean and limbs glistening with anointed oils. At their apex was His Holiness, Akoris, followed by his second in command. Ankhmir's glance traveled over me without acknowledgment. I shivered.

"They stink," said a voice at my side.

"We probably smell bad after our prayers, too," I replied to Selene.

"Nope. We smell like flowers," she said, eyes lighting up. "Portia, look." She pointed past Sikara—busy barking orders to priestesses and handmaidens alike—to House Neberu among the noble families filing inside.

My eyes immediately found Alex. She stood out amongst their servants not because of her face, which was as taut as it had ever been, but her walk. Every prideful movement said she'd never been a servant before, and had no desire to remain one. I willed her to look up, and a jolt of victory shot through me when her eyes flicked to us.

She tilted her head, hair still braided to frame her face, and her expression softened before she mouthed, "Ready?" I nodded and held the basket up. Her smile widened as her house took its place near the chamber door. She gestured toward a pillar at the edge of the room, away from the commotion.

Got it.

I hid my face as I moved toward the pillar, Selene trailing me. When we reached the designated post, I turned to find Alex had slipped away from House Neberu equally as quick. Selene beat me in speaking to her. "How did you get away so fast?" Selene asked, wrapping her arms around my sister.

"Because I'm a ninja," Alex replied.

"Did anyone see you leave?" I asked my twin.

"No, they're all too involved in the ceremony stuff."

"Perfect," I said, putting my basket down. Selene reached in and felt the fabrics. When she gave me a pointed look, I replied, "Even the Hyksos have throwaway piles."

"I *thought* you disappeared while Tasherit was wrapping those girls," Selene said. "Do you think we'll be able to walk out the front door with these? They'll wonder where we're going without the princess."

I shrugged. "It's camouflage, not a free pass."

"We'll leave tonight for the temple of Amun during the feast," Alex explained. "Everyone will be too busy and drunk to notice. Just follow along with all the girls for now." My sister peered toward the gathering. "We should hurry. We don't have much time." I handed both Selene and Alex a few yards of the Hyksos wrap. I coached them through the proper dressing technique and, with a few glances around, took a spot in the back of the handmaidens.

The ceremony began as harpists strummed their instruments, and the royal family ascended the dais, on which thrones of ebony, gold, and precious metals waited. The queen emerged in a kalasiris whose train followed her in a stream of golden linen. Her hair was pulled beneath a metal headdress with splaying wings. Lesser members of the royal family snaked around the stage, along with the kingdom's elite: viziers, ambassadors, architects, and merchants. The rest of the crowd settled in by level of importance, leaving the floor in front of the royal family for the handmaidens. Pharaoh Anen was absent.

The harpists' song slipped into a different, more melodic tune. The Hyksos women began to hum and glide through entrancing movements. Selene, Alex, and I followed as best we could, eyes on the polished tiles. Through the flutter of limbs, servants removed Tuya from her litter, and when her feet touched the ground, she became the halftime show. The melody was just *painfully* slow. The Hyksos procession added to the princess's magnificence, I'm sure, but did nothing for a hammering heart.

Finally, the ladies picked up the pace. Around us, the handmaidens were a marching band, their lines winding gracefully through and around each other as the princess approached the thrones. The three of us stumbled along, trying to follow the white-wrapped forms, but when they abruptly stopped, I almost plowed into the maid nearest me. I cast my gaze up as the princess reached the base of the royal stage and dropped to her knees before the monarchs of Waset.

Our procession had unfurled a Hyksos vizier, an ambassador, and the governess holding a bridal box, and by some stunning failure of luck, the back of the procession had become the front. Alex, Selene, and I stood close enough to the princess that one wrong glance could ruin everything we'd planned. We pulled the linens over our faces as far as they would go.

Even with my eyes cast down, I recognized the leopard robe of the High Priest of Amun as he strode to the dais. His voice rebounded through the hall. "A Hyksos flower will bloom before the gods of Egypt," he began. "Amun's blessing will bring prosperity to this union, the binding of Waset and Avaris, in the spirit of Thutmose's victory so long ago." I glanced up at the dynamic High Priest, who extended his bejeweled hand to assist the princess to her feet.

Silence fell on the hall. It was time for the formal presentation, and the knowledge pumped excitement through me. We'd soon be in the clear. My thoughts were consumed with home and the binding trade. They collided with each other, begging for my full attention, until from my periphery, another man ascended the dais.

With a broad back beneath a soldier's pectoral, he faced the audience. My eyes flicked to him despite myself. He carried a polished tray in both hands, and (to match his military attire) he also wore a soldier's grimace. "The General Raia," announced Akoris as the Egyptian throng nodded in approval.

The High Priest distanced himself as the general spoke. "The Horus Lord will ensure Ma'at, governing the two lands with a secure Southern border and a swift victory in the north." A satisfied whirr of chatter and approval followed. My ears perked—I'd heard that voice somewhere before.

The general stepped down, and the High Priest of Amun began again. "The presentation of the Hyksos princess to the prince of Egypt," he bellowed. "From this day, she will be Tuya, Great Lady of the Two Lands. The son of our Horus Lord will present her with a gift. It is Nekhbet, our vulture goddess, who will offer protection of this royal woman." He raised the tray toward the sky before returning it to chest level. The token was a beaded faience necklace with golden links. The High Priest continued, "The prince welcomes her to this fertile land."

I still racked my brain at the general's voice. *Where had I heard him before?* And then my heart stopped. The general was on the banks during my first night in Egypt, caught in heated conversation. I glanced up again. After receiving the tray with the princess's gift, another man took center stage. Before the elite families of Waset stood Egypt's prince.

Merenptah.

SAHDINA (PART 1)

The boy I'd met on the Nile banks was as I remembered—same features, same movements, same proud if mischievous glint in his eyes. But as my gaze traveled to the striped nemes crown atop his head, as well as Mr. Pomey's rearing cobra on his brow, he couldn't be further from the soldier I'd helped with a rock and a decent throw. His back stiffened as he strode to his betrothed.

And he was freaking engaged.

It probably wasn't customary that princes carry their own trays, but he did. He stopped before his bride and allowed her to glance over the beautiful necklace, nod graciously, and indicate one of the maidens should take it. Cheers soared about the prince and princess as they bowed to each other. I could almost taste the people's excitement.

I placed my hand to my throat, searching for the imprint of the scarab, remembering how he popped the glass wings out of its sides. That kind soldier was engaged to a princess who wore a veil made out of pearls. I must have been so stupid to him. He wasn't out of my league; he was out of my stratosphere.

Eh.

Eh.

My eyes snapped to Alex, whose nostrils flared with a sneeze on the brink of eruption. One that didn't disappoint. Alex's hands flew to her mouth, but the violent sneeze was mighty enough to startle the bridal box from the governess's hands. It hit the floor with a deafening clang, spilling its contents across the tiles.

The weight of hundreds of eyes was on us in an instant. "Down!" I whispered to Selene and Alex, and the three of us dropped to the tiled floor, collecting the scattered contents and hiding our faces.

For the longest moments of my life to that point, awful silence hung in the air. I waited for Sikara or Tasherit to recognize us, and yank the Hyksos imposters away by our collars. But my anxiety was only met by the clack of the High Priest's sandals as he stepped in and continued the ceremony. I exhaled and jabbed Alex in the rib. "Nice, Alex."

"Sorry," she whispered. "All this incense is killing me." When we stood, my sister handed the box to the governess. We took our places again, and Akoris summoned the prince to bow before his betrothed.

I just stared. Somewhere in my mind, even as we plotted to get home, I wondered if and when I'd bump into the soldier again. But watching Merenptah—no, *Seti*—swear his loyalty to the Hyksos princess before gods and country wasn't the reunion I'd expected. He was the son of the Horus Lord, and I crouched in the wrap of a handmaiden. We were equals on the banks. We weren't now.

Alex shoved me, breaking my trance, as the ceremony came to a close. The handmaidens were on the move again. The royal family left the dais, and servants ushered everyone left toward the palace's Feasting Hall. I swallowed hard as we passed the empty thrones where Seti's general and High Priest joined the march toward the feast. The general was as I remembered him from the shore, larger than one of Rawer's Medjay guards, with a steely gaze to match his serious expression. I slowed my pace, falling behind Alex and Selene.

"Portia, keep up," my twin said over her shoulder.

"I'm right behind you," I said. Selene shot me a conspiratorial glance before engaging my sister in a barrage of questions. With Alex distracted, I moved closer to the general and High Priest. Akoris and Raia were only feet away, and I understood why the noblewomen smiled at them.

"General Raia," said Akoris in greeting.

The general returned a warm nod. "High Priest, your words were moving."

"This is an important moment for Waset, Avaris and Seti," the High Priest said. "You see he wears the nemes crown."

The general nodded. "It unfortunately won't be long before Pharaoh Anen goes to the Field of Reeds," said the general, in the commanding voice I remembered from the banks. "He is preparing Seti for the transition. He's already taken on many of his father's duties."

"He will bear it well," said the High Priest. "It is why our gods gave him to us."

"Speaking of gifts," the general said. For the first time, his lips tugged upward into a smile. "My mother sends her gratitude. She found your tonic soothing and has returned to many of her previous duties in the House of Women. She's always loved looking after Anen's wives and daughters in the birthing pavilion."

"I am pleased that Baketamun is in better health."

The general's voice lowered. "I also send my gratitude," he said.

"It is welcomed but unnecessary." Akoris gripped the young man's shoulder with warmth. "I will see you at the feast, general." He nodded to Raia before disappearing among the dignitaries.

"Stop being nosey." The voice came from my side, and I jumped. My twin's sparkling eyes bored into me. She'd broken free from Selene, who mouthed *Sorry* to me.

Before I could respond, hands squeezed my shoulders, nudging me away from my sister and the freshman. I turned to a stern-faced Hyksos girl, not much older than me, pushing me on. I dug my heels into the ground as Alex maneuvered toward us, but before my twin could interrupt, another Hyksos maid stepped in front of her. It was almost like the parking lot again, with Sasha blocking my sister and Smith sneering in my face. "Come with me now, or," said the handmaiden in front of me, pointing toward Tuya's governess, "Nimae will be angry."

Who is Nimae? I wondered, not realizing it was too late. The maid's expression fell as she backed away. Nimae, the charging bull, stopped mere inches from my face. Her brow wrinkled. Her jaw squeezed tight.

"Follow," Nimae instructed. I held my breath. Even Sikara's temper could be matched, and surpassed. Nimae glared at the maid cowering nearby. "Ensure she is in place. Tuya has requested her." The girl nodded as Nimae turned away.

Me? Why would the princess request me?

My escort yanked me forward. "Come on," she said as my feet relented. We pushed through the airy courtyard into the Feasting Hall; I scanned the crowd for Alex and Selene and found them in the middle of the procession, far from me. My companion wouldn't speak further, but she dragged me impressively if I gawked too long in directions other than forward. With Nimae lurking about, I couldn't blame her.

All too fast the plan had taken a turn for the worse. My sister and Selene were nowhere near, and I had no idea why Tuya would want to drag me away from them. Her handmaiden wound me through the rows of maids until we stood directly behind the princess. My heart dropped, expecting her to whip around and force me to explain myself. Instead, she carried on with her back straight and her eyes ahead.

What is this about?

As the Egyptian guests made their way into the Feasting Hall, the handmaidens bypassed it for Tuya's apartments. The princess, her governess, and the higher-ranking maidens split off from the rest of the Hyksos entourage. As much as I wanted to fade into the background, the girl still dragged me behind the princess.

Tuya's apartments were in the southwest corner of the palace, and her chamber was magnificent. The scenes sprawling across the yellow-painted walls were of the Hyksos terrains, serene despite the tension rumbling in her homeland. Linen curtains draped her windows, catching every breeze, and clay oil lamps filled the room with delicate light. The rest of the apartments, where the princess's retinue would sleep, took up two levels of chambers, and all of the rooms surrounded a square courtyard whose trees blushed in crimson foliage.

Tuya and the surly governess disappeared into a private chamber until the time came to attend to the feast. I tried to busy myself, unpacking some of her clothing with the other handmaidens and keeping my head down. The other ladies whispered to each other in the Hyksos language, but I was surprised when I often heard the name Tuya instead of Sahdina. Even in this private space, she had already given up who she once was.

When she reappeared, she wore a tunic of the deepest blue I'd ever seen beneath her shimmering veil. Though I still hadn't seen her face, she was an arresting beauty as we began the long walk toward the Feasting Hall. Gorgeousness aside, I did wait, however, for the moment she'd stop and tell me why she'd picked me out.

As we neared the feast, other handmaids spilled into the corridors with us. I peered over their shoulders but caught no sign of Selene or Alex. At the grand entrance, the maids stilled. "What are we waiting for?" I asked one at my side.

"The announcement," she whispered. "We can't go in until they announce us." As if cued, the grand doors swung wide. Light poured in from high windows above the rows of the tables. Painted gods feasted with the Egyptians through reliefs spanning the high ceiling, and Pharaoh presided over the celebration like a shepherd watching his flock. I turned from the decor as the noble families of Waset shuffled to their feet. Every eye was on the mysterious Hyksos monarch, a Hollywood star glittering on the red carpet.

Tuya reached the raised stage where a steward of the king awaited her. He wore a ceremonial shendyt and a cartouche bearing Anen's insignia on a bronze plate around his throat. She bowed, and upon rising, Nimae handed her another finely crafted wooden box, which Tuya then presented to him. The steward opened the box and inhaled its contents as if he were in a morning coffee commercial. "The spice of your Omnu trees," he said, with a smile. "The Horus Lord will be immeasurably pleased." A murmur of approval rustled through the attendees as musicians took up their instruments. The room soon swelled with music and chatter.

The Hyksos procession moved away from the dais, and though I was surrounded by a hundred other women, I was completely alone. The musicians played flutes and harps while the guests drank beer and gorged on roasted fowl. Dancers pranced in flirtatious troupes around the guests with tambourines. The male entertainers donned short wrapped kilts, and I diverted my eyes from the entertainers wearing nothing but beaded belts.

When the sun hung low in the sky, most of the feasters were completely drunk from pomegranate wine and beer. Nimae, however, was not off duty. As a palace servant presented Tuya with a steaming plate of roasted oxen and fresh vegetables, the governess shot up from her seat, blocking the food as if it were a grenade. She muttered something about having not inspected the platter and marched the servant back toward the kitchens.

Perhaps the other maids were used to Nimae's antics, as they continued to speak about themselves. I couldn't help but watch the strange governess. The pair almost crossed the hall when a man in the blue of Amun entered Nimae's path. She collected herself, still gripping the frightened palace servant, as the temple man whispered to her. I leaned forward until Tuya stood, the maids rising with her. Distracted by Nimae, I was last to my feet.

When she motioned for us to sit, her eyes met mine. "Come with me," she whispered, in a surprisingly sweet, singsong tone. My face burned. *This is it.* She stepped down from the dais when another handmaiden moved to accompany us. Tuya raised her palm. *Not you,* the gesture said. *Her.*

I followed as Tuya slipped through her retinue and out into an adjacent courtyard. The airy enclosure was a welcome change from the crowded aromas circulating the Feasting Hall. I focused on the clacking of her sandals against the stone walkway. My heart thudded. *What could she want with me?*

The princess stopped and stretched her arms. "Can you help me with this?" she asked, with a glance over her shoulder.

"With what?" I asked, before remembering that I should have

just said, "Yes, my lady." She laughed and fiddled with her veil's netting. Before long she had unhooked it, folded it delicately, and handed it to me. "Aren't you supposed to keep it on?" I asked.

"Even Princess Tuya needs a break from being Princess Tuya." Her hair was styled high revealing a swanlike neck as the princess peered around, taking in the exotic trees planted in the courtyard. "I'm sure you've wondered why you've been attending me these last few hours," she began. "I've kept you close because I have a question for you." Her eyes, a collage of brown and green, sparkled. "How did you get the ceremony robes?"

I took an instinctive step away, though her tone was more curious than accusatory, and stammered, "I came with you from Avaris."

"You did not," she replied, shaking her head. "Neither did the other two." I began to speak, but like in the Feasting Hall, she raised her palm. "I know my ladies."

The budding twilight danced over her as my shoulders hunched. *The jig is up.* "Are you going to tell?" I asked.

"I just want to know why. My kingdom has enemies."

"I have nothing to do with that, I promise. I'm not from anywhere near here, and I'm trying to get back."

"Where are you from?"

"It's easiest to say it's too far for you to know. And I have to meet this guy later to help."

"And you trust this man?"

I bit my lip. *Hell no.* "My sister does. She . . . I . . . want to go home."

"With no due harm to the men and women of Avaris or Waset?"

"I'm the least dangerous person you'll meet." Unless you're a cart. "Are you going to tell?" I asked again.

She was quiet for a moment. "How boring would that be for

me?" A mischievous grin crept across her face. "You're the first person I've met in a long time that hasn't been preselected."

"You're a princess."

"And excitement for one is rare." She extended the crook of her arm and after a beat, I looped mine through hers. *Was this happening?* I thought. *Why was the princess of Avaris being kind to me?* We began to stroll as if on a schoolyard. "I know everything about the Egyptians, about Anen and Seti. I don't know anything about you."

"There's not much to tell . . ." *That you would believe.* "I only took the robes because it would be the easiest way to escape."

"*Escape?*" she asked. "And then I called for you." She shook her head before squeezing my arm. "I didn't intend to disrupt your plan. You will be able to leave tonight. I will not stop you."

And as soon as the plan derailed, it was on track again. "Thank you," I said, heart taking flight. I scooped at her veil, which had started to drag when we looped our arms. My smile split my face, but when I turned to her, the princess's was expressionless. "Can I ask you a question?" She arched a brow and nodded. "Have you met the prince?"

"Seti?" She thought for a moment, eyes cast upward. Everything about her shimmered. "I have not. Emissaries were sent to Avaris on his behalf, but until this morning, I never had the pleasure." She pinched my arm. "He's kind of young, isn't he?"

This time I laughed. "They want a lot from you," I said.

"And what do you consider a lot?"

"Marrying the prince." I lowered my voice. "Coming here for the good of everyone. There had to be some other way to get the support you needed."

"I see." She hummed. "I love Avaris—"

"But you don't love the prince."

She tightened her grip on my arm. "Loving Egyptians is never an easy thing." Morse code was less cryptic. "I should return to the feast." She nodded toward her veil. "May I have that back?"

I handed it to her, and she deftly slipped it on. Smile hidden. Sparkle masked. She turned away but stopped herself. "Supposedly there are exquisite gardens in this palace," she said. "If you find them, you may also stumble on a useful set of gates. If anyone stops you, say your princess sent you on a special search and you got lost."

CHILD OF SET

I dodged palace guards en route to the gardens, unsure exactly where to find them. The princess nodded at a set of halls leading toward the western end of the palace before returning to the feast, but that was a hint with incredible limitations. My skin tingled as I willed the gardens to appear. If they did, I would locate our exit route and come back for Alex and Selene.

A turn in the hallway opened into night air. I found myself on a landing step leading onto a dirt path surrounded by manicured foliage. I exhaled at the sight of the palace gardens. Enclosed by the high stone walls, I spotted two guards patrolling the top. Luckily, they moved in sync. When they headed for the western wall, I darted toward the east, seeking any hint of the promised gate. I met a wall of shrubs instead.

"I received a report today, general." The voice carried from the opposite side. I held my breath. Though the thicket separated us, I'd know Seti's voice anywhere. I hadn't overlooked the gates, so they had to be on the other side of the shrubs. I rolled my eyes. *Great.* "The fort we visited was destroyed."

"Destroyed?"

General Raia and the prince stopped abruptly. "Yes, Raia, destroyed," said the prince.

"Are you sure it was the Seafarers? They wouldn't strike with Egyptian aid to the Hyksos, especially a fort granting access to the Iteru, to *us*," said General Raia. "They aren't suicidal."

"The report is similar to notes of Seafarer attacks," the prince replied. "They intended to send a message."

"Then halt any coordination with the Hyksos until this has been fully investigated."

"I can only give you so much time," said Seti. "I cannot tolerate a threat to Egypt, direct or subtle. And without us, the Seafarers will massacre the Hyksos and set their attentions to Waset."

"They wouldn't dare. The Egyptian army would crush a Seafarer invasion."

"It won't come to that if we step in now—"

"Avaris isn't the helm of the world. Waset is. It is inadvisable to lend Egypt to someone else's war."

"Remember yourself, Raia. We are not children learning in the edubba." Seti bristled. "You speak to the future of Egypt." I awaited an all-out brawl until realizing the prince and the general had passed the shrub divider and were on my side of the garden. They regarded the strange girl hiding near the bushes, their measured steps drawing them closer.

My eyes flicked up, missing the general as Seti's gaze tore into me. His eyes widened. *He never thought he'd see me again either.* "If a maid could breach our securities, we are not safe at all," Raia grumbled, scrutinizing the guards I'd evaded.

Seti ignored him. "*You*," he said. "You didn't say you were a Hyksos."

"You said your name was Merenptah," I countered, straightening my posture.

"Merenptah? I haven't heard that since we were children," said Raia, with a short laugh before his eyes darted between us. "You know this maid, Seti?"

"I do," the prince said, turning to me. "Merenptah is my mother's name for me. Formally, I am Seti." He studied me. "A Hyksos? A maid of Tuya, nonetheless? What are you doing here?" he asked. "Were you *escaping*?"

I'd never been a great liar. "No, I wasn't," I stammered.

"Then why are you escaping?" He folded his arms in amusement.

"I'm not, I—"

"Our palace is not to Hyksos standards?"

"No. Yes. I mean, I was just—"

"Speak up, maid," Raia cut in. "If you are not escaping, then why aren't you at your lady's side?" My mouth glued shut, but Raia's scrutiny did not relent.

"General," Seti said. "Please." Raia exchanged a glance with Seti before stepping back, disapproval radiating from him. He was too intense for his age—not much older than Sikara—and scared the hell out of me. But he'd probably seen the world as a soldier and didn't suffer fools or childishness gladly.

"Why aren't you with your princess?" asked Seti. "Is she terrible? She must be if her maids desert her."

"My princess sent me back to the chambers, and I got lost." I backed away from them. "I'm sorry I disturbed you," I said. My retreat, however, was short-lived.

Seti stepped forward. "Stay," he said. "Our palace has bored you and your mistress has obviously abused you. Enjoy the gardens at least." The invitation meant my plan was thwarted.

"The general had a report to investigate anyway." Seti glanced at Raia, his pointed look directing him toward the palace.

"Your Majesty," the general said with a bow. When he straightened, he breezed by us. You'd only catch the terse glance in my direction if you didn't blink.

When he left, I found Egypt's prince smiling at me. "By Amun, this is a good day. I thought you might have died."

"Why would I have died?"

"Plague."

I frowned. "I didn't have plague." A beat passed. "So the prince of Egypt thought about me? *Right.*"

"Of course I did," he said. "You thought of me."

The words tumbled out. "I didn't," I said, hating when presumptuous people were right.

"Of course you did. Why wouldn't you? I rescued you. You owe me your life."

"I rescued you first, and you were really just paying me back," I said. "So you weren't kidding when you said your dad was important."

"Pharaoh Anen is my father, yes."

I lowered my voice. "How is he doing?"

"He wasn't present today." Seti sighed. "It's best to say he is as to be expected." He'd been lighter about it on the shores, but again that was months ago. And he wasn't talking just talking about the father he loved, but the ruler of Egypt, the greatest power in the world. I wanted to ask Seti more about his father's illness, but I could tell he didn't want to talk about it.

I changed the subject. "I see." I thought for a moment. "Can I ask you another question?" He nodded, if slowly. "Why did you lie?" I asked, despite myself. "You said your name was Merenptah. Why didn't you just tell me the truth?"

"That wouldn't be safe in the field. You saw what those men did when they thought I was a rich soldier. Besides," he said, grinning, "you were already sick with plague. To know you accompanied Egypt's prince might have sent you into a frenzy."

I flapped my arms at my sides. "You are such a *brat*. I should have let them steal your money."

He laughed a big laugh, a wonderful laugh. "I'm a what?"

I overly enunciated, "You. Are. A. Brat."

"Are all Hyksos women so difficult? Is this what I have to expect?" he asked, though I was positive he didn't know what *brat* meant. "Speaking of truth, you didn't inform me that you served the highest house of the Hyksos. So we're both despicable liars. And if you sing Tuya's praises, why are you leaving?"

"I'm not leaving," I said. Seti's mouth pressed into a hard line. "I have sisters who need me more than Tuya."

"Is it not a good life, waiting on a princess in a palace? I'm sure any woman on the street would trade places with you, if her sisters needed her or not. Even I'd love to be you. There would be no real responsibilities. I could be hidden from the public eye, invisible."

"You think I'm invisible?"

"There are a hundred of you," he quipped.

"I'm not invisible. They need me, and I'm helping them. You're the one that's invisible."

He straightened his back. "And how is Egypt's prince invisible?" Egyptian rulers were considered living deities in their own rights, something I'd learned in the temple, and something I'd forgotten in the moment. It might not be smart to speak to the next god-king so freely, even if he was just a boy. "No," he said, reading my mind. "Please speak."

Or maybe perceived godliness didn't matter. "Everyone can see that you're a prince, but no one can see whoever Seti is. They see the power, the clothing, the—" His shadow meandered over mine.

I hadn't noticed how close he'd come. Moonlight cast dancing shadows on our skin, and when my gaze was his, those eyes were the darkest obsidian.

"The what?" He asked.

Say something, anything. "The wealth," I piped before withdrawing, willing my heartbeat to slow. "From the temple servant to the farmer to the tomb builder, everyone's too absorbed in their own lives to know yours." From a safer distance, I dared to turn back to him. "What would happen if everyone could see you, if they could see *Merenptah?* Then what would you do?"

He maintained the new distance I'd set, mulling over my words. "You must go? This is what you want?"

I nodded, though that too was a lie. "I have to," I said, by way of an answer.

"Then I would suggest the eastern wall." He pointed past the divider. "Pull the hanging plants back, and you will see a gate. It leads out to the city, and it will be unguarded in one hour." He lingered before heading back into the palace. "I never said thank you."

"For what?"

"My life," he said, and returned to the feast honoring his bride.

"Where are the guards?" asked Selene. "I thought there were guards on all the walls?" As Seti had predicted, the garden's barriers stood unprotected. The three of us were alone as the moon smiled down. "How did you find this?"

I snapped out of my trance as the boom of drums and flutes reached a crescendo behind us. The prince must have returned. Something in me longed to go back to the Festival Hall, eat more fowl, perhaps dance with the entertainers. I pushed those desires aside. "I got a good tip," I said.

"A good tip?" Selene asked. "From who?"

"Friends in high places," I replied. Once at the eastern wall, we pulled the hanging plants back, revealing an elaborate gate that was—to our advantage—unlocked. When we stepped through to a quiet road circling the grounds, our first taste of freedom in weeks washed over us. The elation quelled, however, at the sight of a man waiting patiently on the other side.

Alex's arm stretched in front of Selene, but I recognized him as Ankhmir, the High Priest's second in command. I patted Alex's shoulder. "It's okay," I said. "It's okay." I turned to the priest. "I thought we were supposed to come to you?"

He shook his head. "His Holiness must not wait for the trade. I will see you back to the temple. My litters are near here." For a moment, he stopped and stared at me, namely my throat, and the blue scarab around it. As I had done before entering the temple, I instinctively moved to cover it.

"Follow me," he said. In his stately robes, Ankhmir turned and headed down the dirt path toward the palace docks at the riverfront, where the litters of the Egyptian nobles waited during the festivities. As we walked, I glanced in the direction of the Temple of Isis, and everything I was leaving behind. Not only had we deceived Sikara and Tasherit, but we hadn't said goodbye.

Ankhmir traveled a few paces ahead, until we found the litters near the harbor. Wind wrapped my shoulders. Ankhmir gestured that we remain as he spoke to the watchman patrolling the dock and the carriages, assumedly until he found his own litter. Selene brushed against me. "What are you thinking?" she whispered.

"Why would I be thinking anything?"

"You always make faces when you think." She glanced over

her shoulder. "The museum, after your practices with Sikara," she said. The palace glowed behind us, illuminating the curves of her cheeks. "It's beautiful, isn't it?"

Alex approached us. "What are you two looking at? We should be heading over," she said. "I think he's almost done."

"Just look at it," said Selene. "We may never see it again."

Alex arched a brow. "We don't have time for this."

"But we weren't ever supposed see the world like this," said Selene. She regarded the city as she did the artifacts in the museum, as if she were absorbed. "We've gotten something special."

My sister was scared. We all were. But Selene had a point. "Come on, Alex," I said. "Just look for a second." She sighed before letting the splendor of Waset fill her vision one last time.

Suddenly, Selene grabbed my arm. "Where did Ankhmir go?"

Instead of the glittering city of Waset, the freshman's gaze was on the banks that had somehow emptied. Our fearless leader had indeed disappeared. "I don't know," I said uneasily. "Call of nature?"

Selene ignored my joke. "Why would he just leave us?"

"I don't know," I repeated. "But he can't be far." As I spoke, Alex's scream pierced my eardrums. I snapped around, but my twin was nowhere to be seen. Grains of sand and something lighter— salt maybe—swept across the ground where she had been.

What the hell?

Selene yanked me away as I yelled for my sister. Maybe she saw something I didn't, as the small girl dragged me from where we stood, her curls blowing violently in the night wind. Our feet trudged through damp earth and sand. I grabbed the sides of my head as my dinner threatened to reappear. And then Selene dug her nails into my flesh. My eyes widened as I turned to her, finding she too was already gone.

THE BINDING TRADE (PART 2)

I wrapped my arms around my chest, surveying the beach for something—anything—emerging from the sand. Nothing moved aside from the air snapping around me in harsh, biting winds. My anxious breaths drew silver stripes. Whatever took Alex and Selene left me for last.

I gripped my sides tighter as an icy hand found my shoulder. I turned to Ankhmir. Relief washed over me. "Thank God!" I exclaimed. "I thought you'd left. You have to help me." But Ankhmir said nothing, tightening his grip on my shoulder. Bekmut's touch had been cool. His icy fingers burned my skin. "Ankhmir?" I asked, before yanking my shoulder free.

"You didn't wear that scarab yesterday. You didn't wear the mark," he said, in a voice all wrong. It almost hissed, registering in an inhuman key as he stepped forward. "The heka in you is greater than the binding trade." Wintry gusts billowed from his limbs. I winced at its shrill sting to my eardrums and quickly peered around the beach. Everyone, even the lone dockhand, had gone. "There's more than fire beneath your skin, one that His Holiness demands, that he's sought for many years."

161

I didn't need to stick around to figure out what he meant. Fear sang through my body as my legs launched me away. Reflex wasn't, however, enough. By only raising his hand, Ankhmir summoned the sand beneath my feet to snap around my ankle. Dirt and earth, mud and dread, swarmed around me as he heaved an impossible chain of sand like a whip, reeling me back to him.

Once in range in a bed of dirt and mud and wiry plants, the priest leaned down to me with eyes glowing—a pulsating violet that cut through the dark. Like Bekmut's eyes. Like Ramla's. "The fire in you is the star's heka," he said.

"We've known since Shemu it was here," he continued, "but we thought it was with the princess." He shook his head. His gaze settled on the scarab necklace dangling around my throat. "The mark." He flipped the scarab, studying the markings on the side and the Amun inscription. "The mark is on the star."

"I don't know what you're talking about," I said as Ankhmir suddenly yanked the necklace, pulling until I stood on the very tips of my toes. The links, however, didn't snap. Unaffected by my strained breaths, his curious eyes inspected it, trying to see why it wouldn't break.

I thrust my foot into his gut as he did. The kick was hard, but there was no crunching bone. My foot instead met *harder* bone. As pain stung my toes, Ankhmir's eyes narrowed to slits as he gripped the chain tighter, cutting off my airways. My limbs thrashed against him, but he ignored me, hissing curses in the language he'd spoken the night before.

His face, my instincts instructed as they had so many times since Shemu. Warmth flooded my cheeks. My limbs followed, igniting from the inside out. My hands glowed. The pulsating heat ripped through my veins, swirling beneath my skin, amplifying from distress. *His face*, my instincts screamed now, so I slammed my searing hand, bright in the darkness, against his frozen cheek. Light spread like roots across his skin, burning his flesh. He wailed and dropped me, but it was no time for celebration. Through the sting of cold in what had been a warm, sweet evening, the priest lifted his right hand. My mouth hung agape at his fingers' contortion, bending in ways that should have snapped the ligaments but instead elongated his hand unnaturally. As his eyes gaze met mine in stunning violet, his hands twisted into sharp, deadly claws. "The mark is on the star," he repeated.

He shifted his weight before launching forward. I took off in my best run, but my feet were clumsy over the damp, yielding earth. I fought to scramble away, to fly, but I couldn't outrun the thing that wanted my heka.

And then a bold shard of light sliced the night air. On a collision course with the priest, it hissed through the darkness. My clumsy run slowed as for some reason I glanced back, less afraid. Even from my place, some several yards away, the light had stilled in the darkness, now a single rod that pierced through Ankhmir's abdomen.

I took in the startling sight of the priest motionlessly hovering in the air. Curious, I stepped forward as a groan escaped his mouth. My gaze traveled up to his. The priest's eyes no longer glowed violet. Instead, the empty, gray orbs sunk in his face.

I jumped back as the shining blade retracted from his stomach with a jerk. The priest twitched before crumbling into the ground, no longer a man but a pile of sand-like grains. Green robes flapped in the winds before me. Sikara stood in his place now, a metal dagger—no longer glowing— with a slender dagger in her right hand and the sword in her left. A grin creased her lips.

"You really should play nicely with others," she said, before gingerly stepping over the mound that was Ankhmir. She wore her cloak from the Lotus Ceremony and wiped the long, thin sword on the interior of her green robes. She placed the dagger inside one of the folds of fabric. Her hair was no longer pulled back in tight braids, but hung in wild, loose curls.

I clasped my hands tight to my mouth. "What are you doing here?" I asked, bile threatening to escape.

Her eyes twinkled with flecks of gold as she pointed her blade at my attire. "You stole from the temple this morning," she said. "Thievery is frowned upon in the priesthood, as well as conspiring to do so with others."

"I worked alone," I lied, heart thrumming. Sikara sucked her teeth before turning back to scoop up a delicate handful of Ankhmir's remains. "Sand and salt," she said. She returned to me and blew the grains in my face. My fingers flared at the insult with both light and sparks.

"You've already forgotten," she said, ignoring my hands. "When you simply react, you miss the obvious." My hands flared brighter in warning until a squeeze on my shoulder derailed me.

I turned to my side where both my sister and Selene stood unharmed, if winded and anxious. Alex withdrew her hand from my shoulder, her palm so cold I shivered at her touch. I threw my arms around them. "How did you do that?" I asked Sikara. "Where were they?"

She indicated the pile. "Where the Serk hold captives."

"It was so cold," Selene said. "We were on some sort of bank like this one, and could see you, but couldn't get to you."

"It's like Duat," Sikara said of the Egyptian underworld, "but more of an in-between place than the final."

"And who are the Serk?" Alex asked.

"The priest was a Scorpion," she replied and looked at me again. "And you, fool, were about to become one just like him, and like your friend Bekmut," she said. "We found her." Sikara twisted the sword in the air admiringly. "That was fun. And that terrible Ramla, but that didn't surprise me as much."

"You . . . killed them?"

"I'm sorry. Did you have plans for a Scorpion outing tomorrow? Sail the Iteru together?"

I stammered. "And you're one, too?" I inhaled. "You're a Scorpion?"

"No," she said. Her eyes danced between the three of us. "I'm only here to recover what you all stole." Sikara twisted her sword again, watching its now faint gleam before suddenly bursting with laughter. "By Amun, you should see your faces!" She snorted. "I'm not going to kill you for the robes," she said. "Why save you from a Scorpion to kill you for the robes?"

"Sikara, temper yourself," said a voice at my back. *Who could possibly sneak up on me like that?* They came round to face me, and before I could blink, all six feet or so of the High Priestess Weret stared down at me. If she was a gazelle from afar, she was a giantess up close.

And gorgeous. I could only imagine the beauty of her youth if she was this striking now. A green, patterned headdress wrapped tightly about her crown and piercing dark eyes studied me. "Though we normally kill thieves of a royal bride," Weret added. Her voice wasn't as singsongy as Tuya's, but it had a melodic, soothing effect as well. "You have now learned the business of Amun's temple. I wouldn't entertain their barters again."

I diverted my eyes for a moment. *I knew it wasn't a good idea.* She stepped closer, regarding me carefully. "You are impressive," the High Priestess said. Weret's voice had a way of wrapping around you, quelling doubts and fear, making the corners of your mouth twitch up. It was not difficult to imagine why her temple was almost the richest in Waset. She pointed to my hand. "May I?"

I creased my brow, assuming she would have wanted to see the scarab, as Ankhmir had made such a fuss over it. And though she'd asked nicely enough for my hand, I still hesitated. What if she wanted to do that white-out thing Ankhmir had?

The High Priestess dropped her chin, eyeing me as if I were a cranky child. "If I meant you harm, you would already be harmed," she said. I sighed and opened my hand. The surface had blistered over again from tapping into my heka. She brushed her fingers across my palm, and I winced. "It hurts every time, doesn't it?"

"How did you know?" I asked as Weret smiled. The High Priestess's robes danced in the Nile breeze as she raised her hand to the sky. A rumble stirred above us, clouds forming in what had been a clear evening. Thunder crackled as Weret snapped her left hand toward the shoreline. Lightning erupted from her fingertips, setting fire to a cluster of reeds.

As we watched the blaze with wide eyes, Weret held up her palm. It was near covered in hellish blisters. "She's like you, Portia," Selene gasped.

"Not every gift is easy, and you are very gifted," said Weret.

"My lady, we should go," Sikara interrupted. Her eyes darted over the beach.

"Yes," Weret said, gaze shifting now from Selene, to Alex, and lastly to me. "Please return to the temple with us, unless you would like to remain here and wait for more friends to arrive."

"We'll go," Alex jumped in. She grabbed Selene's and my arms and yanked us forward.

THE BLAZING STAR

"Close the doors," the High Priestess instructed a servant. As the girl complied, I peered around Weret's chamber. It was smaller than I assumed it would be, with elegant images of the goddess gracing the walls. In one relief, the deity stretched to the ceiling to survey the priestesses. A few oil lamps dotted the room, but for the most part, the High Priestess operated in dim light and shadows.

Weret removed her headdress. Thick, silver-streaked hair grazed her shoulders— a deviation from the priestesses who cut theirs short, braided it down, or had none at all. Though decorated headdresses and wigs fit shaved heads best, Weret's thicket of coils reminded me that she was human, despite everything I'd just witnessed.

The servant returned to Weret's side with a cone of incense, which the High Priestess burned on a wooden mantle-shrine to the goddess. She drew a deep breath afterward and motioned to us. "Please, sit," Weret instructed.

Alex and Selene collapsed in sturdy leather chairs near her, but I held my stance. "I can stand," I said.

Alex grabbed my arm and tugged me into the chair with her. "Oh, sit down, Portia. Stop being stubborn," she said. "She wants to help us."

The ghost of a smile traced Weret's face as she approached us and also took a seat. A green jewel hung around the High Priestess's neck, its bronze trim matching the rings in her ears, earrings I'd seen before, though not on a human. I leaned forward. "The cat wore those earrings."

"What cat?" Alex asked me.

"She's known as Bastet in the feline form," Her Holiness said in amusement.

"You know who I'm talking about?" I asked. Weret nodded. "I can't believe I'm asking this, but are you the cat?"

"No," Her Holiness said, and from the periphery of my view a small, feline silhouette slipped through the shadows of the oil lamps. It gingerly trotted into the light, gray as I remembered, though its eyes weren't as abnormally green. It found its way to Selene's lap. The freshman rubbed its head as it purred.

"Hello," Selene said with a laugh.

"Off her, miw," said Weret. The cat rubbed her head against Selene again before hopping off her lap—and transforming into Tasherit.

Completely nude, Tasherit stretched her limbs, "Of course, my lady." The kindly priestess bowed to Her Holiness before the servant who'd brought the incense carried an armful of linen clothing for Tasherit. The priestess plucked a tunic to cover herself and took a seat in the back.

I clamped my hands over my stomach. If anything else happened, I would have a stroke. "But I saw her at home," I said, rubbing my temples. "Why?"

"I know you have questions," Weret began. "And I will do

my best to answer them." The High Priestess peered between the three of us. "I know you aren't from here, or Swenett." Her eyes landed on me, and for a moment I wondered if Sikara had told her the BS I'd said, or by some way, she'd heard when I said it. "You've seen a year far from that of the Scorpion." She paused a beat. "You've swam the Rivers of Time."

I held the scarab necklace up so the great ladies could see. "I think this is why we slipped through the rabbit hole."

"Slipped?" Weret asked. "The heka required to maneuver the Rivers of Time is not ordinary. You are here by Ma'at's will alone, not chance."

"Ma'at wants three girls from the future?" Selene asked.

"Apparently," Sikara said to the freshman. "Our involvement was only to assist what was already happening, when the rivers opened to you in Shemu, Portia."

Shemu, I thought. *The Golden Apple Ceremony?* "You mean everything during that last week at home . . . fainting, fighting the Grizzlies. That was the river?" I asked as Weret nodded.

Alex rubbed her temples, her brain dizzied under mounting questions. "So the Akoris guy isn't the guide?"

"A guide is helping you right now," said Sikara. "Her Holiness is a guide; each head of each temple is a guide by right." She shrugged. "I guess in some way your Serk friend gave you adequate advice."

"Adequate?" asked Alex. "What do you mean by adequate?"

"I mean it was satisfactory, but not exceedingly so."

Alex rolled her eyes. "I know the definition of adequate."

"The High Priests and Priestesses have many duties and many names in Waset," said Weret. "And one of mine is to follow the star."

"Ankhmir said something about a star," I said. "He kept saying the mark was on it, that my heka was a part of it."

"Well," Weret said. "The star has much to do with the current season, Akhet. The Iteru's flood is the blessing of our year. The prince's wedding coincides with it." Weret turned to Alex. "Why does the Iteru flood?" Her Holiness asked my twin. "Surely you've learned from your time here."

If she weren't brown, my sister's face would've burned scarlet. Her light eyes sparkled. "Yes," she said. *Golden Apple Champion strikes again.* "The Nile floods because of Isis's tears. They filled the river after her husband Osiris was killed."

Weret nodded. "When Osiris was killed, Isis scoured the banks to find each part of his dismembered body. Once found, she assembled them to reunite with her husband. The rich, black earth of the Two Lands mimics how sorrow and restoration bring Egypt new life."

"The new life is the harvest after the Nile floods?" asked Alex.

Weret smiled. "That is right. The flood nourishes us all."

"You still haven't said what the star is," I said flatly.

Her eyes fell on my neck. "It's around your neck, Portia." Her eyes lingered for a moment before breaking away. "Ma'at didn't deem you worthy of just any heka," she said. "She gave you the star of our goddess." I touched the scarab. "Isis did not have the power to restore Osiris alone. Her mother Nut—our sky—was saddened by her grief and gifted her a Sopdet—"

"Sopdet?" I interrupted.

Alex elbowed me. "Sirius," Alex said. "Sirius is the name of the star in ancient Greek. Much of what we really know about Egypt is through the eyes of the Greeks and Romans. So Sopdet became Sirius—"

"The blazing star," continued Weret. She didn't appear to understand the Greek words so much as the context of Alex's explanation. "The brightest in the sky."

"It goes black during Akhet," said Alex.

I gaped at my sister. "How the hell do you know all this?" I asked her.

She shrugged. "Just do."

I turned back to Her Holiness. "So my scarab is Sirius, *err* Sopdet?"

"Your scarab has much of its power, yes. Some years, if there is a need, Sopdet doesn't just go black, but sends its restorative power to the Two Lands again, as it did so long ago. And Ma'at picked you to bear it."

I pushed onto my feet, pacing before I'd even realized. *Holy shit.* I'd always wanted to be a special snowflake, especially when my twin became a genius. I should have better evaluated that desire. "Like the *Sword and the Stone?*" Selene asked, interrupting my thoughts. "Portia's King Arthur?"

The reference was lost on Weret, who didn't reply. She instead instructed me to flip the scarab with the twist of her fingers. "The priest said the mark is on the star, right? That is true. You see the markings on its sides around the inscription?"

"How'd you know about the inscription?" I asked.

Weret held my gaze as if she were about to answer, maybe with something I hadn't expected, but my sister cut in. "So why is this a time of need?" Alex asked. "Why would Sopdet need to come here again?"

"The Hyksos, probably," I answered, wanting to say at least one relevant thing. "The princess is coming here because of the fighting in the Delta."

"And the Delta is crawling with them," Sikara said.

"With fights?" I asked.

"With men like your friend," Sikara replied.

I shuddered. "Well, that qualifies," I said as Ankhmir's voice

slithered into my memory. "Ankhmir said"—I glanced at Sikara—
"before you killed him . . ."

Sikara grinned. "You're welcome."

I shook my head and continued. "He said that they knew the
star arrived in Shemu, but they thought it was with the princess,
not me."

The great ladies all exchanged glances. "By Amun," Sikara said.

"What?" I asked.

"Akoris thinks it's with the princess because of that damned
fleet," Sikara said before Weret markedly cleared her throat.
"My apologies, but if something happens to the princess before
we've handled the Serk, then Egypt will sail into a war it certainly
cannot win."

A chill ran through my limbs. I peered around. "We can't just
leave Tuya to get attacked." Ankhmir terrified me, and I had heka
of my own. I didn't know if Tuya had some magical buddies on
her side, but the fight in no way was a fair one. Aside from that,
the princess had been so kind to me when she didn't have to be.
I found a small but present friendship in her I admittedly hadn't
felt with Alex for a while.

Sikara turned to Weret. "We should bring the princess here."

Now Alex shot up. "You want us to go back to the palace, with
those things?" My twin caught my gaze. "We need to be figuring
out a way home. The princess has her own guards, and heka, and
whatever. She'll be fine."

"She won't be fine against those things, Alex."

"*We* barely made it out."

"Though I appreciate that you care about the princess,
Portia" the High Priestess said, raising her hand up as if to give
a verdict, "retrieving her would also keep Waset safe for more
time, which is what we need." A moment passed. "Go to the

palace tomorrow when the sun is highest," instructed Sikara.

"Why?" Selene asked, who I'd kind of forgotten was still in the room.

"Serk hunt from the shadows," Weret replied. "I will already be at the palace to conduct a morning blessing. Meet me and we will speak to the Hyksos governess and princess."

"Good," said Sikara. "The shadows are easy to spot at high sun."

I caught my sister's eyes, but she didn't say anything else, only turning her gaze away from me. Her exhale was long and exaggerated. "Fine," my twin grumbled. "Let's just get this over with."

Alex turned to leave, but Sikara lurched in front of her. "Her? My lady?" Sikara looked at my sister indignantly. "She and the small one were hardly effective against the last Serk."

Alex glared at Sikara. "I'm not leaving Portia alone. Besides, I can help. I . . ." She searched for words. "I'm smart."

I couldn't help gaping. It was the first time she'd ever said it out loud. There was no false modesty. No shyness. No downplaying her abilities to make others comfortable. Egypt was bringing something new out of her, out of all of us, and I wondered who we all might be in the end. "I just won the Academic Decathlon," Alex continued.

Sikara laughed and folded her arms. It was kind of fun to watch. "Fine, then," she said. "Just don't die in my way."

MA'AT'S WILL

Describing the air between Alex and me as tense would be understating it. A barefoot temple servant in a plain sheath escorted Selene, Alex, and me back to Tasherit's chamber. She held a small oil lamp, little more than a bowl with a floating wick, to guide us through the dark hallways. I hadn't taken Alex's side back in Weret's chamber; I wasn't twinning, and it wasn't sitting right with her. It pained me when I'd catch my sister's profile and she'd angle away from me.

When we arrived in the chamber I'd slept in since Shemu, the servant placed the lamp down on one of Tasherit's small ebony tables. She'd already found a mat for my sister, so as Alex settled on it, the servant girl plucked fresh linen sheaths from a pile waiting for us on one of the chairs. She distributed them as deliciously cool night air drifted through the window. I was grateful to peel the Hyksos clothes off my sticky skin in favor of the light fabric. "Thank you," I told the girl. "Where's Tasherit? Is she coming back here?"

"The great lady will sleep down the hall," she said, and nodded before slipping out of the room. The quiet settled in on us anew, with only the night air and song of chirping crickets in the background. I lay on my mat as everyone did the same. Alex, whose mat bed was near mine, rolled on her side, presenting me with her back.

"Look," I said. "I know you're mad."

"Goodnight, Selene," Alex's voice clawed out in warning.

"Night," Selene said, as if she didn't want to get in the middle of it.

"Alex, come on."

"Goodnight, Portia," she said with finality. *Fine, whatever.* I'd try again in the morning. I readied for bed, and though Alex was pissed and finicky, relief washed over me as I eased into sleep. They weren't what any of us expected, but we were finally getting some answers.

Screams tore through the chamber sometime before daybreak. I shot up on my mat, having been in the good kind of sleep that doesn't release your unconsciousness easily. Another shriek tore through the air, sharpening my senses.

The screams came from Selene. When Alex caught my gaze, there was no trace of anger in her golden eyes, and we scrambled from our mats over to the freshman. I hit my shin on one of Tasherit's stupid tables and hobbled as Alex rushed to her side. "Selene." My twin's voice was a sharp whisper. "Selene, wake up."

Still, the freshman did not. She tossed and turned, holding her head and shrieking every few seconds. "What's wrong with her, Portia? You've been here with her all this time."

"I don't know," I said. "Please, Selene, wake up."

"Move back," said a woman who flew through the chamber door. It was dark, but I recognized Tasherit's high but firm voice, the one she used to order servants in the infirmary if necessary.

The wigless priestess, still clad in her sheath from Weret's briefing, maneuvered past us.

"What's wrong with her?" Alex asked Tasherit. The servant also followed the priestess in, once more holding her small oil lamp. She stood beside Tasherit to light her work.

"This happens in the infirmary sometimes," she said, by way of an answer. Tasherit's mouth thinned to an anxious line. "She has these sudden dreams and headaches, or both."

I drew my brows together. Selene told me about her dreams but hadn't mentioned the return of the headaches. *Why would she keep that from me?* "Bring the water over on that table," Tasherit told me, breaking my thoughts. "And the cloth."

Before I could move, Alex rushed over and grabbed a jug of water on one of the little tables. My twin handed it to her upon return. Tasherit took one of the cloths, dipped it in the water, and then wrung it out. She placed the moist cloth delicately on Selene's forehead.

"Come on," Tasherit said, drawing Selene back to consciousness. In response, the freshman's tossing and shrieking lessened to murmurs. When Selene blinked her eyes open, I was ashamed at my relief. Her eyes were still dark brown, not purple.

Panting, Selene's dark gaze traveled between all of us. Alex knelt down and took her hand. "Are you okay?" my twin asked. "You were screaming."

"Yeah," the freshman said breathlessly. "I'm okay." She gently detached from both Tasherit's and Alex's grasps. She scooted to us, her legs bent and back pressed against the stone wall. Speckled light from the servant's lamp danced on Selene's face. She gripped both sides of her head. "Thanks," she said, breath evening. "Thanks for waking me up."

"What were you dreaming about?" Alex asked. Selene took a

moment to respond, inhaling before doing so. *Oh shit*, I thought, heart thrumming. *This is going to be bad.* "What's wrong?" Alex asked her as I leaned forward to hear this.

Selene pushed her draping curls aside. "When the Iteru rose, my headaches started again. And the woman began showing more in my dreams." Selene angled toward me. "We shouldn't go back to the palace."

"But we have to get the princess," I said.

"Portia, the creatures she showed me were the Serk." The freshman shook her head. "And she didn't just show them, but she had me look in the river," Selene said. "I saw everything in the River of Time until the next sun. By tomorrow night, we were still here, but the princess wasn't. She was in Duat," she said of the Egyptian underworld. "It's Ma'at's will."

I held my breath. This couldn't be right. We had to get Tuya. Anger and defiance surged through me. "Damn Ma'at's will," I said, slapping the jug of water over and scrambling to my feet. "Is the woman in your dreams Ma'at?"

My outburst didn't bother the freshman. She spoke to me as calmly as she had the Grizzlies in that parking lot so long ago. "No," Selene said. "I don't know who she is."

"Then how does she know anything about a goddess's will? We're getting the princess," I said. "She's wrong, Selene."

"She's not wrong," said the freshman. "You just don't like it." She focused on both Alex and me now. "Neither of you like the truth when you hear it."

Alex straightened but didn't address the accusation. "Is there anything you do know about this woman?" my twin asked.

"Only that she's hiding," Selene replied as a sudden pain must have rocketed through her skull. Selene grabbed the sides of her head and grit her teeth. "And until we find her," she managed, "we're never going back through the rivers."

For a moment no one in the room breathed. I wished, like the priestess, I could become a cat and slip out into another time and place. "Come on," Tasherit told the freshman. The priestess stood, assisting Selene to her feet. "Let me help you." Tasherit and Selene left, flanked by the servant. Morning light crept farther into the chamber as Alex and I held stared at each other, finally twinning through our scant ability to breathe.

Selene didn't come back that night, nor did I see her at the morning prayers. In a way, I didn't see anyone. Alex and I weren't saying more than a handful of words to each other, trying to function without choking on everything we'd learned. After the morning prayers, we still had some time before the sun crept high in the sky. I desired the comfort of routine and found myself walking toward the training room.

After passing through the entryway, I found Sikara sitting on her dark, wooden desk. With her hair piled high again, she was every bit the straightlaced priestess I'd first met. I crossed the threshold to find a seat in front of her. "What are you doing?" I asked.

She didn't glance up as she attended the fabric on her robes. The long linen covered nearly half of the desk. "Preparing my sword," she said.

"It looks like you're fixing a busted stitch," I said. She didn't answer, opting to hop down from her desk and snatch away the linens covering the rest of the surface. Next to her lay an assortment of weapons, including the sword and dagger she carried the night before. I stood up from my chair to inspect them, wondering if I'd ever see them glow again.

Sikara, on the other hand, propped one leg on a stool beside the desk. Around her muscular thigh was a strap to hold some of those sharp, pointed objects. "I'm doing that as well," she said, and plucked her metal dagger to slide in its sheath.

"You are a terrifying woman," I said with a shaky—if slightly awestruck—laugh. She sheathed her sword next and turned to me, freeing her curls from the elaborate updo. "Why don't you wear the wigs or the head pieces like Tasherit and Weret?"

"The same reason you don't," she said. "They're big and heavy and get in the way." She folded her arms. "You should also know that the Kushite will not come to retrieve the princess. Tasherit reported that she is in the infirmary with head pains," Sikara said. "She is a child, so it's probably better this way."

"She's only two years younger than me and Alex. That's like . . . marriageable here." I turned my lip up at the creepy thought.

"She's small," Sikara said. "Too small to fight if we need her. She doesn't have your heka."

"I guess," I said and sat on her desk, careful to avoid the many deadly items Sikara had displayed like a sandwich spread. "So how did it get bad enough that Ma'at would send for us?"

"It's not in her balance that men fight monsters," Sikara replied. "I said Avaris's Serk problem is worse than Waset's. The Hyksos think they war with the Seafarers, but they don't. I said the Seafarers were weaponized. Well, the Serk were it."

"And how did they get the Serk?" I asked.

"There is a reason you were to complete the binding trade at the temple of Amun," she said. "His Holiness gave them the Serk. Each guide has their own responsibilities. The High Priestess guards the star. And the High Priest had domain over the Serk."

"Then why would he give them away?"

"If you just asked nicely enough, I'm sure he'd tell you." *Okay, dumb question.* "All I know is that he did so about eleven floods ago, and in that time the Serk have almost taken the whole Delta. They're coming south now, as their numbers increase with that damned trade."

I almost made that damned trade. "What would have happened if I did it?"

"Exactly what you think," she said. "Scorpions seek pure heka, old magic. Mortals don't have much, only their souls. The trade gives the Scorpions your ka. They consume it, take your shell, and make you a Scorpion as well. But I'd imagine your heka bothers them. It's not like temple heka, like mine or any of the other great ladies'."

Bekmut's freak-out after the light incident in the temple of Amun started to make more sense. "Your heka is very potent, Portia," Sikara continued. "I felt it when I touched your hand. But it's also strenuous on the body. That's why your hands burn and why you grow queasy. It's heka sickness. It lessens with time and use, but never completely leaves."

As she spoke, footsteps traveled through the doorway. We turned. Alex stood there, her arms folded and bright eyes roving from me to Sikara. Her mouth curved downward at the priestess. "Tasherit told me where to find you, Portia. We have an hour before we need to go," she said, before turning away. Her last instruction echoed back at us. "Tasherit laid out some clothes in her chamber for us."

Sikara sucked her teeth when she'd left. "And your sister needs to stop her moaning and prepare herself," she said. "Scorpions aren't an everyday adversary, even with your little piece of jewelry. They don't like light or fire and are brutal warriors that hunt in the dark. The only forewarning that one is near is the cold, dimness, and maybe their tails."

"Ankhmir didn't have a tail," I said.

"Believe me," Sikara replied, "he had a tail." She angled toward me and smiled. I couldn't tell what was behind it. "High sun is coming. Be ready."

SAHDINA (PART 2)

Akhet season was truly upon us, and it was never more apparent than as Sikara, my sister, and I discreetly wound through Waset's backstreets toward the palace. Most intelligent people had left the market and other work until later in the afternoon. We were the only idiots walking around in the grueling heat. Despite the swelter, Selene's words still rang in my head. The princess would already be in Duat, in the Field of Reeds, no matter what we did here today.

That couldn't happen.

I wouldn't let that happen.

The priestess yanked my arm, and I stumbled to face her. "Hide that thing," Sikara said, shoving my scarab necklace beneath the linen folds of my sheath. Sweat rolled down her brow, and she blinked the beads out of her kohl-trimmed eyes.

"Do you need some water?" I asked. Those vivid specks in her irises flared as she wiped her brow. Priestesses of her rank rarely dabbled with the unmerciful high sun, remaining mostly indoors until daybreak or twilight. And when they did venture out, as Weret did earlier that morning, servants carried them in litters through the city streets. Our mission, however, didn't require such attention.

Sikara also didn't like asking for help. "I have no need," she said. "Mind your necklace. You don't know who's watching."

"We actually do," Alex retorted.

"And do we want them to know that, oh wise Hyksos maid?" asked Sikara, eyeing Alex and my clothing. My sister glared back. A jade cloth wrapped Sikara's kalasiris, while my sister and I wore Hyksos robes to maintain the fiction of being the princess's attendants. The ping-pong match of nastiness between Sikara and my sister had only intensified since the previous night.

"Relax, both of you," I said, before turning to Sikara. "Why would the Serk be looking for the star? If all they want is ka, I'm sure the High Priest gets them enough."

"Prevention, I'd assume," she said. "He gave the Seafarers the Serk because no one can stop them. The only heka that rivals theirs is around your neck. If I were on his side, I'd want to hold the star as well." She stretched a moment. "You both can be so obtuse sometimes."

Alex smacked her lips. "I thought priestesses were always nice," she said.

Sikara grinned like an animal baring its teeth. "To *you*?" We stopped for a moment as Sikara adjusted her linens and what I assumed to be a weapon hidden beneath. "Damn sword is heavy, but it's the best backup for prayers."

The priestess's pace increased. Her wild, dark curls blew in the wind as we cut through the streets, following her path toward the palace's stone walls. Though we'd all changed in a night, it hadn't. Its encasement was still strong and imposing, with guards at every checkpoint. The only welcoming image, however, was the splash of green at the entrance.

The High Priestess stood with one arm to her side, and the other in its linen sling, holding it tight against her body. Her robes of bright white made her a beacon against the mud brick and stone. A green wrap adorned her head, and thick, bronze necklaces danced up to her chin. She scanned the three of us as we approached, and I was unsure of the thoughts brewing behind an otherwise impassive face.

A guard came to her side with a sword not meant for ceremony. Despite this, she only glanced at him. "They are mine," she said. He peered between the High Priestess and the rest of us, but he turned. Sikara bowed to Weret, and we followed suit, but the High Priestess didn't speak, not even to her second-in-command. She turned on her heel, and we followed her gleaming robes up the entryway of Egypt's elite.

Once inside, the High Priestess led us back through the winding halls until we reached the Hyksos apartments. Weret's snake-charming voice wafted to my ears. "The princess's governess, Nimae, is expecting us," she said as we arrived at the grand entrance. "None of you may speak. We cannot squander this opportunity."

She glided across the limestone floor, eyes on the princess's governess standing in the middle of the hallway to greet her. Nimae bowed to the High Priestess. "My lady, the princess is pleased to grant you an audience." Weret nodded—her only acknowledgement of Nimae. When behaving as the High Priestess, Weret rarely responded to anyone. It was incredibly unnerving.

Nimae scrambled to compose herself. "This way," she instructed. Weret and Sikara passed her en route to the chamber but, as Alex and I followed, Nimae grabbed the back of my linens. "What are you doing here?" she spat. She trudged into the chamber, holding me tighter than expected. "You both should be at the baths with the others," she said when we'd entered.

Lying was never my strong suit. Earlier that morning, Sikara had come up with some rebuttal if this situation presented itself, but of course my mind went completely blank when I needed it. "We, well, we were—" I said, and she threw me to the floor. I hit the ground and slid across the polished tile, but that didn't stop Nimae from charging forward. Heat rushed to my face, and my palms responded with soft light. I shook them to quell my heka response before tucking them in the folds of my clothes.

"I dismissed her," a voice said from a corner of the room, and we turned in its direction. The princess sat on an embellished cushion by a window overlooking the Nile, enjoying a tray of fruit and the breeze. She wore a casual sheath dyed Hyksos crimson, with her long, sheer veil sparkling atop it.

Nimae's back straightened. "You knew of this?" she asked the princess as Alex helped me up.

"My ladies will serve the goddess whenever the High Priestess deems necessary," the princess said, finally turning to us. She rose, and in turn, we all bowed. Well, I bowed and scrambled behind Alex. I steadied my breathing as best I could, and the wash of light across my palms dimmed. "Please," she said, instructing us to rise.

When Weret approached her, she nodded graciously. "High Priestess," she said, awe coloring her voice. "You will have to excuse my lady." She waved toward the governess. "She is very protective." Nimae collected herself before taking her place behind the princess. "How may I assist you?"

Weret drew a breath before unraveling a tale of desert mercenaries in Waset, of traitors, thieves, and murderers bent on breaking the union of the Egyptians and the Hyksos. It was so enthralling that if I hadn't already learned the backstory, I wouldn't have known she bent the truth. Her story excluded the

Serk, the goddess's star, and the pendant whose power exploded fire and electricity from my limbs. The princess rose and clasped Weret's hands. "If the goddess wills it, we will leave and take refuge in the temple," she said.

Nimae darted to the princess's side. "We cannot just *leave*," she objected, grabbing Tuya's arm. Weret's impassiveness yielded to a wrinkled nose. Royalty wasn't touched in that way.

The princess shrugged from the governess's grasp. "*Nimae,*" Tuya said.

"You are young," the governess insisted. "You do not understand how this will look. Pharaoh must not think we are insulting him." She squared her gaze. "We cannot flee like peasants. We must collect your best servants and your finest clothing. You are the princess of the Hyksos."

Tuya's voice was edged. "It is the will of the goddess, my aunt," she replied.

"We will leave tonight and no sooner."

Tuya returned to the High Priestess. "We will leave this evening," she said apologetically. "We most certainly appreciate your warning."

As the High Priestess took Tuya's hand again and clasped it, a voice snapped through the chamber. "That can't happen," my sister interjected. She stepped forward, hands shaky, but face resolute.

Shit.

Her light eyes appealed to the High Priestess and the Hyksos princess. "It's safe now, but tonight there will be shadows everywhere. We couldn't possibly get her out then—"

"Heed your lady's concerns," the High Priestess cautioned. Her Holiness's voice dropped an octave, and my sister's mouth snapped shut. She held the gaze of the High Priestess, only to glance away and step back. Her jaw and fists clenched.

Weret turned to the governess. "Forgive her," she said. "We have spoiled her in the temple in one evening. But I agree with your maid. I respect your decision but do not advise it." She began to leave. "We will return in the evening."

Sikara, Alex, and I hurriedly bowed and funneled into the corridor behind the High Priestess. I planned to scream at Alex, but Nimae followed us out, spewing her own venom before I could. "*You*," she said, pointing at Alex. "I need assistance with the princess's food for tonight." Nimae waved her over. "Come, now. The women of Isis can hold on to the other one for the afternoon." Nimae pointed dismissively at me before taking Alex's arm.

"I am *not* leaving my sister alone," Alex said, struggling against Nimae's ironclad grip. "She'll be a sitting duck for Scorpions."

As I rushed over to help Alex, palms tingling again with heka, Sikara called out to us all. "I'll stay with Portia," she said, gliding over to the display. She glanced at my hands, and I shoved them behind my back until the familiar tingle dissipated. "Let's make this go smoothly so that the temple can help you," Sikara said, though I wasn't sure if she spoke to Nimae or my sister. "We want to help you."

I couldn't name it, but a subtle shift happened between my twin and Sikara. Maybe it was Weret's authority back in Tuya's chamber. Maybe Alex decided she needed allies if she was going to speed this up, that this wasn't her decathlon team who followed her commands. Whatever it was, Sikara's sudden niceness disarmed my sister. Nimae's grip relaxed as my twin sighed. "Come with me," the governess said, and began toward the kitchens.

"I won't be far, Portia," my sister said, wariness in her voice as she followed her.

"Portia," Weret said when my sister had gone. "Stand guard for the princess until the evening."

Sikara removed a small blade from her robes and handed it to me. I held it out like rotten fish. "What am I supposed to do with this?"

"You're so strange," she said as the pair turned to leave. "I always love a new sword."

Weret continued. "We will take the princess to the temple after the reception tonight, when there are no disturbances. Do not deviate." She motioned as Sikara adjusted her sword in her clothing.

"I thought Sikara was staying with me?" I asked the lower priestess.

She grinned before adding, "I lied."

BENEATH THE OMNU TREES

We need to go.

We need to go.

We need to go . . . now, now, now.

The sun descended that evening in a last burst of orange, red, and pink before it gave way to the stars. Egyptians considered Ra's journey a life cycle: birth at daybreak in the east and death at sunset in the west. There would be plenty of shadows from which the Serk could hunt soon. Dread crept up my spine.

I stashed the blade Sikara had given me in a basket near my chair as I waited outside the princess's door. I didn't know who exactly would appear first. Neither Nimae and my sister nor Sikara and Weret had returned from their activities. "Shh," someone said, their hand landing on my shoulder. I jumped before looking up at the princess. No veil covered her face, and she smiled in defiance. "We'll just be in the guest quarters. No one will see us," she said, and breezed by me, heading toward the courtyard I'd watched all afternoon.

I followed her into the enclosure, a sweet evening breeze already dancing around the Omnu trees edging the garden. Unlike the bountiful tamarisk and sycamore trees, their thin branches coiled like smoke from a cigarette. At the tips, red blossoms shook in the light winds. I touched one. "These are the famous Omnu trees?" I asked.

"You like our saplings," she said. "Their addition was a very kind gesture of the palace. When I'm homesick, I can look out here and see a little piece of what I've left behind." She also had her governess, but I doubted that she filled the princess with warmth or fondness. "The Delta is a beautiful place, despite the troubles."

"Does it make you angry?" I asked. "Are you angry with the Seafarers for the attacks?"

"I was so small when they arrived that I don't know a time without them," she said. "No, I don't hate them. That would take too much energy." She thought for a moment before a smile crept on her face.

"What?"

"Even if I hadn't stopped you, you wouldn't have gotten far pretending to be one of my maids. You look very Egyptian."

I sighed. "So they tell me." A beat passed. "Where's Nimae?"

Tuya arched a brow. "You are the first ever to inquire about her welfare." The princess pointed up to her dark room. "No lights yet. I assume she's still fussing in the kitchens about my food. I will admit I'm glad this reception is only for the Egyptian monarchs. It took her so long to test my food last night, my arm started to look appetizing."

"Is she always that fun to be around?"

"You've actually caught her in a good mood," the princess said with a wink. "She can be much worse. I've heard that she was pleasant in childhood, before my mother married my father, King Ashmar."

"She's jealous of your mom's marriage?"

"Yes and no. My grandfather was an advisor to my father's predecessor. He was an extremely wise vizier and an honorable man. The only problem was that he had an abundance of daughters. As the eldest, my mother and aunt were both eligible to marry my father. My mother is not nearly as beautiful as Nimae—" I coughed a bit. I couldn't imagine Nimae being much of a beauty. Tuya laughed. "She is very lovely when she isn't frowning."

"She's always frowning."

"Therein lies the problem. But the king chose my mother for Prince Ashmar. This sent my aunt into near madness with jealousy, so much that no other man wanted her. Thus, my grandfather insisted Ashmar wed both."

"Wait, your aunt *and* your mother are married to your father?"

"Yes, of course," Tuya said as I suppressed my horror. "But Nimae was not satisfied, because her children would not be Ashmar's heirs. My mother's would; my brother is next in line. Thus, Nimae squawked and squawked until she attained a more considerable position."

"Your nurse?"

"Yes, for quite a few years now."

"Why would she want to follow you around?"

"My mother is the only royal wife. Being my nurse gives Nimae great status in our home, and still more when we travel. It was a well-played move. But lately she's been so angry . . ." Tuya shook her head. "One would think she'd be happy now. She has her position and this relocation in Egypt." Tuya looked to me and shrugged. "Perhaps she misses her children."

"I'm sorry," I finally said.

"My thoughts are not consumed with Nimae," Tuya replied.

"I actually gave a great deal of thought to what you asked the other night."

"Me?" I creased my brow. "Wait, what did I say?"

"You've forgotten so quickly?"

"A lot has happened since yesterday."

"You asked me if I loved the prince." A lump caught in my throat. *Oh, that.* She didn't seem very interested in him beyond her duty.

"I could. I will have to, even if it's not . . ." She stopped herself.

"If it's not what?"

"Well, we all dream about being like Isis and Osiris when we're little girls, don't we?"

"Really? She had to piece him together. It's kind of disgusting."

Tuya laughed. "I've never heard it put like that. But every little girl dreams of their love story." I shrugged, a bit uncomfortable. I hadn't taken the princess for a romantic. Maybe I was uneasy because I hadn't thought much of love stories until that moment. Jason was a crush. What she had in mind was nowhere near that. "Their love watched over the Two Lands, but love also separated them, tore them from each other's arms."

"Is this the difficulty of loving Egyptians?"

"It is the difficulty of truly loving anyone. My mother first told me of the goddess; how Isis really fell in love with Osiris in Avaris and the Egyptian empire sprang from it. But don't say that to anyone here," she said with a chuckle. "The goddess saved her husband for their love and for our world." She plucked a blossom from one of the Omnu trees and held it in her palm. "We even owe them for the Omnu."

"Why?"

"Well, the young saplings sprang beneath their lovers' embrace."

My face burned with embarrassment. "Oh, I see," I said, eyes falling anywhere but Tuya's knowing smirk.

Again, she laughed at me. "But unfortunately, it's the Omnu spices that the Seafarers so badly want." She handed the blossom to me.

"They are really pretty trees."

"Yes, they are. We wanted to make the Seafarers comfortable on our lands. But some people are insatiable." She shook her head. "You'll have to forgive me. I've been speaking so much over the past days, and I don't even know your name."

"My name is Portia," I replied, bracing myself for her inevitable confusion. I could be smarter and pick an Egyptian name, but I hadn't. I wanted to hold onto something from home. To my surprise, she didn't ask for an explanation, so I continued, "I'm sure it's not easy to stay in Egypt with people you don't know."

"Every Hyksos has a role to play in easing the suffering of our home. This is mine." She was thoughtful before speaking again. "When you came to me last night with those curious eyes, I wanted to help you. I assumed you had a home, and as I cannot return to mine, it pleased me to help you."

"You know you don't have to do anything you don't want to," I whispered. Words tumbled out as we continued to walk. "That's what my dad always said."

"I see," the princess hummed. She wasn't the easiest to read as I offered my counsel.

"You don't even have to be an Egyptian princess," I said. Her stride stopped, but the words scrambled out now. "There's always another way."

She turned to me, pity in her eyes. "Oh, Portia," she said.

"Even your name," I said. "Really, Sahdina—"

She only touched my face. "*Tuya.*"

The sound of footsteps interrupted us. The princess straightened her back, asserting her regality, before walking in the direction of the noise. I followed, my gaze diverted slightly as I realized how childish I must have sounded to her. General Raia came into view first as we neared the voices that now filled her courtyard. Akoris followed shortly after. They were like the holiday season: when Thanksgiving pops up, Christmas isn't far behind.

As they neared us, the pair abruptly stopped and turned away, as though they'd caught Tuya coming out of the shower. I'd forgotten the princess's face was uncovered. This didn't stop her from approaching them, however. "Princess Tuya," General Raia said with his back to us. "Your veil. We thought you'd accompanied the maids to the baths, or else we would not have used this route. We apologize for this impropriety."

"Am I so repulsive that you should turn away from me?"

"It is improper—" the general began.

"It will be improper *tomorrow* at the ceremonies. Let's leave now to now. I say it is fine."

It took a moment, but the two slowly faced her again. Akoris pulled off his leopard fur and draped it around her shoulders. "There is a chill to this evening," Akoris said.

She drew her fingers along the fur before her eyes flicked back to him. "I doubt I look like myself now," she said.

"It is my honor to see that you are well," replied Akoris. "The prince is favored by the gods. We'd all rejoice for such an honorable wife."

She looked to the general. "Is that true, General Raia? Would you rejoice for a wife like me?"

Raia shifted, if imperceptibly, and cleared his throat. "To acquire a wife and create a family is a duty of manhood," he said, as if reading from a textbook. Raia's eyes landed on me and narrowed in recognition. "Princess, are your maidens often alone in the palace gardens?"

"My maids?" her voice twinkled in amusement. "Sometimes they get lost, as ladies do in strange, new places."

"Of course," said Raia. He watched me for a moment longer before regarding the princess. "Why don't I escort you both back to your wing?"

"That would be very kind of you," she replied. I expected the princess to say her farewell to the High Priest, but instead she looked at me. "Would you please tell the prince about the temple move?" she asked. "I'm not positive that Nimae had the message relayed."

"My lady," I said with a bow, one discreetly hiding the blood draining from my face. *The prince?* I didn't want to go anywhere near the prince. I would have rather asked Pharaoh to jump our Civic than find the prince. I rose as the general and princess disappeared into the palace.

"What a handsome pair." I turned slowly to see that the High Priest hadn't left yet either. His mouth twitched upward. "And she kept my fur." His eyes fell on me as my body tensed. I managed a small bow. He studied me, and I wondered what he might say, until: "Follow me. I will show you to the royal wing so you don't get lost with this"—his words turned pointed—"important temple business."

HIS HOLINESS

I wondered if he could sense my heka as we walked, if he was somehow aware the star he wanted was right beside him. With each step, I reminded myself that neither Tasherit nor Sikara had known heka was in me until they touched my hand. Still, my blood was ice. The man in the blue robes of Amun had done so many terrible things, and these tales made him almost omniscient in my mind, maybe even capable of listening to my thoughts.

The royal apartments lay secluded on the far southeast side of the palace. Every servant that passed us eyed the High Priest and me, but none were bold enough to question the odd pairing aloud. "What's your name?" he asked, breaking the silence lingering since we left the courtyard of Omnu trees.

It was an odd inquiry to a servant. We were nowhere near equal rank. For once, a lie came quickly. "Sahdina."

"Like your princess." The side of his mouth crooked up. "How appropriate," he said. I glanced up at him, not expecting the softness of his voice or the warmth of his eyes. Like Weret's, his gaze sparkled with intelligence, with the gods' secrets only he was supposed to bear. Myrrh, not as overwhelming as Ankhmir's scent, wafted from his clothes, perhaps with hints of sage.

It was my turn to eye him now. He seemed like an alright guy, like he could be friends with my dad and talk about his weird artwork or sports highlights. I knew I should hate him, that I should conjure my heka while he didn't suspect it, but I was actually enjoying the walk. "And what occupation does your family hold, Sahdina? Merchants? Viziers?" He angled toward me. "To wait on the princess, you must come from a noble house."

"My mother is dead," I said. "And my father doesn't belong to any house."

Akoris narrowed his gaze. "You don't come from a noble house?" he asked, maybe more himself than me. "Then you must be ambitious to have gotten where you are. I admire your fortitude," he said. "There is a chill in the air. Had your princess not taken my leopard fur, I would let you wear it."

"Thank you, Your Holiness," I said. His robes were woven with fine linen that draped his shoulders, torso, and floor-sweeping shendyt kilt. Jewels glittered on his hands and around his neck, adorning his clothing layered in blue. We continued through the hallways, entering one with elaborate oil lamps on the walls. They brightened the darkness with tiny balls of light, some that illuminated the High Priest's shoulder and on it the marred—if healed—flesh of an oblong scar.

"Is that a brand?" I asked despite myself. He glanced at me peculiarly and I diverted my eyes. "Forgive me, Your Holiness," I said. "I had no right to ask."

"Don't apologize," he said, and focused on it for a moment. "My fur usually covers it. Anen's father outlawed marking slaves long ago, but when the decree first came down, not all sepat governors paid it any mind."

It came out as a whisper. "You were a slave?"

"Surprises you that a High Priest was born lower than a rekhet?" he asked. "It is true. Even you can become more than a servant bearing her mistress's name."

"I enjoy my duties to Tuya," I said. "She's good to me."

"She's a kind woman," Akoris said. "Which is good. Most of her ilk are not." I wondered what he meant as he then smiled at me, and I found myself smiling back. There was light from him that made me feel like he understood me and that he could fix my problems. Was this really the man I was supposed to fear, that let monsters loose on the world?

The High Priest's stride stopped at the end of the hall. "Down that way," he said, pointing. "Deliver your message and tend to your princess." He began to turn from me. "I wouldn't wander about at this time of night, Sahdina."

I bowed and silently watched him disappear in a sea of blue. When he'd left my sight, I turned and prepared myself for the task at hand. My head was spinning, whether from the confusing encounter with the High Priest or being near the royal wing, I couldn't say. I laid my hand across my chest, taking deep, unhelpful breaths.

Two burly men guarded the hall leading to the royal chambers. Each carried a large spear with a bronzed point and had the type of discipline that didn't allow for flinching or shifting their weight. "Hyksos maid," one said, scrutinizing me as I approached.

"A message from the princess of the Hyksos," I said, before explaining the new arrangements. When I finished, he gestured to the man on the left who summarily disappeared down the hall toward the royal wing.

"Your message will be delivered," said the remaining guard. "Return to the Hyksos apartments."

I sucked my teeth at his curtness but turned on my heels.

Message delivered. *Check.* One step closer to securing the princess. *Check.* One minute closer to home. *Check.* That relief lasted only a few steps as the clack of sandals trailed me.

One pair belonged to a guard.

The other didn't. "I thought you'd left us," he said.

I glanced over my shoulder. My smile curved upward. "My plans changed, Prince Seti."

"A short trip," he replied as I faced him. The prince of Egypt grinned at the entryway with his bearish guards. He wore another dark kilt, and sweat and grime coated his brow. "How are your sisters?"

"Fine now," I said.

He angled his head. "Fine in one night?"

"In one night," I parroted.

"I thought the other maidens were off somewhere? The baths or something like that."

"I have been assigned personally to Tuya."

He clapped his hands. "A promotion!"

"No. Well yeah, kind of," I stammered before straightening my back. "I came to deliver a message for her. Which I did." I turned. "And now I'm leaving."

"Wait," he said. The word echoed a few million times in my head before I turned back. He stepped toward me. "You're always in such a rush." My face warmed. *Had the Seti–Portia tango started in the garden, or maybe when he was only Merenptah?* "How long have you been at your post?"

"Why?" I wrinkled my brow.

His voice softened. "You look tired."

A weak smile tugged at my lips. "I've been there since the high sun." My body suddenly weighed a thousand pounds. "And yes, I am tired," I replied. "It's just not my priority."

"Are you hungry?"

"What? I mean, yeah I am, but—"

"That's treasonous," he cut in. I arched a brow. "All servants in the palace must be rested and fed. Come with me."

"Merenptah," I said, and didn't move, opting to stare in moronic disbelief.

"What?" he asked. "You've already left your post."

I began a protest that slunk into a stammer. "You're hungry," he said. "Come on." He turned swiftly toward the gilded royal wing. I glanced to Bear #1 and Bear #2, but neither spoke. With a sigh, I followed the prince.

LIKE THE SUN

The royal wing stirred with activity, but Seti didn't flinch at the servants buzzing past with trays and other wares. He didn't have to. Walking with the prince of Egypt was like accompanying a lion in the jungle. He was the king, or would be soon, and his every movement was deliberate, purposeful, and slow. I, on the other hand, moved as if dodging pedestrians on city sidewalks.

"Don't worry about them," he said, indicating the servants. "They'll move around you." Small oil lamps sat atop ebony tables with lion's paw legs. The prince scooped one up as we entered a long hallway. The constricting space didn't keep my eyes from a mural with painted Ma'at watching over Anen's family. I rolled my eyes. *Ma'at . . . ruining my life since Shemu.*

My gaze drifted up, where Nut spanned the entire ceiling, her body an expanse of glittering stars above us. Many other gods stood on either side of the walls around Seti and me, feasting in reverie. The starry hall opened into another passageway and another, and the pleasant echo of harps and strings met us more distinctly with each new chamber. "We must be near the reception," I said. "You're not going?"

201

"I hadn't planned on it. There will be many parties this week." Finally, the hallways ended at a cedar door, painted gold and red with carvings of Horus's wings along the arch. He tapped it once before a servant in a cream linen tunic swung the heavy door wide.

My breath caught as we crossed the threshold into a lavishly furnished room. Couches and ebony tables were strewn across the polished tiles, and reliefs of the cow goddess Hathor with her golden horns and sun disc graced the walls. Wicker chairs clustered near the cushions and tables, and invitation to relax in this space.

I thought I understood luxury. I had seen programs on television where celebrities showed off their homes and cars. Personally, I wouldn't call our Hyde Park home luxurious, but we didn't want for anything. But this room was not luxurious. It was otherworldly. "What is this place?" I asked.

"This is where my family eats, if we wish to do so together," he said, as if the chamber held some ordinary dining room set from Ashley Furniture. He signaled to one of the servants with a flick of his hand; the man scurried away. "They'll prepare the room for dining," he said.

"I couldn't—"

"You aren't hungry?"

"I am, but *Meren*—" I caught myself. "Seti, this is your family room."

"And both you and I need to eat. I've hunted much of today. You've tended a royal bride, which I imagine is more tedious work. Come. I won't be convinced otherwise."

I subdued a smile. "So you're a brat used to getting your way?"

"You sound shocked," he replied. I laughed and walked over to one of the couches, whose cushions were lined in crimson silk.

Alongside the cow goddess, the flickering oil lamps illuminated murals of Egyptian women singing, dancing, and playing with their children. I noticed a scene of a young boy hunting near the Iteru. Seti, I assumed. This was a glimpse at the royal family's private life.

Servants entered the room with trays of food balanced on their shoulders. When they reached us, they bent low to lay them on the ebony tables and not make direct eye contact with the prince. The aroma of the dishes was intoxicating. I couldn't help but smile. "What are we having?"

"I'm sure some of the food from tonight's reception." Seti glanced at one of them, and before he could speak, the servant stood before us. "What have you brought us tonight? It smells as if fit for Amun himself."

The servant bowed. "Thank you, your approval is an honor. The kitchen has prepared tiger fish in spiced broth with pomegranates and cheese." He pointed to attractively shaped clay jugs at the end of the table. "And there you'll find the best wine in the Two Lands."

"Thank you," Seti said, and the servant bowed again and disappeared to the outskirts of the room. My stomach growled as the food's aroma played tricks on my nose. I was probably supposed to ask to eat. Seti was a royal, and they more than likely should eat first. But the food before me, smelling so wonderful, kept me from caring. I tore a piece of bread and dipped it in the broth before devouring it. I repeated the motion until the bread vanished and Seti's laugh filled the chamber. "And you said you weren't hungry," he teased. "Did they not feed you in Avaris?"

I wiped my mouth and laughed as well. "I didn't think I was this hungry," I admitted. There'd been so much excitement— Scorpions and binding trades, heka and prophecies, rescue attempts—that I'd forgotten to eat. "So are these paintings of you and your parents? Who are the girls over on that one?" I noted of the murals.

"I have sisters. My oldest often used this room to gossip with my mother. Then she married a Babylonian vizier."

"She is in Babylon?"

His features twisted. "Egypt does not give away her princesses."

"But you'll take someone else's princess."

"Most would rather be the queen of Egypt," he said as feet shuffled into the room. I turned to a harpist, carrying her instrument folding into a low-backed chair in the corner. Once seated, she plucked the delicate strings.

"You always have music while you eat?" I asked Seti, turning back to him.

He glanced at the harpist as if he'd never given it much thought. "Yes, usually," he said. "Your princess doesn't employ musicians?"

"Not for every meal," I lied. At least four people accompanied us in the chamber. This didn't include the men standing guard in the halls. "How do you live your life with so many people around?"

"This is what the gods intended for me," he said, leaning back contentedly.

"Are you full?"

"Yes, thank you." He thought for a moment. "And speaking of music, are the dances of Avaris like those of Egypt?"

I thought of the Egyptian dancing I'd seen, their professional troupes with musicians, jugglers, and acrobats. It was admittedly not what I knew, especially outside of a circus. "No," I said.

"Then teach me one."

I crooked a brow. "You want to learn one of my dances?" I asked.

His grin turned rakish. "I do."

"You are very demanding today."

"They should have never told me I'm a prince." He stood up from his couch and planted his feet in the ground. "Show me."

I smirked and stood up as well. "Alright." We moved to an open stretch of glistening tile. "Okay, this is the wedding feast dance of my people," I began. "So you move to your side like this for four counts." I snaked to the right, crossing my leg back in a grapevine on the second beat. Seti clumsily mirrored me.

"Good, now take four steps to the left," I said, again crossing my leg on the second count. "Great, now stop. So here you're going to step forward on your left, and tap your right foot in. Then step back on your right and tap in with your left. Now do that for eight counts, then swing your leg around, and start the whole thing in the opposite direction."

The harpist tried to keep up with our fluid, if ever-changing motion. Seti's brow creased so tight a bead of sweat trickled down, and I had to hold everything together so as to not burst out in hysterical laughter. "This is a dance for wedding feasts?" Seti finally asked. "It's exerting. What is it called?"

"The Electric Slide," I said, unable to contain the laughter anymore. "We like it for special occasions: weddings, birthdays, anytime *Just Like Candy* by Cameo plays."

His confusion was so apparent he'd stopped moving. "Are all the dances in Avaris exhausting?" he asked.

"You want to learn an easier one?"

"Please," he said.

"You'll have to come closer."

He held my gaze before asking, "How close?"

"Closer than that." I laughed. "There's a foot of space between us."

He neared me, and for a moment, I thought the soon-to-be Horus was just a boy at a Sadie Hawkins dance. "This close?"

I peered up into his dark eyes. "That's fine," I said quietly, and took his hands. I placed them on my waist, closing the remaining distance between us. His eyes flickered in surprise, wary of dance but intrigued by my boldness. My arms slid his neck. "And now you sway with the music."

"And what is this dance for in Avaris?"

"Egyptian princes," I said. His laugh was a burst of color to my senses, full of amusement and warmth, and the harpist had an easier time following these movements. He pulled me closer. The sweet scent of cinnamon and sage filled my nostrils, and I was aware of every breath he took.

We danced for some time, enough that I'd barely noticed the sun slip away. When I glanced out the windows, a clear and perfect night had taken over the Akhet sky. I bit my lip, guilty that I was having been too good a time to race against Selene's prophecy, to find a way home for my sister, to admit that I had enjoyed my walk with the High Priest.

My movement stopped. "Is something wrong?" he asked.

"I have to go," I whispered.

"The princess?" He released me only to crook a brow. "Oh yes, how else will she survive? She's only traveled with ninety-nine other women."

I narrowed my eyes. I liked him, but he was still a presumptuous prince whose gilded world circled him. "Believe it or not, I'm as shackled to my duty as you are, *Prince Seti*," I said.

"How?"

Because I have the star around my neck, I wanted to say. *Because if I don't get Tuya out of here, you'll go to war and get blown to smithereens. Because I was born the less impressive twin of Alexandria White, and there's nothing I can do about any of it.* "Have you ever heard of an underdog?" I asked. He shook his head. "Well, an underdog is the person that everyone expects to fail."

"And this is you?" he asked. "This is why you run?"

"No, I'm worse than an underdog," I began, and Alex's face came to mind, my sister born a genius. I loved my twin, but it was sometimes hard to like her. "People don't expect me to fail. People don't expect me to do anything at all."

Seti's expression softened. "And why is that?" The prince anticipated my honesty, but I hadn't been honest with myself yet. Alex had never barricaded me in the house, belittled me, or sabotaged me. If I had found something that I was good at, she would have been my biggest cheerleader. But I never gave her a chance to support me. It was easier to think she eclipsed me.

"It was me," I said. "When I really think about it, it was me."

Seti extended his hand. "Come back, if only for a moment." I came closer, though not into his embrace. He slowly touched my face, letting his callused fingertips trail my jawline, chin, and the curve of my lips. I wouldn't expect a prince's hands were callused, but he was Merenptah as much as Seti. "But there is something I cannot understand."

"What's that?" I asked.

"I can't see you as an *underdog*. In the garden, all I could think about was the fort, how I'd missed something. And every moment has been consumed with preparation for the Horus Throne. Anen united Egypt. He brought her peace, stability, untold wealth. I can't afford mistakes. I can't squander our legacy."

"Ever heard of Xanax?" I asked. He narrowed his eyes, but I shook my head again. "Nothing, keep going."

"And then you appeared again from nowhere, and—" He cut himself off, searching for words. "I could see only you. You are like the sun."

My thoughts scattered. Despite my bravado, which pulled the prince of Egypt into a slow dance, I still wasn't used to being the center of attention. This was a feeling for my sister, not me. "I wouldn't say that."

"So you would call me a liar?" he asked. "That is punishable by death." I tilted my head to him, and his lips grazed my brow. "Is this all right?" he whispered. "You see me as I see you?" I nodded before I'd even realized. I peered up to him now, knowing my eyes were moons, swallowed in the reflection of his. I'd only kissed a boy named Benjamin in the sandbox in kindergarten, but this wouldn't be a sandbox kiss.

Our lips, however, didn't meet. Someone banged their fist against the door, and we jerked apart. The harp music slowed as Seti glared at the door and launched himself toward it. When he swung it open another servant scurried in, followed by a burly guard. "Yes?" Seti growled.

"Your Highness, we thought you'd attend the reception. When you didn't come, we searched your chambers for you but you weren't there."

He peered at each servant in the room. "You don't all talk to each other?" The bowed to assuage the mistake and muttered apologies. Seti rubbed his temple. "Well, you have found me," he announced.

The guard wasn't one of the two I'd met at the chamber entrance, but he was large enough to be one of them. The servant's gaze flicked to me, eyes wide in understanding. "Your Highness, we were only ensuring your safety—"

"And you have ensured it. Now, please return to your post."

"Yes, Your Highness," he said. Seti watched the servant and guard leave before glancing back to me. I couldn't hold back my laughter.

"This isn't funny," Seti said, though he was laughing too.

"I think I should go, *Merenptah*," I said.

He smiled at his family name, though displeased with my retreat. "Why?" he asked.

"I'm full," I said. "And it's late. Do you know if Weret is still in the palace?"

"The High Priestess?" Seti was bewildered. "The temple litters were still outside, so I'd assume she's at the reception."

"Thank you," I said. I came to his side and pressed my lips to his cheek. He caught my hand and squeezed it before I pulled away. I turned from him, disappearing as Cinderella would, but with both slippers in tow.

SHADOWS

I dashed toward my post, leaving a bemused Seti behind and nearly mowing down a few palace servants. With the moon high, Weret would be ready to collect the princess. I needed to be at the chambers when she arrived. I passed the burly guards at the entrance of the royal wing and rocketed through the confusing halls toward the Hyksos apartments. I followed Akoris's route as best I could until faint string music caught my attention.

My feet slowed at the entrance of a reception hall, presumably the one Seti had ditched. I peeked in the direction of spilling light before a gentle hand tapped me. "It's the reception."

A small girl carrying a tray of fruit stood beside me. Her angular eyes, golden skin, and delicate features were accentuated by kohl and rouge. With a wig of neat plaits cascading down either side of her face, she couldn't have been more than eleven years old. "Come with me if you'd like," she offered.

I peered inside again as she stifled a yawn. "You're working late," I replied. A few moments wouldn't hurt. "I'd like that," I said.

Her large tray wobbled in her tiny hands as we made our way inside, and a few figs toppled onto the limestone. She froze. "I

210

don't want your lady to be offended. I see you are a lady of the princess. I'm not usually so clumsy."

I reached down and picked up the fruit for her. "Don't worry about it," I said with a wink. She grinned, exposing her small teeth.

This reception lacked the grandeur of the Feasting Hall and the warmth of Seti's family dining chamber. But a painted dais stood at the front with a vizier to oversee the event in both Anen and Seti's absence. In a floor-sweeping shendyt, he perched on a cushioned chair near the empty Horus Throne.

"My lady," said the girl. She held out a hand. "I can take those now—unless you're hungry."

"No, no," I said, handing over the figs. "Thank you." She showed all of her teeth again and trotted off. Unlike the audience chamber, this room was circular with benches and backless chairs for the guests. The servants stood around the perimeter holding bronze platters, while musicians strummed lyres at the foot of the dais. I hung near the outskirts, blending in with guests and servants.

I scanned the crowd until my eyes landed on General Raia standing with Pharaoh's stewards, and Weret and Sikara chatting at a table near them. I tossed around the idea of approaching them—they'd either welcome or smite me—when Akoris breezed into the hall. His sharp features flattered his face, and he'd acquired a new fur to drape his marked shoulder.

Akoris bypassed the partygoers for General Raia, who had the air of a chaperone at a junior high school dance. Raia warmly greeted Akoris, best as I imagined that he could. The stewards bowed to the High Priest before excusing themselves. In the meantime, the High Priestess pushed her food forward and rose from her seat. *Follow*, she mouthed to Sikara, and they disappeared down a side corridor. I maneuvered along the edge of the room until I noted the High Priestess was already being followed.

Akoris excused himself from the general to discreetly trail them, so I did the same, moving with delicate steps. The robes of blue and green swayed in the near distance until Weret abruptly spun. Akoris stopped as I edged into the shadows. "High Priestess," Akoris called out.

Weret inclined her head toward the Hyksos apartments. Sikara eyed Akoris for a beat but followed the instruction. "Doting on your princess?" Akoris asked when she'd disappeared. "You are devoted, my lady."

"My vow has been to serve Isis. The Hyksos princess is a faithful worshipper."

"*You* are a faithful worshipper," he said. "But we should be so much more than this, Weret."

"Your ambition is not Ma'at's will." The words settled. "And as your wife, I only wanted you, not to claim the Horus Throne."

I blanched. *His wife?* "You don't think you'd be a better fit for it?" The High Priest nodded toward Weret's arm, the limb always wrapped close to her body. "After what they did to you?"

"I do not." She shook her head. "The Serk are here."

"Of course they are," he said. "It was only time until they made their way to Waset. You should know this. You were there when I traded the knowledge."

"I was there," she said, "when you forgot those who loved you most."

"Forgot? The only reason your temple stands is that Iuli assumed correctly; I'd never destroy it under your supervision. But the moment you step down as High Priestess, it will be ashes. Iuli's defiance is inexcusable."

"And what about Preneb?" she asked.

"I betrayed His Holiness to save you. My patron wanted the Serk. Your princess wanted your head," he said. "This has always been for you."

"For me?" she asked. "You wanted your revenge against the nobility"—she glanced at his shoulder—"not for hurting me, but for branding you." She wrapped her free arm around her waist. "It's a sickness in you I can't heal."

He stepped closer. "Before the next flood, there will be a new Horus Lord on the throne, and it will not be Seti. Pharaoh Anen will die, as will his court and line. We'll start a new Egypt. It may not be Ma'at's will, but it's mine. Rule the Two Lands as my queen."

He loved her. His compelling words said as much. And she wanted to go with him, just like I enjoyed his company on our walk to the royal wing. The yes was a quiver on her lips.

But the High Priestess stepped away, and pain tore through her husband's eyes. "Preneb didn't want this for you," she said. "He wouldn't have taken you to his temple had he known what you'd become."

Akoris's gaze flamed. "You came from a high house," he said. "I was born under the cruelty of noblemen, something you didn't know until you served them." Disgust tinged his voice. "Preneb is gone, and the past is unchanging. For the last time, join me, wife."

Her words crashed down on us all. "The past *is* unchanging, Akoris," she said, widening the gap between them. "And so am I."

My feet flew. I ignored the burn in my shins, telling myself to focus on the original plan: get Tuya, go to temple, and tell Ma'at's will to jump off a bridge. But that intention, and the entire evening, had become a jumbled mess. Everything I'd learned wedged in spaces where it wasn't designed to fit.

I turned rounded the corner to Tuya's chamber, knowing that at least Sikara would be waiting for me. I was surprised, however, to find the entryway empty. Alex and the princess spoke by her balcony as I entered. My sister's arms wrapped around her abdome, distress coloring her expression. Before I discovered the cause, someone snatched me up by my linens.

I dangled in Nimae's grasp. *Again.* "How dare you leave the princess!" She shook me as Tuya and Alex dashed over.

"I ordered her to go," the princess exclaimed.

Nimae still flung me about. "Speak up for yourself, girl!" she said, as the scarab's chain snagged and tangled in my clothing. The ornament that usually dangled on my chest was now tight on my throat, cutting off my oxygen supply.

"You're choking her!" Alex screamed, reaching for Nimae's hold.

"By Isis, let her down," Tuya insisted.

The governess grunted and shook me one last time before flinging me away. I was grateful to slide across the floor as my lungs clawed for air. "Wouldn't want that, would we?" She stalked off.

I covered my scarab as I coughed. "She's psychotic," Alex said.

"And I thought she liked me," I replied. Alex rolled her eyes and helped me up. "Man, she's strong."

"Where'd you go?" Alex asked. "I thought Sikara was staying with you."

"Something came up," I said. Alex's expression screamed *I'm-calling-Sikara-a-bitch-in-my-head.*

"Your sister?" Tuya asked me, stepping into our conversation.

"Twin," she corrected herself. "I didn't notice earlier." The princess smiled. "I always wanted a sister. The rest of my mother's children are boys."

I nodded, but Alex tapped her foot, ignoring her. "Nimae is ridiculous," Alex said. "Where's the High Priestess? We should all be gone by now."

"Alex, you can't say that in front of the *princess*."

"It's fine," said Tuya. "Nimae is like this sometimes when she's not getting her way." She called after her erratic governess and made her way toward a corner of the room enclosed by delicate, hanging draperies. "I'll speak to her," she said, and vanished into a changing area.

"This is taking too long," Alex grumbled.

"We're almost done," I replied.

"We've been here . . . what? About seven hours? It's like we're just sitting around waiting for"—her voice dropped to a whisper— "a *Scorpion* to jump out and kill us."

"We'll be out of here soon," I said, as the clack of Tuya's sandals stole our attention. The princess backed away from the dressing area. Her hands clasped tight over her mouth. "Tuya?" I asked. The princess barely acknowledged me. Her entire body shook.

"Portia, the lights," Alex whispered from behind me. Darkness seeped into the chamber, pushing light from the corners first and heading for the room's center. "It's so cold," Alex said, silver stripes dancing from her lips.

My heart raced. "Help me get Tuya back," I snapped at my sister. But Tuya's shaking only intensified as we tried to tear her focus from the curtained nook. And then Alex froze as well. I said, "We have to get her to the door, Alex."

"Nimae," Alex said. My gaze dragged the governess, who crawled from the dressing area on all fours, those fours being pointed claws. Each movement ripped her sheath along her twisting, elongating spine. Alex slapped my arm. "Ankhmir didn't look like that!" she yelled.

I could only imagine what Tuya had seen when she went after her aunt. Maybe one claw, and then two and three, had sprouted from Nimae's hands before she folded into herself as though she'd never been a person at all. But as Sikara said, the Serk weren't an everyday adversary. Nothing made that more obvious than the dark, waxy shell hardening where her skin had been, where she grew a Scorpion's exoskeleton.

"By Amun, every time I leave you, you bait one of these disgusting beasts." My gaze found Sikara stepping through the doorway, sans Weret. Her eyes danced from me to snarling Nimae.

"A little help here, Sikara? *Please*!" I shouted. She grunted, already reaching for a clay oil lamp that had been sitting on a table near the door. It was something a genie should have popped out of, with two holes for the oil and the flame. Sikara moved fast, almost too fast to recognize, and slid the lamp to my feet. I didn't think. I just picked it up and threw it at Nimae. The top fragmented on impact, its oil smearing the floor, flickering with hungry embers. Nimae staggered.

"Give her to me," Sikara said, pointing at Alex. "And get the princess."

The flush across my face ran down my limbs, swirling electricity beneath my skin. My hands brightened as the white-gold sparks burst from my fingertips. I slapped my palms together, concentrating the heka into a line, into a whip. With a breath, I hurled on instinct around my sister like a lasso. "Ow, shit, that stings!" Alex yelped as I flung her toward Sikara.

The young priestess snatched her quickly and pushed her through the door. "Hurry up," the priestess shouted as she followed my sister. I could hear Alex's protests, trying to fight Sikara not to leave me, until they finally disappeared.

Princess next, I thought, but when I peered to my side, Tuya was no longer near me. She'd approached Nimae, who was still staggering back from the oil surrounding her, and the fire dancing across it. Nimae's eyes flicked from Tuya to the fire, and back to the princess. More of the thick, shiny shell covered her body, making her appear as human as an actual Scorpion in the sand.

"What have you become?" Tuya asked her.

"You look like your mother," Nimae replied, her voice as layered as Bekmut's had been. "I was supposed to be chief wife," she said. "But my father threw me away. Your mother threw me away. Avaris threw me away, but I don't need them. I will have an Egyptian line, a *royal* line. All the High Priest needed was the trade and the mark. The mark is on the star."

"What star, Nimae?" Tuya asked and begged at once, "Let us take you to the temple. No one has to know about this." But Nimae hissed in an awful key, and I couldn't tell if she was angry, laughing at Tuya, or both.

"The star of Isis. You arrived on the Iteru. He thought you it was you," Nimae said. She made that awful sound again. "But it wasn't. It was *her*." Her eyes snapped to me. "I almost just choked you with the mark, girl."

One of my guesses had been right. Nimae hiss-laughed, and chills ran down my spine. Tuya's eyes darted to me, pleading that I go, but I couldn't leave her. Nimae inched closer to the flames, wincing at them but defiant. "You should have let me choke her, Sahdina," Nimae said.

"I'm your problem, not her," the princess replied, approaching the fire between them. "Stay back," Tuya warned. The princess overturned more of the oil lamps in the room. They crashed to the ground, smearing the tiles black with oil. Hungry flames danced atop.

Nimae recoiled. "You stupid girl," the governess spat as the fire grew near them. Tuya only shot her chin in the air. She covered her mouth as best she could from the thickening smoke, and overturned another lamp. Heat billowed toward the entrance as flames flicked across the spattered oil, reaching out to the drapes of the changing area.

The flames burned faster than I'd expected them to, as if moving with a purpose, with a ka, with Ma'at's will. Nimae and the Hyksos princess were in a fire dance they'd brought from Avaris, one that could engulf everyone in the room.

Enough of this. I pressed my palms together again, intending to recreate the lasso of heka I'd used on my twin to tug the princess away. But I hadn't moved fast enough. Time slowed as Nimae sprang over the flames and descended with a single claw that pierced her niece's abdomen. I screamed as her body jerked, absorbing the impact. The princess stilled.

My gaze traveled up to the Scorpion. With hungry fire surrounding us, Nimae's eyes undulated violet as she threw the girl off her claw. My heart was tight, stomach in my throat. "No star," Nimae hissed into the night air. She was more Scorpion than Nimae, more creature than human, the thing that killed Sahdina.

My hands sparked with rage and sorrow. The Scorpion noted my heka, and with a hiss-laugh, she leapt into the air. My head shot up to the painted ceiling that she scuttled across.

Flames danced around us, and I shoved my arm across my mouth to keep from choking on the thick smoke. "You are . . ." She dropped to the floor behind me. I snapped around as the limestone beneath my feet rumbled. " . . . the star." Her claws cast wild shadows in the moonlight as she lurched toward me.

Am the star? I thought. *I wear the star.*

I didn't have much time to dissect her meaning, as the Scorpion sprang again, this time at me. Drawing the best breath I could in the clouded air, I stilled. A rush of power erupted from my hands, a lightning bolt bursting through the Scorpion. She teetered back, hissing and clawing at the air. With throbbing and bloodied hands, I stepped forward and watched in amazement as Nimae dissolved into a mound of sand and salt.

My head began to throb as my light dulled to nothing. "Don't move!" yelled voices behind me. I glanced over my shoulder to find Akoris in the doorway, surrounded by Pharaoh's guards. They took in the flames and wreckage. Two remained at the entryway as the others rushed into the room and stamped out the dancing flames. Others flew in with containers of water.

I didn't move. I couldn't. Their voices were slow noise in the background of my head pain. I took a step forward but stumbled, vaguely aware that the guards had boxed me in. Not too far from us lay Tuya, lost in the debris. I brought my hands to my face. *Blotchy. Red. Bloodied.* I dropped them as my gaze drifted from each face until I found a familiar one. Akoris inclined his head toward my neck, where my exposed scarab dangled. And he smiled.

GIFT OF HORUS

The General Raia pushed through the guards. They'd doused most of the flames, but smoke still rose from the charred wreckage. The general shivered. Whether from the sight or, with the flames stamped out, the odd chill wafting through the air, I was unsure.

Raia's hand found the hilt of his sword. "General," said a guard. Raia snorted in reply and pointed at the High Priest, chummy rapport gone in the wake of the attack.

"Remove him," Raia said, striding in resolution and authority. With Akoris gone, the general surveyed the chamber until he found the Hyksos princess. She lay near the dressing nook, her body covered in shredded linens. His gaze lingered before turning to me. "You are never where you're supposed to be," he said.

I stepped forward, though the room spun. "General, please—"

"Do not speak!" His timbre was as imposing as his physicality, almost larger than the thief Seti fought so long ago.

"But I didn't do this."

The general kicked at the sand and pillar near his sandal. "Your guilt is not the question," he said, jaw clenched. "The only question is whether you'll die by Egyptian hands or Hyksos." He indicated the guards. "Seize this woman!"

My head was a pressure cooker, multiplying the guards in my sight. I backed away as they charged, eyes dancing around the room. When the night breeze shrouded me, I remembered Tuya's balcony at my back. I raced to its edge. The guards' voices fell away as I hopped onto the ledge, and leapt.

I was a falling star in the night sky. Adrenaline rushed through my veins wind whipped against my face. I was perfect in flight, against all that I had seen and the traumas colliding within. In seconds, the ground would shatter me. In seconds, I'd have an education in landing.

The will of my heka took over, my limbs like an expert acrobat. In a splash of green and a thud, I landed. My body rolled forward into a cluster of lilies, breaking my fall like a baseball fits into a catcher's mit. I should have broken every bone in my body, but aside from a throbbing elbow, I was miraculously all right.

An arrow plunged into the dirt beside me. "Shit," I exclaimed as someone plucked me from the lily patch. Sikara steeled her gaze despite a gash running down her shoulder and neck.

"They've called the archers."

"No shit," I said as she released me. We dashed for a sliver in the palace wall, an exit shrouded in fig trees.

My sister met us there, but it was no time for hugs. We raced for the temple, and the distance seemed no shorter despite our quick pace. We said nothing as we darted through Waset's backstreets, until the temple rose above the mudbrick homes, gleaming under the moonlight. We hauled ass down the pathway beneath the sycamores until the ascending steps lay before us.

I grabbed my knees, forcing air into my lungs. The head pain had subsided, so I focused on breathing evenly. Sikara breezed by me. "Don't die," she said, heading up the steps. I lifted my eyes after her, unable to ignore the scarlet stream trickling down her arm.

Alex shook me so hard, I nearly tumbled over. "Are you crazy?" she demanded. "You jumped off the balcony! Didn't you see how far up you were? I thought you'd committed suicide."

"The guards had blocked me in," I said. "What else did you want me to do? Let them kill me?"

"Of course not, just . . . are you hurt?" She grabbed my right arm to inspect it, and I yelped.

"She just ran across the city," Sikara interjected. "Stop your moaning." Alex sighed as we climbed the temple's steps. I glanced over my shoulder to the House of Rejoicing. In the distance, the palace brightened like a jack-o'-lantern.

Ma'at's will had won after all.

Alex and I arrived in Tasherit's chamber as the priestess trailed us. Though she wore a wig with heavy beading, her steps were light and agile. "Sit there," Tasherit said to me and pointed to one of the stupid, little chairs littering her already cramped chamber.

I found a seat near her slanted bed. "Where are Selene and Sikara?" Alex asked.

"The great lady is having an audience with Her Holiness," Tasherit said. "The child still suffers with head pains. You just ran a long way, Alexandria. You should sit as well."

Alex nodded and approached me slowly. I watched as she plopped onto Tasherit's bed. Neither one of us had slept on it—the slant in the bed wasn't easy to get used to—and I opted for the reed mats. Alex's hand found my shoulder. "What happened in there?" she said. "What happened with the princess?"

It was the only question that mattered, and the only one that ate my words. The sobs clawed out of my throat as I found her twinkling eyes. "She's dead," I replied. "Just like Selene said, just like Ma'at wanted." I turned to the priestess. "Why would Ma'at do this?" Sympathy filled Tasherit's gaze, but she said nothing as my sobs choked out.

Tasherit sat beside me, now with a small bowl on her lap containing ointment for my throbbing elbow. Like most of her treatments, it smelled like exotic death. She spread it across her hands before working it into my throbbing elbow. "This will help with the pain," she said. "The great lady and Her Holiness are considering our next action against the High Priest. You will stay in this chamber until they're ready."

I jerked my hands out of Tasherit's grasp. "The princess is dead," I repeated. "And the guards think I killed her."

"Why?" Alex asked. Fear tinged her voice, though it was steadier than mine.

"I was the last one in the room with her," I said. "I killed the Scorpion, and it vanished. The guards only saw me and Tuya's body."

Alex turned to Tasherit as the priestess stood from her chair. "Can't we just tell the guards what happened?" Alex asked her.

"The guards don't know of the Serk as we do in the priesthood," Tasherit said, voice softer than normal, if at all possible. "I doubt they'd believe you."

The room quieted, though the tension and sorrow lingered. "I'm not concerned with the guards anyway," I said. "Akoris saw my scarab. He knows I have the star."

The priestess's eyes snapped to mine. "Surely you're joking," said Tasherit.

"I wish I was," I replied. "He released the Scorpions, he wants to rule Egypt, and only the star can get in the way of that.

Everything is just going wrong." I fixed my gaze on the priestess. "You didn't answer my question, Tasherit. Why did Ma'at bring us here if not to save the princess?"

Tasherit took a deep breath. "You did not save the princess because it was not Ma'at's will."

"Portia." My twin gripped my shoulder. "It's not Tasherit's fault."

I ignored Alex. "So Ma'at doesn't want to do the right thing?"

The priestess shook her head. "You still don't understand Ma'at. She is neither cruel nor kind, good nor evil. Ma'at has no side. She is only balance."

"Didn't *she* bring us here to beat the bad guy?"

"She brought you here because the Serk magic entered the world and yours had to as well," said Tasherit. "You aren't here to rid us of trouble. There is no world of only light, Portia, or darkness."

When Tasherit left us, my sister and I sat up most of the night, me in my chair, Alex on Tasherit's bed. Twinning. And with no lamps to brighten the room, we stared into the chamber's darkness and our own grief.

"They were married." My voice twisted out low and scratchy, having weakened some time ago under all of my heartache and helplessness.

"Who was married?" Alex asked.

"Weret and Akoris," I said. "I overheard them tonight before the princess died. He asked her to come back to him"—I paused for a moment— "so they could rule Egypt together. He said that by the next flood, the Serk will have cleared out all of the power players in Waset, and he'll claim the Horus Throne."

I wished I could have seen Alex's features, but we were still twins. I knew the horror that spread across them. "And did she say yes?"

"Would you have told Jason yes?"

"Jason?" she asked, chuckling. "Maybe," Alex admitted. "He's so damn fine."

I laughed a bit in return. I needed to. "She turned Akoris down." The bed rustled as my sister shifted. "I need some air," she announced and swung her legs over the side. Her feet touched the floor. "I'm going to that big window. You want to come?"

I shook my head until I realized she couldn't see me. "No, that's okay. I'll be here," I said as my twin slipped out of the room. When she'd gone, I peered into the darkness until another pair of feet shuffled toward the entryway. "Short walk," I called out to Alex. "Was Rawer guarding the window?"

The glow of an oil lamp filled the doorway in response, and it didn't illuminate Alex's form. Wearing a linen tunic, Selene held a small lamp as she walked into the chamber. Her dark curls hung over her face. I straightened in my chair as she crossed the floor and took Alex's place on Tasherit's bed.

"Are you okay?" I asked her. "Are you feeling better?" She scooted closer, allowing the soft glow to dance on her face. She pushed her curls back from her brow and peered around the chamber. Finally, her gaze locked with mine. Her eyes were not their usual soft brown, but milky and clouded. "What's wrong?" I asked, recoiling.

"Nothing's wrong," she replied. She placed the oil lamp on a nearby table and touched my shoulder. Her skin was clammy all over, perspiration beading on her neck and brow. "When we walked together today, I saw a bit of myself in you." Selene glanced over her shoulder before returning to me. "Perhaps it was narcissism to see yourself in a common girl with a royal name."

"Akoris?" Selene was the same, but completely different. She had an air of importance, of regality, that she hadn't earned. She wasn't the fourteen-year-old who hadn't grown into her graces yet. I could faintly smell myrrh on her skin.

"But Portia is also a lovely name," Selene continued by way of an answer, "and the Temple of Isis is almost as marvelous as Amun's." Heat swirled beneath my skin. When my hands glowed, Selene shook her head. "Your defenses are not needed. If you try to harm me, your friend will bear the brunt of it."

"How do you know my name? And what have you done with Selene?"

"I have done nothing with the child."

"You're speaking through her!"

"This is nothing she can't do. If only she knew her true capabilities."

I drew a breath. "What do you mean, she can do it too? She can get into people's heads?"

"She's not just a strange girl with dreams and head pains." The freshman shook her head. "She is gifted, like you. No, she doesn't have light or fire, but her talents are highly coveted in the priesthood. Selene is an Eye."

She continued. "We don't access everyone's minds, but we can see through *each other* when our abilities have matured. Which is, consequently, how I know your real name now." She inched closer. "A few Eyes are born per generation. We can feel when another is near. I have known for some time that one was close, though their abilities were still underdeveloped."

Maybe that's why her headaches got stronger in Akhet. I furrowed my brow. "So why are you here?"

"Your friend's abilities have matured," she said. "And her

memories have been very helpful," she said. "For instance, I saw your trip through the Rivers of Time. And that we were supposed to meet when I still had the service of Ankhmir."

She cleared her throat. "I am here because I saw you with our princess tonight, as did our guards. And it was at that time you saw me admiring your beautiful necklace. It's very important to me." She smoothed a wrinkle in her sheath. "I intended to enter the temple myself tonight, but then I sensed that Eye again, stronger now. So instead of entering the temple, I just accessed the child's mind. I am very happy that I did. The High Priestess really should have—"

"Leave her out of this," I warned.

Selene only grinned. "I did not mean to displease you." She ran her hands to a link of jade beading around her wrist. "I'm sure the High Priestess has not painted a flattering picture of me."

"My opinion of you doesn't matter."

"Oh, but Portia, it does. As I told you, I was born a slave and my mother worked her way into a noble household. I served the noble boys in the edubba, learning what I could between bearing their cups and swatting their flies. But my work was difficult because often I suffered terrible head pains without any idea why."

Selene continued. "I thought that I was cursed. But then the High Priest of Amun, the great Preneb, visited the household, as he was a cousin of some sort. Preneb was also gifted by Horus, and when he felt the presence of another, as I did with your friend, he wanted to teach me to control it. He arranged for me to leave the household and become a scribe at the temple of Amun."

"This has nothing to do with me or Selene."

"Patience, Portia." She angled her head. "Priests are the mouths of the gods. We protect divine knowledge on papyrus scrolls, on the temple walls, and sometimes elsewhere."

"Like the Serk," I said.

"Like the star," she replied.

"And did Preneb . . ." I asked. "Your shoulder? Did Preneb give you that mark?"

Selene's jaw tightened. "A year before I left for the temple, my gift as an Eye matured. I didn't know what was happening at the time, as your friend has no idea why her headaches are so strong currently. I couldn't serve those boys for a month. They didn't want me to forget why I was there, so the day I returned to work, they seared my flesh with a reminder that I'd be a slave no matter what station I reached."

My heart tightened. "I'm sorry," I said.

"It is of little consequence now. Before the next flood, Egypt will have a new vision, a new monarchy, new leadership."

"Yours?"

Selene's mouth quirked up. "Portia, tonight I would like to offer you a trade. I want the gifts of Isis's star. For it, I will give what *you* most desire: to make this simply go away. I'll return you to your time."

I narrowed my gaze. *It's good that he came to me and not Alex. Alex would have put a bow on the scarab and asked him if he wanted overnight shipping.* "No," I replied. "I didn't want the binding trade, and I don't want this."

"Don't answer in haste," she said. "I will receive your answer in the morning. I plan to return to this temple then with the general and Anen's guards. Without my influence, they will seize you as a murderess."

"I didn't kill the princess."

She flicked her hand. "It's such a confusing mix-up. The Serk can be unmanageable." She trained those eyes of white on me. "If you accept my offer, then you will not have to worry about imprisonment. Perhaps death."

I touched my scarab, for the first time seeing Akoris in totality, even if through another person. He was charming, gifted, kind . . . and mad. "Ma'at gave me the star for a reason," I said.

"*Gave* you the star?" Selene peered quizzically from me to the scarab before wrinkling her nose. "By Amun, you don't know."

"What don't I know?" I asked, dropping the scarab.

Her smile was crooked as she rose. "The mark is on the star."

"What does that mean?" I hopped to my feet and squared my shoulders.

She leaned forward. "Ask your priestess," she almost hissed, and collapsed to the floor. I dropped, catching the freshman only before she slammed her head against the tiles. The freshman coughed, clinging to me as if I'd fished her out of the river. Sweat poured down her face. Sikara was right. It was difficult to move heka through the body.

Selene blinked her eyes wide, clear and brown again. "How did I get in here?" she gasped. I didn't answer, only stroked her hair. It would be time for the morning prayers soon, but I didn't care. I wanted answers now.

Trapped in Flesh

We found the doors to Weret's chamber unguarded. I clenched my fists as my eyes danced over its markings to the goddess. A singular thought had mocked me since I'd grabbed my sister from the window and stormed over with Selene: Weret had done nothing to protect us. She'd *chosen* not to.

My knocks went unanswered, so I pushed the doors open as Alex and Selene trailed as best they could. The High Priestess's chamber was still its own world, a room of lavish furniture and idols to the goddess. Tonight exhaustion hung heavy in the air, perhaps blotting out any chance of brightness. The few lights casting shadows in the chamber came from sparse oil lamps. She stood in the middle of the room with her salted hair freed. It rested on her shoulders as she spoke to Sikara, who sat nearby. Though resting beneath her linens, for once Her Holiness's arm was not in its sling.

Despite our intrusion, the High Priestess did not speak. It was Sikara who straightened in her chair and turned to us. "The High Priestess will speak with you in the morning," she said. Her voice was hoarse and her eyes were heavy. She'd never seemed so young or so exhausted.

"There's no time for that, Sikara." I stepped forward. "Akoris will be here in the morning, and we're all going to talk right now." I approached and though Sikara may have been tired, she was still *really* fast. She'd swept between me and the High Priestess before I blinked. Sikara squared her shoulders, burning me with her gaze. "Do not test me, Portia," she growled.

"That is enough," said Weret. "Sikara, let her speak." Her voice was rich with authority as Sikara reluctantly withdrew. "To what do we owe this pleasure, Portia?"

"Akoris came to me." I pointed to Selene. "Through her."

"Sooner than I thought he would," Weret replied as Selene caved in on my twin. "I'd left Selene without wards. An unwarded Eye would prove very tempting to him." Alex couldn't support her full weight, and knelt down with the freshman as Selene slid to the floor.

The High Priestess gestured to a servant waiting in the shadows of the chamber. The attendant deftly took Selene up. She swooped in so quickly I'd barely heard her feet against the stone floors. "Sit her over there," the High Priestess said, pointing toward a collection of wicker chairs by her window. "And give her water. She needs to replenish." The servant nodded without making direct eye contact. "Heka sickness is an awful thing to watch."

"Akoris could have killed her," I said.

"He wouldn't kill another Eye," Weret replied.

"Why? What does that mean?" asked Alex, placing her hand on my shoulder. She'd returned to my side when the servant took hold of Selene. She squeezed my shoulder, signaling that I could step back; that I didn't have to be so . . . on. "What does it mean to be an Eye?"

"It means that, like Akoris, Selene is tuned to the will of our gods. Upon her son's birth, Isis bestowed Horus with a gift: clarity and sight of the mind. Perhaps it would be the All-Seeing Eye to you. Sometimes divine gifts find their way to men and women."

"My dreams and headaches—" Selene began from her chair before a wave of heka sickness set in. The attendant quickly pressed a cup to her mouth.

"Please, just drink now. But yes, Selene, your gift came first," she said, peering between Alex and me. "I mean, of the three of you."

"Of the three of us?" Alex asked.

"And how do we know this doesn't have anything to do with you and Akoris?" I said. "I heard your conversation tonight at the palace." Weret smiled at me, though something in it showed Her Holiness's dilemma: whether to address me as a child or a woman.

"Portia said you two were . . . *are* married," Alex said.

"I wouldn't use any of you against my husband," she said. "And I wasn't always the High Priestess. I was appointed by Iuli, the High Priestess of Isis before me. When I met Akoris, he was favored by Preneb, the High Priest of Amun. I was the handmaiden to Pharaoh's eldest daughter, Neferure, who'd recently accepted a marriage proposal.

"Preneb often counseled Pharaoh's sons, and Iuli counseled his daughters, but Neferure was not satisfied with her wisdom concerning the betrothal. She had a hot temperament and sought out Amun's priests by inviting herself to one of her brother's sessions. Preneb, however, wasn't there. He'd traveled north on temple business, and Akoris filled in that day.

"I was in her retinue, of course, and thought him stately," she continued. "He advised my princess to bring offerings to Amun during the entire Ahket season that year, and I often escorted her to the temple to pray. It was there that Akoris first spoke to me. It was there we fell in love.

"As the unclaimed son of a slave girl and a nobleman, Akoris naturally wanted his mentor, Preneb—the only father he'd known—to marry us, but he was still away. So we postponed the ceremony until his return."

She peered at my necklace. "I enjoyed serving Neferure, but before my parents sent me to wait on her, I was a highborn daughter myself. I had many fine things at home, and I missed them, especially as my wedding approached. While Neferure was off to the baths one night, I tried on her betrothal gift—a lapis scarab with glittering wings from Swenett."

I touched my neck. "My scarab?"

"Ma'at has a sense of humor," Weret said with a weak smile. "I only wore it for a moment, but my lady returned early and flew into a rage, believing me a thief. She had me arrested, and ordered that I go before Pharaoh's stewards to beg for my life."

"Akoris tried so hard. He went to the stewards, but their mercy only stalled my punishment." She drew a breath. "And when Akoris gave up hope, a man came to him, one I'd later call his patron. He had no great house or family name, but he said he could free me. He'd do so for a small price, for something only the temple, only Preneb had access to: the Serk. As Preneb was an Eye, like Akoris, he was warded. This man needed to get around that."

"So why bring it to him?" Alex asked.

"Because Akoris was not just any Eye," Weret said "He'd become the most talented Eye in Egypt, his natural abilities surpassing even those of Preneb. Akoris was tortured whether to betray his master or save me, but in the end, you know what he decided."

"So they let you go?" I asked.

"I was released, but not before Neferure's personal guard gave me her farewell." Weret removed her arm from the shield of her clothing, revealing her right hand for all to see. I then understood her reclusiveness concerning it. Her hand bent too far in all the wrong ways, having been shattered and never set properly to heal.

Weret's eyes saddened. "Preneb married us when he arrived from the north and that night Akoris took his wards. It sent the old priest into state of nothingness." *A coma*, I thought.

Weret's gaze landed on Alex. "You asked me what I meant when I said of the three of you," Weret said to her. "I will explain this now, but you'll have to forgive me. Iuli instructed that I wait until it was absolutely necessary to say this." She turned to me. "Your scarab is powerless."

"But you said the star's power is in this necklace," I said.

"Your necklace is not the star," she continued. "The last star emerged as always from the Iteru, right after Akoris took Preneb's wards and became High Priest in his stead. Previously it had been a jewel, a weapon, or some other token. But this one took the mortal form of a Mitanni princess."

"Anen's father had annexed the Kingdom of Mitanni, and her princess Ashkai floated up the Iteru after the campaign with her husband, a respected Egyptian general. She wore cultural marks on her skin; all Mitanni of her age would have them. But the star's mark was amongst them."

Weret continued. "Soon after the general's welcome feast, he was stricken and succumbed," she said. "While everyone else wondered why the healthy, young general's ka would give out, High Priestess Iuli already was certain of the answer. Knowing of the star's involvement in this—"

"She confronted Akoris?" Alex asked.

"She confronted me," Weret replied.

"But wait," Alex said. "Did you . . . did you know what Akoris was doing?"

"I was there when he conspired with his patron and provided him the knowledge of the Serk. I didn't know all of the details, but yes. My husband had saved my life, so I turned a blind eye."

"And what did you say to Iuli?" I asked.

"She'd told me that if Pharaoh took this wife, if the star fell into the hands desiring its power, there would be no future for Egypt or the goddess."

"And?" I asked.

"I told her it wasn't my problem," Weret said regretfully. "I told her to leave us alone. But that evening Akoris gave me a gift, the scarab that belonged to Neferure, now inscribed: to my love the blessings of Amun. He said he told Neferure of the inscription the scarab would bear, to whom it would belong, as she took her dying breaths."

"It was a horrific act," Weret said. "I was no longer looking into Akoris's eyes. I was looking into his swelling rage, the pain bleeding into every decision he made. Not even my love could heal him. Iuli and I took the princess to the Iteru. We evoked the Rivers of Time to protect the star and summoned the heka to transport them—"

"Them?" Alex cut in.

At this, Weret's smile returned. "Ashkai's children had been hidden in Egypt for months, as she'd been warned to do before arriving. The campaign at Mitanni lasted seven years. Ashkai's marriage to the general had produced . . . daughters."

My spine prickled. She was going somewhere with this that I didn't want to follow. "You aren't saying . . ." Alex said.

"Yes, that scarab is only the mark. You are the star. The woman, heka trapped in flesh, was your mother, who passed the magic of our goddess to you, and you will do to your children."

The mark is on the star, I thought. The phrase didn't mean the symbols on the scarab. It meant the scarab on me.

Weret turned apologetically to Selene. "We knew the Rivers required special heka, but we thought Ashkai would be fine. Only she wasn't. She was spent, and the heka sickness came too severely for her to last long after." Weret turned to a piece of lapis, fashioned into a face, hanging on the temple wall. Though it had seen wear and tear, it was still mostly smooth, and blue as a tranquil sea. She extended it to Alex. "Ashkai's death mask."

And Alex slapped it from the High Priestess's hand. It fell to the floor, a new piece splintering off from its side. No one moved. "No," Alex said. "My mother is Sandra White. She died of an autoimmune disease in Chicago."

Weret met her storm gently. "Your mother was a Mitanni princess who died of heka sickness."

"But we have photos with her, birth certificates!" Alex countered as nausea coursed through my body. It was all too much. We were the relatively normal daughters of Richard White. We didn't have another sister, and we most definitely were not ancient Egyptians. There was no reality to accept other than what we knew.

Still, Weret shook her head. "You don't understand the ways of heka or the River. You were born of Ashkai, and your heka belongs to the goddess."

"I don't have anything that belongs to anyone. Portia has lightning. I don't have anything like that."

"Of course you do. When heka is passed from mother to child, it sometimes has to be triggered. Your journey through the River started yours as it did Selene's. The mark began Portia's. Why do you think you have your aptitude? Your propensity to learn was the first of your gifts." Alex inhaled sharply. Weret had attributed her intelligence to something she feared more than anything. A kick in the stomach would have been easier to take.

Alex's voice was barely audible. "You're wrong," she said.

"I was there, Alexandria. Why do you think Iuli made me High Priestess? She installed me to wait for you," she said. My twin backed away, but Weret still came forward. "You weren't stripped from your home. You were returned."

"Stop lying!" Alex yelled. "Stop . . . just stop all this!" She turned and dashed out of the room, her footsteps disappearing down the hall.

"The truth may be necessary, but that doesn't make it easier to bear." She turned to me and whispered, "You should go to her."

DIFFERENT WAYS

I wove through the temple, though I did not particularly want to speak with my sister. *Could I have a moment to figure it out for myself first?* No, not when you have siblings. Not when you're twinning. Not when Alex needed me. She'd always been worse with change.

I fought the knots in my stomach and followed her into the corridor, but she was already gone. Shrieks at the private entrance, leading toward the Hypostyle hall, let me know where to find her. "Let me out!" Alex yelled at the temple guards blocking her way. The large wooden barriers were rarely guarded from this side, but the guards remained steady, backs to the door, spears raised.

"We are only commanded by the High Priestess," one said.

"Alex," I interrupted.

She didn't turn. The dance of torchlight played shadow tricks on my eyes. "I'm not staying here, Portia." It was as much a warning as a declaration.

"What about Selene?" I asked.

"Go get her, and we'll leave. But I'm not staying here another minute."

"Alex, just wait," I said, gently touching her shoulder. She spun around as if I'd broken a rule and she had no problem ratting me out to Richard. My words didn't come fast enough.

"I am not going back in there," Alex said. "I don't have to do anything that I don't want to."

"You think you'll find home out there?"

"You think you'll find it with them? They want us to be some weapon for Egypt. That's not who I am, Portia, and it's not who you are either."

My mouth clenched. It was rare that my sister was ever angry, let alone furious. But she annoyed me more in that moment than she frightened me. Alex was so resolute that she was presumptuous. Sure, she usually knew everything, but that didn't include how I felt. She hadn't known that for a while. "And how would you know who I am?" I asked, folding my arms.

"Because I'm your twin. If there's anyone who knows you, it's me. You're not some cosmic warrior." Her eyes narrowed, trying to convey what she found obvious. "You *have* a home. Dad and I love you. There's nothing else you need."

"But what if this is something I *want*?"

Horror colored her expression. "What about Dad and me? What about your life with us?"

"I've had sixteen years of it! You're the smartest person to ever set foot in Roosevelt, maybe to ever exist. But who am I? I'm the twin waiting by the car." I was flying and drowning all at once, clawing for the right words. I wanted her to hear me, to understand. "It only made sense for you, Alex. Why wouldn't you want to go back? The decathlons, prom, Jason—"

"I told you Jason and I weren't going!" she almost screamed, but neither of us budged. "Then what's it really about, Portia?"

I hesitated as I searched her eyes, so brilliant in the shadows of the temple. "This is the first time I mean something," I said, my voice cracking before I could get all of my words out.

"You've always meant something to me," she said.

"But I didn't mean anything to *me*, Alex," I replied. "I didn't mean anything to me."

My sister said nothing, staring as if I were a stranger. Something in me shattered as she turned on her heel. This time the guards parted before her. She didn't look back as she pushed the doors open and disappeared into the night. Hot tears welled in my eyes. "Do you wish the doors closed, my lady?" a guard asked. His eyes weren't on me.

Weret's hand landed on my shoulder as she moved from the shadows. "Yes," she said.

"You told the guards to move?" I asked, and she nodded. "Why did you let her go?"

"You need different things, and you will find them different ways," she said, and the guards shut the entrance door.

DEATH MASK

Selene left the infirmary to stay with me in Tasherit's chamber. By some stretch of the imagination, I actually slept that night. Without my twin, however, it was nowhere near pleasant. I had one dream. Alex and I stood at the temple door as we'd done hours before, but I was now as much an outsider as a participant in our fight. Each time the dream recurred, Alex left me standing in the stone hall with the temple guards. I never chased her.

Someone shook me as I opened my eyes. "Portia," a voice—Selene's—said. The freshman sat the end of my reed mat. "Get up."

I groggily obeyed, stretching my limbs and standing. I slipped a jade robe over my sleeping sheath and peered around the room. Morning light poured through the windows, making something blue gleam brightly from Tasherit's dressing table: Ashkai's death mask. *The hell?* I thought. *Who brought it up here? And why hadn't it been entombed with her?* As I walked over to inspect it, Selene grabbed my arm, stopping me. "Do you hear that?" she whispered.

I stilled as the echo of hooves traveled to my ears, shortly followed by men snapping orders. "Akoris," I said. "Come on."

We flew out of Tasherit's chamber, my thoughts crashing against each other. *Why hadn't we come up with a plan last night?* I thought as we found the hall leading to the temple entryway. The echoing voices swelled in number and intensity as a figure blocked our path. Rawer's chest rose and fell as if he'd also been tearing through the halls.

"Not here," he said, voice hushed and quick. "The temple is filled with Anen's guards. And they've taken Her Holiness and the great ladies. You must come with me now." He was wearing a simple headdress and a shendyt of a rekhet, and turned to slip through another set of corridors, expecting no reply but obedience.

He was wearing camouflage. He was going to sneak us out.

We obeyed. My heart raced as we attempted to match his swift run. "Why would they take the great ladies?" I asked the Medjay's back as we rounded another corner.

"Because they wouldn't tell them where to find you in the temple," he said, without turning to me.

"Is Akoris here?" Selene asked. At her voice, Rawer's gaze flickered back.

"I've only seen General Raia," Rawer replied, winding us through a final hall that opened into the kitchens. Another of the Medjay temple guards already waited for us, relief flooding his eyes at the sight of Rawer. The head Medjay nodded toward the side door that once only contained the merchant Neben. It was like a lifetime ago.

I was distantly aware that Rawer spoke again. "Her Holiness has arranged for us to take you to a safer temple in the south. The Medjay will protect you at all costs." He turned to us again, to Selene. "That is our vow to you." Despite the fight with my twin, I was relieved she wasn't here for this. I wished Selene had been so fortunate also.

Rawer and the guard slipped through the side door of the kitchen out into sunlight, and we followed. A cart pulled by two horses waited for us in an enclosure merchants and servants used for their temple dealings, resembling the one I'd burned down. A dirt road snaked around the yard acting as a barrier to the modest wheat field that grew beside the temple. Rawer quickly helped us into the bed of the cart before climbing into the driver's seat with the other guard. The Medjay snapped the reins, signaling for the speckled horses to push forward. "Through the wheat field," Rawer instructed. The guard clicked his tongue and pulled the reins. The horses wound off the road into the bending wheat stalks.

It was still Akhet, so the wheat wasn't extremely high, but there was enough to shield the cart from view. "Sit low," Rawer said as the cart divided the rows of plants. I nodded, forgetting that his back was to us, and he probably couldn't see it, before turning to Selene.

"You okay?" I asked her.

The freshman squinted in the morning glow, but it couldn't hide the fear dancing in her eyes. "Tasherit warded me this morning, before I came back to the chamber from the infirmary." Her gaze bored into mine. "And now I know who the woman in my dreams is," she said. "She told me afterward."

"Well, she's no dummy," I said. "Who is she?"

Her voice was a whisper. "The goddess."

"*What?*" I screeched. Rawer peered back, narrowing his eyes at me in urgency. I lowered my voice. "Like the one with her own temple?" Selene nodded. "Why is the goddess hiding?" I asked while the cart slowed to a stop.

We'd cut through the field to make it to another road at its side. The Medjay guard sat straight despite the winds picking up,whipping the wheat stalks to and fro. The men slowly climbed out of the cart, sliding out spears I hadn't realized were under their seats.

"Why are your weapons turned against me?" the voice called out. My spine pricked. "I bear no arms," said the High Priest. "I'm not tearing through your lady's holy temple." The horses grew restless under the increasing winds.

Rawer spoke clearly. "Be still, High Priest." The winds whipped at Akoris's heavy robes, but that did not stop him from moving. The Medjay trained his iron-tip spear on him. Akoris grinned.

The High Priest slipped into movements as fast as they were soundless. The best of what I could distinguish entailed the High Priest grabbing each guard by the shoulders, and at his touch, they dissipated into mounds of grain. There wasn't so much as a scream.

Without the guards, without the rush of urgency, it was oddly quiet until: "Portia." The High Priest called out to me.

"Stay here," I said to Selene as I climbed from the cart. She grabbed my hand and stopped me. "What?"

"Wait," Selene said, and searched my face. "Take this," she said, scrambling for something in her robes. Her fumbling hands landed on whatever she searched for, soon producing Ashkai's death mask. "You need this," she said. "You need her."

Portions of the mask had splintered off over the years. The crash against the floor after my twin slapped it from Weret's hand hadn't helped either. None I'd seen during my temple work were like it. Usually the entire mask was solid and painted for the afterlife. But the eyes on this had been cut out, almost like it was never meant to lie quietly for all time.

I took it and secured the odd mask over my face, as if it could protect me from the High Priest. The broken guise covered only my brow and the top of my nose, barely reaching my mouth. I left the cart and approached the High Priest. He'd moved from where he made mounds of the temple guards. "A death mask," he began. "Theatric."

As the winds thrashed at my jade robes, I raised my chin and glided nearer. "You should know this one," I replied. His jaw clenched though he said nothing. My eyes cast down toward the remains of the temple men. "Where are your guards?" I asked.

"Anen's men fill the temple," he said. "I am faster alone." His eyes flicked behind me, and his face split into a wide smile. I turned, following his gaze to Selene who'd left the cart and cautiously approached us. "Selene, what a joy. I see that you've been warded." I thrust myself in his view, blocking the freshman. He laughed and waved his hand at me. "She is not my concern at this instant," he said. "Are you prepared for our trade, Portia?"

"Never," I said, summoning all the courage I could.

His eyes flickered in amusement. "My deal was more than reasonable," he said. "Oh, the vast self-righteousness of youth. Portia, I will have the star's power"—his tone dipped viciously low—"even if you come to me in pieces." Heat flared through my hands, brightening them to near translucence. Sparks burst through my fingertips. "Ah, *that*." Akoris eyed my hands. "Have a taste of real heka."

Akoris rushed forward and clamped down on my hands, squeezing the bones in his grasp. If I thought my newfound speed was impressive, his was far superior. My scream stuck somewhere at the base of my throat. Once, when I was about seven years old, Alex dropped a box of canned goods on my foot. A few of my toes turned black and blue, and I hobbled on crutches for a week. This was much worse. The pain didn't throb. It was sharp and hot, ripping something out of my skin, out of my ka.

The light and fire.

My lightning.

I tumbled back as he released me. "I will borrow this for a while, Portia, thank you," he said, shooting frenetic sparks from his fingertips. "It is quite marvelous."

I pushed onto my feet and lunged, but Akoris sent a bolt into my shoulder with an amused flick of his hand. I staggered back, something around my neck breaking. My scarab necklace lay near him in the dirt, split into the halves I'd first seen it in. Akoris noticed as well, scooping up his wife's gift. "It's the mark," I managed.

"I added the inscription," he said by way of a response. The wind rushed around him. "For Weret." He threw the pieces as Selene came to my side. The *palace* guards had joined the High Priest. Through the pain's delirium, it was as if they'd materialized from nowhere. Akoris gestured to a guard near the field, and Selene shrieked when one swooped down and hauled her off. Her arms flailed, reaching back for me.

Rage coursed through my body. Selene was kicking and screaming, and without my lightning, I was useless. But I wasn't going to let this happen without a fight. A guard approached me and I pushed back from him, scrambling toward the mound that had been the Medjay. I plunged my hands through the sand and salt and found one of their spears. I snatched it up, and with anger and sorrow surging through my ka, I angled it at the guard trying to detain me and ran him through. I glanced at him for a moment, knowing I'd hurt someone, really hurt someone, but I didn't have time to dwell on it. I pushed him (and the weapon lodged inside him) away, but not before snatching his sword—a preferred weapon.

Akoris left my sight as another of Pharaoh's soldiers ran

toward me. When I swung the blade at him, another met mine with a fierce clang. My eyes locked with the swordsman's and my heart dropped. I knew his grace, his skill, and his coal black eyes. He must have accompanied the palace guards to the temple.

Seti.

SWORDPLAY

I was the Sword, a protector of Egypt, unlike any Medjay or Pharaoh's guard. But my weapon was drawn against the prince of the Two Lands, as well as the boy I'd met on the Nile banks. Wearing a leather pectoral reinforced with rows of small, bronzed plates like those he'd worn the night I met him, the prince stood before me without a crown or helmet. The iron blade he yielded was prepared for a dance. "Drop the sword," he said.

I didn't. I willed down any heka sickness from the removal of my lightning, and my eyes flicked behind him. "You are the prince. Why fight me? You have less important men for that."

He lowered his tone. "You killed my princess," he said. "A personal offense to Egypt." He jabbed the blade, and I hopped back. "And a personal offense to me."

I dragged the tip of mine across the stone step in response. An awful scraping noise followed it. I cast my eyes upward with a small smile. "Then you are my executioner?"

Why am I baiting him?

Why am I enjoying it?

Seti's eyes hardened as a soldier came to his side. "Your

248

Highness, please, let us take this witch now," the soldier said, more insulted by my insolence than the prince. Seti only held up his hand, a decisive no, and returned to me as the soldier backed away.

"If you don't stop this, I will show no mercy for the weakness of your gender," Seti continued, angling his sword at me. He wanted me to obey, lay my sword down. A piece of me wanted to oblige. But I couldn't jeopardize the star because I liked the prince. "You are outnumbered."

I raised my sword, so he gritted his teeth and swung. I readily blocked him. His soldiers called out in support of their prince—they encircled us now—and I glanced at their closeness as Seti reevaluated me. "Why do you hesitate?" he asked.

"Because I would rather not harm you," I said.

"You can't," he replied, and I frowned. His wariness billowed off him, but his pride wouldn't let this go. I swung so close to his skin that my subconscious, the part of me that was only the Sword, purred. Though stripped of my lightning, I was still a deadly warrior. But the goddess gave talent, not control. I would have to discover that for myself.

The prince was on the offensive now, but every time he struck, I evaded. I wouldn't hurt Seti. I *couldn't*. I concentrated on anything other than how easy it would be to kill him until the prince's blade found my injured arm. He sliced the tender flesh and sent white-hot pain shooting down to my fingertips. I unraveled.

The fight became a symphony of scraping metal, surefooted sandals dancing across stone, of dust rising beneath us until, as soon as it began, the fight was done. We stood. Now the tips of our blades pointed at each other's throats. "Do it," the prince said. His eyes were steady and face expressionless. Only his dilated pupils indicated real fear. "You know you have the advantage."

I tightened my grip on the sword. "A small one," I said. My blade slightly raised his chin. He swallowed hard, eying it and then me. Heka swirled beneath my skin, even without sparks, telling me what to do, how to end this. But I was more than what Ma'at, or the goddess, made me. I wasn't just the Sword. I was still Portia.

My blade hit the ground.

Seti stared as if he'd calculated every outcome but the one that had happened. His soldiers rushed in, and the one who'd so badly wanted to arrest me yanked my sore shoulder. "This is the woman?" another asked as the guard shook me. I flopped like a rag doll. "I imagined that she'd be much larger."

"You thought she'd be Sekhmet?" asked another, laughing.

Seti raised his hand. "Stop that," he commanded, and the taunting ceased. He narrowed his eyes, not understanding my surrender. I waited to be hauled away, but instead the prince scrutinized me. "Pull the mask off," Seti finally said.

My stomach dropped. I stupidly turned my face. "Yes, of course," said the soldier holding me. He reached for the mask, and I jerked away. "Your Highness, she will not hold still."

"Move," he said to the guard. The man bowed and scrambled back as the prince stepped forward. "Be still," he told me, his voice firm but without edge. My gaze found his dark eyes, allowing him to pull the mask from my face.

It dropped from his hand, further splintering as the guards jeered. "You are much too pretty to be a killer," said one. The others laughed, if under their breath, but Seti was not among them. He did not laugh. He did not blink. He did not breathe. He was stone, a replica of himself like the statues that guarded the palace.

"Yes, this is the woman from the princess's chambers," announced General Raia, swooping in from the ranks with a searing glare for me. "Who sent you?" I didn't respond. My eyes were on the prince, and I would only answer him. This flustered the young general. "You will look at me when I speak to you," he demanded. I glanced at him. "Who sent you?"

"Isis," I replied.

Raia's face tightened. "Blasphemer." He turned away. "We'll return to the palace immediately. Bring her," he said. I glanced at Seti as he sheathed his iron sword and watched his men take me away.

CAUGHT IN THE RIVER

The cell was as hot and terrible as I'd imagined it would be. Sweat dripped down my skin, making a sticky paste of the dirt on my brow. Though exhausted, I couldn't sleep. After watching Ra's full journey through the room's tiny window, I now lay flat on the floor, staring at the moon.

I'd never thought I'd be captured. I'd never thought I'd see the inside of the palace again, certainly not rotting in a cell. No one had spoken to me since my arrest. Waiting without knowing why is a recipe for insanity, especially when your life is at stake. I tried to focus on the clear Egyptian night outside my window, but the moon only reflected Seti's face, marked with betrayal.

The cell door swung open. Light cut through the darkness, and I turned away to shield my eyes. Feet shifted in the doorway. A loud sigh followed. "I knew there was something wrong with you in the gardens."

"To what do I owe this pleasure, general?" I asked the flat voice. I slowly sat up to face him, folding my legs beneath me on the floor.

General Raia crossed his arms and leaned on the door,

eclipsing the light almost entirely. His hand rested on the hilt of his sheathed sword. "You're a spy."

"Then I'm not a very good one."

"You are trained better than any soldier, any man."

"Then you should improve your army's curriculum."

"*I* train the soldiers," he growled. Raia tempered himself before speaking again. "But of your many virtues, I would also call you benevolent. You spared our prince today."

I bit my cheek as my face heated. "Do you have some news for me, or is your company the standard punishment?"

"There is no news yet," he replied. "I just found it interesting that you could have easily killed one of Egypt's most skilled swordsmen—and I wouldn't say that lightly—but you didn't. You chose to let us take you."

"I didn't choose."

"Don't insult my intelligence. I saw your skill, and I am not prone to embellishment. A swordsman of that caliber is only arrested on purpose." He focused on me. "Why?"

"General," I sighed. "You look like the type who's usually right."

"I am," he said.

"Accept that you are wrong about me. You'll have to trust that."

"Trust?" He angled his head. "You're a man caught in the river, and you'll say anything not to drown."

"I'm no man."

He frowned. "You're right; you're a murderer. Did you let us arrest you to reenter the palace? Are you helping our enemies prepare an attack on Egypt?"

A strained chuckle rose from my throat. "I jumped off a balcony last night to get out of here. I wasn't trying to come back."

"I don't believe you." He stepped forward. "Is that why you killed the princess?"

My voice caught. The accusation pinched my airways with grief. "I didn't kill the princess." I diverted my gaze, only returning to the general once I'd collected myself. "She didn't deserve to die, especially like that."

"You're right." For once, the general was also solemn. Something passed over him, but I couldn't tell what. It also disappeared just as quickly. "She did not," he said, studying me. "You are a very good actress."

"You don't know what happened in that chamber. I was there. You weren't." I glared at him. "Why bother with this? I'd tell you everything if you could believe me, but you're a soldier. You don't think for yourself."

"No one tells me what to think," he said.

"Then believe me when I say this kingdom is in my blood."

He was quiet for a moment, but those granite eyes would not soften. "Your eloquence is distracting," he said, and I laughed uneasily and muttered *thanks*. A sardonic insult from Raia was as close to a compliment as I'd get. He stepped only inches from me. "You will not topple this kingdom. Not while I am here."

I narrowed my eyes and pushed onto my feet. "I'm no threat, general," I said, brushing myself off. "You know that."

He blew out air. "I only know that Egypt is not safe." He turned for the door, which he left open. "Follow." The word hung in the air.

I walked behind him, my simple tunic and green temple robe swaying with each step. "Wait, what?" I asked. "Follow you?"

"Is there some other murderous Hyksos maid in here?" He turned away as I rolled my eyes.

We moved in silence down dark and ominously quiet corridors

until reaching what appeared to be the audience chamber. Beneath the veil of night, everything was indistinguishable, but the large doors, arches painted with reflections of discernment, were wide open, and I remembered the reliefs of Ma'at and Thoth from Tuya's presentation ceremony. "Just so you know," he muttered. "I advised against this."

He sharply nudged me inside and I stumbled over the threshold, glancing back in enough time to see the chamber doors slam shut. I rolled my eyes again at his terseness and moved forward. Before I could say *hello*, just to hear the echo in the empty room, something told me to peer at the thrones. On a normal occasion, Pharaoh would sit on the middle, the Horus Throne, with his chief wife on one side and Seti on the other. His viziers stood below the royal dais and screened petitioners, the most important of whom would go before one or all of the royal family for judgment.

Now, however, only Seti sat before me, in his father's place. He still wore his pectoral and kilt of bronze, with his iron sword across his lap. The last embers of a torch glowed near him, though his face was still blanketed in shadows. The prince was judge and jury of whatever grew between us—and possibly my life.

His voice pierced the quiet. "So I take it you are not just a handmaiden." He leaned forward. "A spy."

My only movement was my pounding heart. "I'm not." He grunted in reply. For some reason, I stepped toward him, the clack of my sandals like thunder against the tile floor. The closer I came, the harsher his stare. "You don't want to use that thing, do you?" I asked of the sword.

"I will if you attack me, Spy," he said. "Raia determined it must be the Seafarers who sent you, or a traitor amongst the Hyksos. But I won't rule out one of our own nobles, wanting the Horus

Throne for his akhu, to honor his family and ancestors. You've never looked foreign."

"I would never attack you," I said. "I'm not here to hurt you."

He ignored me. "Which one hired you? That governor, the tjati Nebsenmut? He's always been a trouble to my father. He probably sent you to infiltrate the palace, to finish off my father, to usurp the Horus Throne."

"I don't want your throne."

His voice crashed down. "You face death, Spy," he said. His every word was meant to burn, and they fulfilled their purpose. He spat the word *spy*, and I never thought I would have preferred for him to call me maid again. "When I gave you safe passage from the garden, you should have taken it."

"It wasn't enough."

"What else could they want? The nobles? The Hyksos? The Seafarers? What more could they want from me?" he asked. "What do you want?"

"I don't want anything from you."

He flew to his feet, fire in his eyes. The sword crashed to the ground. "We're sending you back to Avaris," he rushed out. "We'll let King Ashmar decide what to do with you." The words struggled out of the prince's mouth. "He *will* kill you."

"And would it please you?"

"Would what please me?"

"Sending me to the Hyksos." I was on a roller coaster that did nothing but drop, again and again. "Sending me to die." I had to hear him say it. I'd hurt him. His eyes said as much. Seti rubbed his hands together, too tight, too fast. His thoughts were crashing against his skull as well. "I don't want anything from you," I repeated.

"Why should I believe you?"

"You shouldn't. I just want you to. I need you to."

"You need me to? My father is dying. Egypt could rip apart under a weak transition to a new Pharaoh." He paced. "I owe nothing to you as Horus Lord, but you dare ask me . . . no, *tell* me that you need something of me."

I stepped forward. He angled away but didn't step back. His face was twisted in betrayal and pain, but also something I hadn't expected. Dread swirled in his eyes, violent and demanding. Fear of toppling the kingdom. Fear of being the weak link. Fear of losing his father, and what his life would look like after. "I know what it's like."

"What was it like?" he said, exasperation tingeing his voice. "To rule from the Horus Throne? You can't possibly."

"To lose a parent."

He quieted. This time he did step back. "*Don't.*"

"I'm sorry," I said as he picked up the sword and sheathed it. "But my mother is dead, and I miss her."

"It is Ma'at that he goes to the Field of Reeds and I take my place. I've known this my entire life."

"That doesn't make it easier. If no one else knows, I do."

The prince sighed and descended the dais toward me. "Who are you?" he asked, more curious than accusatory. I bit my bottom lip. But his face was no longer stone. Pinched maybe, but not stone. "Tell me the truth, all of it."

"My name is Portia," I said, instantly weightless. I'd freed the most basic truth. He finally knew my name.

"What language is that?"

It would take way too long to explain Latin. "I'm Mitanni and Egyptian."

"Your name is neither Mitanni nor Egyptian."

"It's a long story."

He approached me, closer still, studying me. "Did you kill the princess?"

"No," I said. "I'm trying to protect Egypt from war."

"War with the Seafarers?"

"From your High Priest of Amun."

"Akoris?" he searched my eyes. "Akoris has been nothing if not loyal. Tell me why he would betray me."

It wasn't what I'd expected. "Wait," I stammered. "You believe me?"

"I want to believe you. Raia wanted you sent to the Hyksos hours ago."

"And you didn't?"

"Of course not."

"Why?"

"Because I am the child of Set," he said, a corner of his mouth turning up. "I am a selfish prince used to getting his way."

It wasn't the time to smile, though I wanted to. "The High Priest wants the Horus Throne," I said. "But he needs me, and he needs Selene—my sister—the other girl he arrested before he can do it. I need to know where she is."

"I'll take you to her. She is with the palace guards."

"Oh, Seti, thank God," I said, relief washing over me. I expected him to speak again, but he only blinked. "What's wrong?" I asked. "Did something happen to her?"

A Cheshire-cat grin spread across his face. "No," he said. "She is fine."

"Then what?"

"My name is better when you speak it."

When Jason Jones called me Miss White, the sound reduced me to shapes and colors. It was strange to have that effect on someone else. Seti stepped even closer, too close not to touch. My arms wrapped tight around his torso as his grabbed my back. It was the hug I'd needed since I'd arrived in Egypt, comforting everything in me that was soft, malleable, and deliciously weak. "Portia," he said, running his hand into a thick lock of hair and twisting his fingers in the curl. "Do you feel that?" *Do I feel heavenly? Why yes, I do.* "Do I feel what?" I asked, my eyes turning up to his. He shook his head and breathed a smoke-like coil into the air. My heart dropped as a new chill wound about the room. I didn't want to speak them into existence, but they were already there. "Scorpions."

WARDS

"What is it?" Seti asked as my gaze darted to each shadow of the audience chamber. His hands cupped my face, searching my eyes. "What is it?"

"Scorpions," I said, though my words were tangled, "killed Tuya. They belong to the High Priest." My breath curled up in silver stripes. "They're already here." Seti's hand found mine before we bolted toward the chamber's heavy doors. In this moment, he was no longer the prince, but the boy I'd met on the banks, whose instincts were on survival.

The wooden doors—painted with the knowing eyes of Ma'at and Thoth—were as sealed as they'd been before. The thrum in my heart was also a pounding in my ears, only giving me vague awareness of Seti slamming his hands against the unyielding wood. "What is this?" he shouted at himself, now thrusting his shoulder against the wooden barriers.

Flecks of paint splintered from the doors' surface, chipping under spreading frost. He'd barely seen rain. *What would Seti know of ice?* "It's iced shut," I said, though he wasn't listening. He no longer fought the sting of cold. Instead, his back stiff,

Seti's dark eyes shifted upward.

"Do you hear that?" Seti asked as I followed his gaze to the ceiling. Shadows and frost-slicked reliefs of Nut's blinking stars met my sight. The rustle had come from overhead, from something scuttling across the tip of Sopdet. Seti shook me back into the moment. "There's another way, behind the thrones," he said, pointing across the chamber.

We dashed across the freezing tiled floors. It didn't last long, as a rush of motion and power fell before us, blocking our escape. The force knocked us back onto the floor as the Scorpion unfolded before us, one nightmarish leg and pincher at a time. Terror welled so greatly inside I could barely move my limbs.

The prince's face went slack. "*That* killed the princess?" The Scorpion's legs shattered whichever tile bore the brunt of its weight. The creature was its namesake in every sense of the word, with eight legs—two of which were oversized pinchers—jutting from its sides, a long abdomen, and dark, waxy skin covering its body. Its girth blocked the royal thrones from view. Glowing violet eyes studied us, perhaps searching for the ka inside.

"Welcome to my world," I said, wondering which palace guard or courtier bartered their soul to become it.

The Scorpion watched as we scrambled to our feet, its stinger waving back and forth in the air, tempting us to guess who it would strike down first. "I'll distract it," the prince announced. He drew the sword at his waist and angled it at the Scorpion. "You get to the thrones and out of here." It stabbed at the air in response. It wanted Seti.

"Not without Selene," I said.

"That was not a request!"

I grabbed his arm. "Not without *you*."

For a lone moment, his mouth twitched up. It was a short, sweet instant quelled by his eyes shifting away. "What's happening?" he asked. "What is it doing?"

Instead of jabbing the stinger again, the Scorpion's body had begun to slowly rock. Tile smashed into bits beneath its girth as those deadly eyes stayed trained on us. "Something's not right," I whispered.

The slow rock became a senses-assaulting hiss. Both Nimae and Ankhmir hissed as they spoke, but this full-body vibration echoed in a pitch reserved for the most sensitive part of the human ear. It needled all of my senses, forcing me to squeeze my palms to my head to block out the painful noise.

The Scorpion's sudden shriek was as unexpected to me as it was to the monster. The cry shook the palace walls and knifed the once unbearable hiss. The thrum ended as sharply as it began. I peered up from my crouch to the Prince of Egypt. Seti panted as blood trickled from his ear. His sword was gone. "Are you alright?"

"I'm okay," I said. He took my arm and helped me up. "What did you do?"

"Lost a sword," he said. "And made it very angry." The Scorpion yowled and thrashed at itself—at Seti's sword more precisely, lodged in its side. It was enough to end the hiss, but the Scorpion was nowhere near dead.

"It's still blocking the thrones," I said, my own uselessness in every word. If the High Priest hadn't taken my lightning, I could save us both. But at this moment I was as human as the prince, and as fragile. My gaze darted around the room until an ember gleaming behind the royal thrones caught my attention, a lifeline I'd somehow overlooked. "Light!" I yelled, gearing up for a sprint toward the Scorpion.

Seti grabbed my hand, stopping me. "What are you doing?" he barked.

"There's a torch behind the thrones!" I said, twisting out of his hold. Seti's brow knotted together. *You're running toward the Scorpion. You're being crazy*, his face said. "They hate light. Trust me, the light will move it." And then I dashed toward it, hoping my adrenaline was enough to wind me safely around.

As I reached its underbelly, I noticed its eyes shifted opposite me. Enraged, it had given up on removing Seti's sword for a chance to remove Seti. The headstrong— perhaps as much as me—Prince of Egypt yelled after the Scorpion like a mad man. His distraction gave me the break I needed, but I wished there was some other way.

Move faster, damn it.

The torch hung on the wall, high above Pharaoh's throne. The flame had guttered as Seti and I spoke about our trust issues and shit that didn't matter at all right now. I hadn't cared then, too engrossed in mending the rift between the prince and me. But now it was our best chance of making it out alive. Fixed a foot or so above the top of the throne, the torch was a curse to my lack of an eighth-grade growth spurt.

Pharaoh's throne was a beauty of fine wood and precious metals—gold mostly— as overlay. Impressive from afar, this detail slicked its surface as chill stung the chamber. The combination of sleek metals and abject cold made the Horus Throne nearly impossible to maneuver. My flat sandals found no purchase; they had to go. Cold nipped my toes immediately after ditching them, but even barefoot, I lost footing every time I attempted to balance and reach for the torch.

I also made the unfortunate mistake of peering below the dais. The Scorpion's stinger jabbed at Seti again and again, and my heart raced as the prince scrambled to keep it from impaling his body. I snapped my head up. I couldn't get distracted, or we'd both die.

A gentle breeze shrouded me. It twined around my body, encouraging an otherworldly stillness to seep in. My heart rate slowed from its touch, and I knew instantly that my world had vanished. There was no audience chamber, no Scorpion, no prince. "What is this?" I asked the void.

Light finally sliced the nothing, at first too brilliant to discern until finding a preferred form: burning green eyes. *Cat eyes.*

"Tasherit?" I asked. The eyes didn't respond, only uniting into a single ball of light. I'd seen its hungry flicker that night, I'd thought the sun burned my bedroom walls. But it wasn't the sun. It had always been this: Sopdet, the blazing star. I stretched my hand out, allowing my fingers to graze the flaming surface, and as quickly as my world had lulled, it was again chaos. I was still in the audience chamber, balanced on the Horus Throne.

Only now I grasped the torch. Victorious, I launched off the throne toward the Scorpion nightmare but stopped short as my knees locked me in place. He'd heard me coming. He'd glanced over his shoulder, at the weird girl from the banks, and then at the torch. And as slowly and lightning fast as I could register, the Scorpion plunged its stinger into the prince's neck.

Something in me exploded.

I launched the torch through the air before I told my body to do so, before the ancient monster understood what I was doing. The torch found its target, but only punctured the Scorpion's face, inches from its eye. It reeled, jerking its stinger back and slamming its body against the walls. Stone pillars snapped like twigs, breaking under its erratic movements. I ignored the Scorpion, walking to Seti as if the prince weren't convulsing against the tiles from its venom and heka sickness. Black lines branched out from the puncture. I knelt down and cupped his head on my lap.

The ghost of a blade sliced past me, and shortly after the Serk's stinger flew from its body midstrike. It bellowed as my head shot up. General Raia stood above me. He held a hooked sword, the largest I'd ever seen. The monster thrashed around, crashing into the thrones and walls. I thought I was in a dream, at least until Raia yelled at me.

"Grab him!" he barked, indicating the prince. "*Now!*"

I shook off my surprise, and we each took a shoulder and pulled Seti toward the shelter of the columns that outlined the room. Raia shoved the sickle-sword at me and began to check Seti's wound. I watched the Scorpion with Raia's sword in my hand. It made a final scream and collapsed into sand and salt.

"He needs the temple," he said, without turning to me.

"Why did you come back?" I asked.

He glanced up. "I ordered the halls cleared when I brought you to Seti. But when I left you, there were no guards at all in the palace. There was, in fact, no one anywhere. When something isn't right, you aren't far."

I frowned. "I didn't call that thing." He glanced at the Scorpion's remains and averted his eyes. It was not a look of shock. "You've seen one before," I said.

"I saw a lot when I was in the Delta," Raia said. "I didn't want to believe they were in Egypt. But when I saw the sand and salt in the princess's chamber, I thought you'd brought them here."

"It wasn't me. It was—"

"The High Priest," Raia cut in. "Before I returned to the audience chamber, I went to the High Priest's quarters, determined we'd remove you no matter what Seti said. I thought the prince would accept reason with Akoris's support. But when I arrived in his quarters, no one was there. But his tables were littered with Hyksos reports and—" His voice caught. "Sand. Frost." His eyes flicked up to mine. "Desert scorpions."

Raia shook his head. "It finally made sense." His voice lowered. "I'd told him about the beasts, and he said he would handle them with the gifts of Amun. But now I know he commanded them." He whispered now. "In this I have failed Egypt."

"You haven't failed Egypt," I said. My eyes glanced over his weapon. "But you should give me one of those. What kind of sword is that?"

"A special khopesh, a sickle-sword. This type of weapon is good for removing the tail. Doing so is . . . helpful."

"You trust me now?"

He frowned. "No," he said. "But Seti does. I'll take the prince to the temple. I know you want to find the other girl."

"Where is she?"

Raia didn't return my gaze as he spoke. "The gardens."

The palace had indeed grown eerily silent, with no guards or servants or lights to be found as I cut through the winding passageways. Finally the dimness of the stone halls gave way to clear evening light beyond the garden's entrance. I stepped my bare feet onto the dirt, surrounded by frost-slicked shrubs, and growing winds at my back. *Akoris is here*, I thought as the hair on my arms stood on end. Wherever I found him, I'd find Selene.

I moved out further into the garden, holding my arms and shivering. I could have called out for him, but instead I waited. He would come to me. I was sure of it.

"When I unleashed the Serk, I didn't know the extent of their nature." His voice suddenly echoed everywhere at once, but the High Priest was nowhere to be found. I turned each way. Maybe I'd been right about his omniscience. "Looking back, it's almost comical that the Seafarers would want them. With no heka of their own, how would they ever control them?"

The winds whipped faster now, and I shielded my eyes from the flying dirt and twigs snapped from the frozen plants. "There's old heka in Avaris that—barely— protects the Hyksos against the Serk. But the Seafarers—"

"Where are you?" I interrupted him.

Light streamed through the darkness. Akoris emerged from it, stepping before me so close I shivered. "Offer someone's greatest desire and they never ask *why* or *how*. They never want the cost." He still wore his cerulean robes of Amun and the dark cloak from the temple steps.

"The binding trade consumes a man's ka. Depending on the soul's purity, it can be a slow process with few signs. Or it can be quite quick and frightening." He smiled weakly. "Often loved ones think this man has gone mad, especially if he comes into contact with pure heka like the star's. You three are extraordinary irritants."

For a moment I thought of the whiteout in the temple of Amun, how my power knocked Ankhmir from his chair, and Bekmut from her shell. "What happened to the Seafarers?" I asked of his earlier mention.

"There are no Seafarers left. They, as well as many of the Hyksos and some Egyptians, are Serk now."

It didn't add up. *What did he want?* "And you did all this because you were asked?"

"Portia, I've always known the cost, and I made my peace with it a long time ago." He angled his head. "My patron is the reason you exist. We released the Serk eleven floods ago, and then your mother appeared with the mark in Ma'at's balance. And now the three of you followed her. Well," he amended, "two."

"My sister left," I said. "I don't know where."

"It is my favor with the universe that the star became three young women." His gaze narrowed. "Prone to ridiculous squabbles."

"Why do you want the star?"

"Only the star can face the Serk. It's in my best interest to secure its power," he said before opening his palm to me. "But the star is not my greatest concern at the moment." From his brown skin, a staticky ball of light hovered.

It sang to me, though I couldn't reach it, as it was my stolen energy—the star's energy. His lips pursed before he blew it into a dark corner of the garden, where it disappeared to return just as quickly, Selene now caught inside like a tiny fly in a sticky spider's web. "For our other matter," he said of the freshman.

"Let her go," I warned. "She doesn't know where Alex is either." He ignored me, instead inhaling the light back like a drag from a cigarette. Selene's floating trap went with it, and the freshman dropped onto the ground. She batted the curls from her eyes, but aside from a disheveled appearance, she was otherwise as I'd seen earlier.

"You claim you are ignorant of Alexandria's whereabouts, and I will accept that as truth. But I don't need Selene to locate your wayward sister. You and Selene were born in the heka of Isis. You have no idea what that even means." He shook his head. "Selene has great abilities that have created an unforeseen complication."

"And what is that?" I asked, afraid of the answer. He didn't respond but fixed his gaze on the freshman. In response, her skin took on an iridescent glow of white. The brightness was like staring into Cecile's headlights. I shielded my eyes until the glow flared before wavering on Selene's skin. When I turned back to her, she was normal again.

"*That*," he said. "That is the complication. The child has been warded. Normally I could take down any wards, but the perfection of her vision hinders me."

"Perfection?"

"Yes," he replied tersely. Selene caught my eye before dashing for me. Akoris just as quickly stuck his hand up, his heka holding her in place. She didn't even get close. "For my loyalty, I will rule from the Horus Throne with the might of the Serk and the star," Akoris said. "But I need the location of the goddess to complete this task, something only she knows."

Oh yeah. *That*.

When Selene told me at the temple, I didn't know why it hadn't quite registered that this was valuable information. "So basically, you can't hack into Selene's sight?" I asked.

He narrowed his eyes again. "Only she can remove her wards, and she is a mule of a child," the High Priest said. "My patron wishes an audience with Isis, but she has not revealed herself for years. We couldn't use the Serk. Even they couldn't smell her heka. I realized only Selene, an Eye of her creation, could find her."

Her? "She's just a freshman." *A clunky fourteen-year-old. A kid.*

"She is an Eye," he said. "The Eye we need." I shivered at Akoris's words. This conflict was more than a High Priest and his wife, I realized. It was more than the Serk in the Delta, or three girls swimming the Rivers of Time. This was gods and goddesses, myths and legends, and very old magic.

His blue robes flapped in the steady winds as he addressed

Selene. "I will be plain with my intentions. If you do not remove your wards, Portia will die. I have no further use for her," he said. "It will not be swift. You will see every bone snap. You will hear every cry for mercy."

"Listen to me—" Selene's voice croaked out.

"Do as I've asked, and she will live," he said. Selene turned to me, ripping in half like dried papyrus. It was almost ironic, really. I'd come to the gardens to save the freshman, but she was the only one who could save me. "You don't want her to die for you, Selene," Akoris warned.

Selene turned back to him. "I won't," she whispered. Her defiance pushed the High Priest into that vicious place I'd been afraid of. He whipped a bolt of lightning—*my* lightning—around me with the snap of his hand. I screamed as the charge seared the exposed skin of my arms and legs. "You think I have limits." He summoned another bolt and held it high above his head. "I do not."

I shook my head at Selene, willing her to hold her ground even as the second bolt crackled around me. It was worth keeping this knowledge hidden. But Selene's choice was based on her own logic, on watching her friend suffer when there was something to be done about it. I knew her answer when her voice cracked.

"Stop. I'll do it," she said. "Just don't hurt her." The lightning withdrew, and I buckled into the cold earth, my limbs throbbing with burns. "Is she all right?" Selene asked.

His voice was flat. "Wards," he said.

"Is she all right?!" Selene howled.

"*Wards!*"

She cast her doe eyes to the ground and shut them. Light emitted from her in undulating waves as she concentrated. When it finally dissipated, Selene straightened her back and returned her gaze to the High Priest of Amun. "They're down," she whispered. Akoris said nothing, only placing his hands out flat. Eyes closed, unmoving as a statue, he murmured in the Serk language, with incomprehensible inflections and breaks. As he did, perspiration rose on Selene's brow. Her eyes took on the white film I'd seen in the temple. Her body shook. One Eye speaking through another was creepy enough. This was much worse.

"I have seen the world, but what you see is magnificent," Akoris began, breath catching in apparent wonder. "And the goddess—" he said, though never finished his thought. His hand slammed against his chest as the High Priest suddenly gulped in air.

The freshman, for her part, ignored the High Priest. Selene shook her head, blinking, eyes brown again, and ran to me. She linked her arm with mine. Her skin was clammy again, as it had been the first time Akoris spoke through her. The trance for some reason was over for both of them.

I should have asked if she was alright, but it wasn't my first thought. "Why is he looking at you like that?" I asked, pulling her back. The High Priest's breathing evened slightly, but it was his new, unsettling focus on the freshman that gave me pause. Akoris stepped toward us, barely blinking, jaw tight. He wore Tuya's expression had when her aunt crawled out of the draping curtains on pointed claws.

And then of all strange possibilities, Akoris extended his hand. "You must come to Avaris, Selene."

She gripped me harder. "Get away," she said, though he ignored her, hand remaining outstretched. She pulled me back with her now, repeating, "Get away," like a religious chant. I had been afraid of Akoris slipping over the edge, but Selene—she was still only fourteen years old. Akoris might not have had limits, but she did.

The High Priest was still, so I shook her arm. "He's not moving," I said. "Let's go." But the freshman's feet were planted. Her chest heaved as if she'd outrun a pack of wolves. "Selene?" I whispered as she now returned Akoris's frightening focus. A choking gurgle rose from his throat as his eyes filmed over with white.

"He's not the only one who can take down wards," she said as she clamped down on my hand. Pain shot through my bones, little shards of magic sliding back beneath my skin and into my ka. Akoris had taken my power. Selene, however, was returning it.

I peered at the High Priest, whose toes barely touched the ground. Selene held him in the air as she turned inward, losing herself, disappearing somewhere I'd never know or see. Just as when I set the cart on fire, she swam in the depths of her emotions, her pain. It was the place Sikara had called reactionary and dangerous.

Blood trickled from the High Priest's nose and stained his mouth. If Selene didn't let him go, she would kill him. And despite facing imminent peril, the High Priest's clouded eyes remained locked on her. He might have deserved Selene's ire. He might have deserved it many times over. But it wasn't our call to make.

"Selene," I said, gently shaking her arm once more. "Don't."

"Why shouldn't I?" she choked out.

"Because you're not him," I said. A moment passed before her eyes found mine. "Let me help you," I said as new tears rolled down her face. The High Priest collapsed to the ground amidst a cacophony of gasps.

"Alright," she said before what appeared to be a crushing wave of heka sickness slammed into her. Whatever power she'd found was too strenuous for her body. Surprisingly, she smirked as I steadied her balance. "This is probably what it's like to be hungover," she said.

I had a joke in response, but didn't get it out. The High Priest was like sound or light. Even bloodied and breathless, Akoris fixated on the young Eye before him, the brilliant girl who knew something very old and very secret. He moved time and space with his hand, snapping a gaping hole from thin air. He snatched at Selene with an impossibly fast, near-invisible grasp. Her nails clawed my skin as he ripped her from my side. They disappeared in an explosion of sand and salt.

SPARKS

I peered out over the helm at the gathering crowds. Women balanced wicker baskets overflowing with lotus blossoms on their shoulders and hips. Children, bursting with giggles and weaving through their mothers' legs, played nearby. A spectacle shaped up, anticipation rising as we neared the mouth of the Hyksos-controlled Nile Delta.

I leaned on the ship's railing, gaze now on the three boats ahead. The smaller two vessels, crafted of thick reeds and curved at each end like breakfast croissants, drew harsh ripples in the waves. The third was a barge like the one I traveled on, carrying men and women more important than me. I'd counted seven boats behind. I hadn't bothered to guess the number Egypt sent in the fleets that followed.

We'd sailed most of our journey under a glittering turquoise sky. But the further into the Delta we sailed, the more overcast it had become. It wasn't pretty, but it was welcomed. I'd grown used to the warmth, but I wasn't sad to see Akhet go. It was quickly becoming Peret, the planting season, which brought some relief from the humidity. The rich, black soil of the Nile banks was ready for sowing as we neared what would be about September in my time. The people of Waset rejoiced at the successful flood. I could have cared less.

Weeks had passed since that night in the garden, weeks without Selene or Alex, and a seventeenth birthday I celebrated without my twin. Only months before, I wanted to go to college as far away from Alex as possible. Only months before, I wished the weird freshman would just stop popping up in my life. Now I woke each day hoping at least one of them would reappear—not an outrageous thought, considering we'd found a hole in time. But each day the sun rose and set without them.

They'd disappeared under such different circumstances. Alex left in the night, refusing to be part of something she couldn't understand, something bigger than any of us had imagined. My twin—the Golden Apple Champion—was content as a winner of the genetic lottery. She'd never asked why she got the winning ticket. And Selene, the girl from the Randos perfectly designed for Waset, had been snatched by the High Priest of Amun for seeing something no one could, for knowing something no one else did.

Sailing the Nile on this day was déjà vu, though it was the Egyptians traveling north instead of the Hyksos princess coming south. We'd made the trip through Lower Egypt toward Sahdina's capital city, and the war was more guaranteed than keeping Ma'at. "You miss her."

She always did that. She always just appeared. I turned at the High Priestess's voice. "I thought you were on the other boat," I said to Weret.

"I was, but now I'm here," Weret replied simply. She ambled along the railing, arm wrapped tight again, approaching me. She wore a headdress that fanned out like vulture feathers along the sides of her face. Thick kohl rimmed her eyes, keeping the sun out, and her gold earrings dangled, reflecting light on her skin. Regality was never her issue.

I, on the other hand, had discovered an unattractive penchant for seasickness soon after we'd left Waset. I turned my eyes past her to the crowds again. Wind danced across my face as the priestess came to my side, although I barely reached her shoulder, and we stood in silence. I knew Akoris would make good on his promise to take Selene to Avaris, so it was a logical place to start my search for her. I just hadn't expected the Egyptian army to follow me.

Once Seti had healed, he and Anen's stewards determined that only the Seafarers could have attacked the palace and Princess Tuya. In the name of the Horus Lord, they dispatched half of the Egyptian military fleet to the Hyksos capital. The prince and General Raia would oversee the new station and crush any Seafarer rebellion.

Weret and Sikara traveled as well, reinstated to the temple shortly after the events in the chamber and garden. Raia, of all people, commanded their release that evening, as only they could tend to the puncture on the prince's neck. For this journey, Pharaoh's stewards requested their presence in Avaris, for Seti would also attend to diplomatic matters during his stay—like marrying a new princess. Weret left the temple to Tasherit's care.

"I miss them both," I finally said. "That's why I'm doing this." My sigh was heavier than intended.

"Blowing your air like a hippopotamus is unbecoming," said the High Priestess. She took her time before speaking again. "I know my presence brings you comfort as we travel to Avaris, and believe me when I say that I'm happy about this."

I waited for it. I waited for the *but*.

"But you must also make peace that you are on a road I cannot travel."

"You can go wherever you want." I shifted my weight. "You're the High Priestess."

"I am not the star. I *follow* the star. That is the sum of my duties."

I clutched my arms, though I wasn't cold. She was still staring at me, maybe through me, seeing every embarrassing vulnerability. "But you're the only one I have left," I said. "I don't want to be alone."

"You'll travel your own path," Weret said, "but you're never alone."

I diverted my eyes. I didn't know what she meant, but it calmed me somehow. "You know exactly how to make me feel dumb."

"Well, on most occasions, you are being ridiculous." I narrowed my eyes at her as she smirked. A smile tugged at my lips in return. Weret glanced over my clothing. I wore a fine cloak with patterns of yellow, red, and blue over my kalasiris. Seti had given me the cloak for the trip, and I clung to it like the last bits of my sanity. With all the arms at the prince's disposal, I hadn't anticipated the unexpected gift to be his weapon of choice. "This looks lovely on you."

"Thanks," I said sheepishly and ran my fingers over the tender flesh on my arms. My burns still healed, a physical reminder that the night in the garden wasn't a bad dream. A strong breeze crossed the waters now, and I readjusted my cloak about my shoulders. "The wind is picking up."

"The Iteru anticipates our arrival more than the Hyksos," Weret said. "We're close." We both stood at the helm now, peering out. Children ran parallel to the boats along the banks, waving and throwing lotus petals. I smiled at a little boy flapping his hands for my attention, spilling all of his petals. He was adorable, like a fat cherub on a Valentine's Day card, but I was still more than a bit cautious. Any one of them could be a Scorpion.

The strengthening wind cleared out the mist that had followed us for the latter part of the journey. The Hyksos palace was not far, and as we approached, the Egyptian influence was truly evident. Painted reliefs and hieroglyphs decorated the stone buildings. Imposing statues of angular gods guarded temples. Though proud, the Hyksos lands were still annexed property, and at first glance, the only difference between Waset and Avaris would be the blossoming Omnu trees that dotted the sky with scarlet.

"I brought you something," Weret said, interrupting my thoughts. She held up her left hand and dangled a blue ornament from it.

My scarab. I touched my throat.

"I believe you lost this," she added. Near the water, the beetle was bluer than I remembered, with a better shine than when it gleamed in Pomey's class. "Take it." Weret didn't waver, so I reluctantly accepted it, running my fingers over the engravings.

"It was yours before it was mine," I said. My fingers curled around its flat underbelly. "Why are you giving it back?"

She nudged my hand. "You should keep it safe." My lips tightened, but I placed the scarab around my neck. "It is very beautiful," Weret said.

She turned to admire the crowds, though she did not wave. Her eyes fell on a woman bouncing an infant on her lap near the riverbank. She watched a second too long. Weret knew so much about me, and I knew so much about her, but in some ways we were strangers. There was a lot to the High Priestess—discipline, austerity, mysticism. But she was still human—sort of—a woman who never got her happy ending.

"I'm sorry."

She turned to me, confusion in once-peaceful eyes. "Why do you apologize?"

I lowered my voice. "Akoris said I exist to fight the Serk, but I feel like I exist to make a big mess out of everyone's life, especially yours." I angled away, tugging the fabric of my clothing absentmindedly.

"Oh, Portia." She wanted me to look back, but I couldn't make eye contact with her. "*Portia*." My eyes reluctantly drifted upward. "Selene is a talented Eye, more so than Akoris but—" She shook her head. "You don't have to apologize. You are such a brave girl. I cannot compliment you enough for what you've done."

"Lose Selene and Alex? Get Egypt into a war?"

"You've grown when so many people do not. The High Priest is the same person now as he was then, despite all that has happened. You're a wonderful person, stronger than you realize." She squeezed my shoulders before glancing away, as we'd both felt the sudden presence of eyes on us.

"But you will never be safe with rogue princes wandering about," she said.

Seti was in nondescript dress, appearing more like the boy I met on the Nile banks than the prince who'd rule the Two Lands. I held the cloak tighter, thoughts wandering through our meet-cute in Shemu, as he bowed to Weret. "High Priestess," he said.

"Prince Seti, why is it that wherever my young apprentice journeys, you are not far?"

"That's a matter of perspective," he said. Weret's face was hidden to me, but I imagined her amusement.

"Please remember we'll reach the Hyksos harbor shortly. Take too long and the guard will forcibly remove you." She walked away without a glance for me, disappearing to another cabin on the boat.

The prince stretched as I eyed his clothing. "Slumming?" I asked.

He crooked a brow. "I do not understand, though I think I should be insulted."

"I mean you look like Merenptah."

"In this moment we are the same."

"Well, Merenptah," I said, cocking my hip. "You can't just come here whenever you want."

"Then what's the point of being Egypt's prince?" He moved closer, squaring off with me in amusement.

"Oh, my mistake," I said, before launching into a dramatic bow. "You rang, Your Highness?"

"That's better." He touched my shoulders before squeezing them, as Jason Jones had done in the stairwell at school. Again, I drew a breath. He didn't notice, his hands running over the cloak, and the length of my arms beneath it, before returning to his sides. "I have to say you look much better as an Egyptian than a Hyksos maid."

"Half Egyptian." *And half time traveler.* I hadn't told him the truth of who I was yet. To him, I was still a strange girl in the Temple of Isis's keep, the daughter of a foreign princess who was entangled with powerful enemies of his kingdom. I'd left out that I was about three thousand years younger than him.

First things first.

"When Egypt is in your blood, there is nothing else to claim." I rolled my eyes before laughing at a phrase only he'd say. The prince was soulful and caring, but in the same breath, reminded you that he was heir of a superpower. He was worldly, but only from the perspective that mattered to him: Egypt's. Despite that, he *did* make me forget that I was alone, even if I felt guilty over our growing friendship.

"Don't worry about what lies in Avaris." He'd read my mind. "We'll find your sister." Meaning Selene.

"And what about the other one?" I'd meant Alex.

"We'll find her as well."

I smiled, if weakly, and searched his shining black eyes. He'd bounced back well, his wound healed to near seamlessness, but it was sometimes hard to shake the memory of the stinger piercing his neck. "Don't make promises you can't keep," I said. "You have more than me to think about here."

Something flashed across his eyes, a memory, a sense of duty perhaps. Leaving his father wasn't easy, as it would likely be the last time he'd see him alive. "I keep my promises, particularly those made to you."

"Do you say that to all the girls?" I asked.

"Yes." He laughed as I groaned. "You're right. There will be many new feats in Avaris. Which concern you most?"

"War and marriage."

"Egypt is not made of fishermen," he said, with a wink. "You've seen our might. I am confident this fight will be quick." The Egyptian navy was intimidating. Even when they sailed peacefully, their presence alone demanded obedience. And he hadn't completely answered my question.

"And marriage?"

To this he shrugged. "Another princess, another marriage. That was the agreement."

"The princess is a big part of keeping peace."

"You'd be more useful with your sword."

"We can't all be me," I joked.

He didn't laugh. "I am aware," he said, motioning for me to come closer. I did. Matters of state had kept Seti and his father busy, so busy that we'd barely been alone since the audience chamber. This was not lost on me as my heart struck up a drum solo. "This pleases you?" he asked when I settled next to him.

I hesitated. "Sure."

"You are a terrible liar," he said. The crowds swelled as we neared the harbor, perhaps all the people of the sepat welcoming our arrival. Their excitement reached us like electricity. "I'll be out there soon," he said.

"As Seti."

"Yes, to meet this new princess." The Hyksos were not pleased to have lost beloved Tuya, but they were grateful that the Egyptians were now irrevocably in the war effort. In the wake of the arrangement, though, the Egyptians insisted that some of the Hyksos traditions be broken. The Hyksos consort would marry Seti soon after his arrival, to ensure that nothing could go wrong. She would even greet the prince with King Ashmar on the shores before the presentation ceremony. "What do you say of this?"

"Does it matter?"

"Your prince has asked."

"I really hate it when you talk in third person."

"Then answer me, please."

I shrugged. "I'm sure she'll make a great chief wife."

"And would you?"

"Would I what?" I knew what he meant.

"Make a great chief wife?"

I swallowed hard. "I don't know," I said, that drum solo hitting a crescendo. "Little girls want to be a ballerina or a teacher or an astronaut when they grow up. Not chief wife." He laughed, though I knew he didn't quite understand what I meant by ballerina or astronaut. He had a *wonderful* laugh.

I angled my head away, trying to deflect his seriousness. Pharaoh had many wives, and one day Seti would, too. But it was clear he was asking me to be not a wife, but his chief wife. He wanted me to be the woman carved next to him in stone, wearing the royal diadem, the consort who wouldn't be lost to history. But I'd never been on a date, let alone entertained offers of marriage. Not so long ago, Portia White would have given anything to go to prom with Jason Jones. Portia White sailing the Nile with the prince of Egypt didn't make sense. I was suddenly overheated under the cloak and his gaze. But Seti's index finger found my chin and gently directed my eyes back to his. "I don't know. Maybe one day," I finally said.

"One day?"

"Not everything is at your beck and call."

Again, his face was blank. "*One day* is not the concern of Pharaoh."

I sighed. "What do you want me to say?"

"I want you to say, 'Yes, my handsome prince, I would make an honored chief wife.'"

"I can't say that."

"Really? It's only eleven words."

"Get over yourself," I said with a laugh. "There's more than just us to think of. Selene is here somewhere, and then we have to find Alex—" I cut myself off with a shake of my head. The thought of everything to be accomplished was overwhelming, and worst of all, I didn't know if I could do it. Seti had been trained his whole life to a prince, a war king. I'd known I was part of the star for a few weeks max.

I expected a frown when I glanced back at the prince, but his mouth only tilted upward. "We will find them," he assured me. His eyes traced my neck, stopping on my scarab. He smiled as he touched it, and my breath caught as he read the inscription. "You wore this when we met."

"From Ma'at," I whispered. He nodded again, allowing the cold scarab to lay against my flushing skin once more. It was strange that I could be so hyperaware of him and yet barely notice as his lips dusted my forehead.

"Then you are favored."

"Yeah," I said. My voice was even, considering my surging thoughts.

"Then it wouldn't be difficult for you to be my princess. You could say it's in your blood," he said. He twined his arms around me, holding me close. *If you tilt your chin up, he's going to kiss you.*

But there was only one problem, and it wasn't that I hadn't kissed anyone before. The flush beneath my skin had become more than awkward anticipation. It was swirling heka, causing electricity to brew more literally in me than figuratively. We'd gone over every means of controlling my heka, except when the Prince of Egypt wants to kiss you.

Great.

Our lips touched before I could warn him of the real possibility of electrocution. And as I thought, a sharp spark leapt from my skin, nicking his bottom lip. He jumped back. I touched my mouth as he stared in awed fascination. *I shocked him. I'm an eel.* "I'm sorry," I said. It was all I could say. "I'm so sorry." This would be the part where *I* turned into sand and salt, purely of mortification, but the wonderful swell of his laugh rose through the air.

"You," he said, with genuine delight. His arms wrapped around me again, as well as in our sudden burst of hysterical laughter. It was a dance, him leading the way with his big, relieving, exuberant laugh. "For you, I will wait for *one day*," he said through now shock-less kisses. "For you, I would wait every day."

Raia led the procession perfectly lined up on the ship. Other military personnel stood close behind. The prince overlooked his men from his central seat at the highest point of the boat. He was Seti now. He wore ceremonial dress, gold ornaments at his neck and wrists, the blue khepresh crown on his head. The khepresh meant that this ceremony, and those that followed, would eventually lead us into battle. Even so, my mind was elsewhere. I tried to be discreet as my fingertips trailed my mouth, fresh with the memory of our kiss. I wished Seti would glance back at me, but as the boats entered the Hyksos harbor, he looked ahead, resolute and regal.

I stood behind Weret and Sikara on the royal boat, closer to the back of what would be a large procession. My scarab dangled around my neck as my eyes danced across the faces in the Hyksos crowd. Raia had overseen the placement of the Egyptians on board, taking special care not to speak to me around his subordinates. He was not as open as he'd been in the audience chamber. As he issued orders, our eyes did catch briefly. They flickered before the general turned from me. If there was one thing I could always get from Raia, it was a reaction.

The harbor of the Hyksos palace opened up from the water. Detached from the rest of the structures in the city, the palace was a spectacle appearing to float above the waves. The royal family stood at its shoreline, some dignitaries positioned on the docks. Despite the mist rolling across the waters, it was hard to mistake the princess perched in front of a host of royal children. She was dressed as Tuya had been, wearing a sparkling veil in the Hyksos tradition. I wondered if she felt like the fifth or sixth bride of Henry the Eighth, knowing that great things didn't always befall those who wed into power.

The boats docked, and after Seti and his military escort disembarked, the rest of us followed. Our legs were shaky after days on the water. Between the green robes of the priestesses, I caught glimpses of the goings-on, of Hyksos viziers approaching Seti. Behind them was a man I assumed to be King Ashmar, and another, his son, Sahdina's brother. A new governess stood beside the Hyksos princess, and when Seti caught sight of his bride, he bowed. She returned the favor before moving along to the Egyptian priests and nobility. I rolled my eyes, wondering how long I'd have to suffer through the pomp and circumstance of the betrothed.

Sikara drew a sharp breath. "What?" I asked, turning to her. She didn't respond, eyes locked ahead. I followed her gaze, and air caught in my throat. Standing behind the new Hyksos governess, the first of the princess's maids, was my twin.

Her eyes were cast anywhere but at the Egyptian fleet pouring into the harbor, but I willed her to see me. I willed her to glimpse at my mouth agape. I willed her to feel my heart pounding. And through that strange, dense mist, not knowing if Alex even acknowledged the boats, it crashed down on me: Ma'at needed us to do more than find Selene and this goddess to get back home. Ma'at needed us to twin again. And if there was anything I'd learned in Waset, it was that Ma'at's will could not be ignored.

ACKNOWLEDGMENTS

This is the part where I run screaming and tell everyone thank you?

I can do that. 1, 2, 3 . . . go!

Firstly, thank you to Laura, who has helped this project grow from a scrawny 55,000-word prayer into a book baby! Thank you for being a wonderful Virgo.

Thank you to Amy and Dara for creating Wise Ink and answering my freak out calls. And thank you to Dara for telling me to just do it (and for also being a Virgo, because Virgos obviously only belong in publishing).

Thank you to Patrick for the wonderful proofread and Steve for having a strong artistic vision for this story. The cover is more gorgeous than I could have imagined. And speaking of gorgeous, thank you to Tamyka for lending her face to Portia's character.

Thank you to my Bison sista, Rhea, for the new author photo, and thank you to Rachael for the PERFECT author website.

Thank you to my extraordinary mentor, Shveta, for teaching me about wish lines and the value of short stories. And thanks for always making me hungry when I read your work and for being supportive when I went indie.

Thank you to Kellie for editing that ugly first draft and loving Sikara as much as I do. More cowbell! And to Amanda for a merciless edit and teaching me not to rely on voice. And for being really British.

Thank you to every agent that passed on this book.

Thank you to Billy for making the Introvert Problems podcast come to life, sticking with me from my pageants days to now, and for being excited about the million ideas I've had in the interim.

Thank you to my wonderful interns McKenna and Jasmine for working behind the scenes. And thanks to McKenna for more Virgo power.

Thank you to Angelica for being the bestest best friend ever, and to Cierra for believing in my work. You are both my favorite Cancers in the world.

Thank you to Erica for beta reading and for our heart-warming Starbucks gabs. And for being an overly-competitive August Virgo.

Thank you to my mom for loving words, investing in sturdy bookshelves, and writing "pugnacious" on the back of my baby photos.

Thank you to my dad for always supporting my dreams, whether they led me across the country to undergrad, to the NBA court as a cheerleader, to a Big Ten campus for grad school, or onstage in tiaras. Thank you for bringing home our first computer and letting me tinker with it, and willingly typing the John Baker Mysteries on Corel Word Perfect. Thank you for still having a copy.

Thank you to my aunts Shar'Ron, Connie, Coco, Janet, and Patricia, and to my grandparents. These women are the best cheerleaders a girl could ask for, and I cherish all of you.

Thank you to my sisters, Nekesa and Maya, who are both

brilliant, lovely, ridiculous, hilarious, and appear in the book in their own ways. Don't sue me. I ain't got no money for you. Thank you to my pup, Thor, for sitting with me while I type. And for chewing on my shoes when you get bored.

And Colin, my midnight sun, a little bit of light when it's challenging, the brilliant burst of Aries magic when it's hard to believe in possibilities, thank you for . . . everything.

photo credit: Rhea Whitney Photography

Imani Josey is a writer from Chicago, Illinois. In her previous life, she was a cheerleader for the Chicago Bulls and won the titles of Miss Chicago and Miss Cook County for the Miss America Organization, as well as Miss Black Illinois USA.

Her one-act play, *Grace,* was produced by Pegasus Players Theatre Chicago after winning the 19th Annual Young Playwrights Festival. In recent years, she has turned her sights to long-form fiction. She now spends the majority of her time working on backstory, teaching dance fitness classes, and cuddling with her American bulldog, Thor. *The Blazing Star* is her debut novel.